"I'd like to marry you, Marisa Reynolds.

"I know we could have a wonderful life together."

She looked up at him and shook her head. How could he possibly think she'd take his suggestion seriously? "Oh, Josh. This whole idea is...is crazy. It's ridiculous."

"Why?"

"Why rush into marriage, Josh? We could just—" she shrugged, trying to give her heart time to calm down "—see each other and find out what happens."

He exhaled heavily. "For me, this isn't rushing. Once I thought I'd do things the conventional way." He frowned with frustration. "I counted on it. And that's been my mistake. I've waited for it to happen instead of deciding it was going to. I've always gotten whatever I wanted. I want this. And I've never failed."

Dear Reader,

This month, Silhouette Special Edition presents an exciting selection of stories about forever love, fanciful weddings—and the warm bonds of family.

Longtime author Gina Wilkins returns to Special Edition with *Her Very Own Family,* which is part of her FAMILY FOUND: SONS & DAUGHTERS series. The Walker and D'Alessandro clans first captivated readers when they were introduced in the author's original Special Edition series, FAMILY FOUND. In this new story, THAT SPECIAL WOMAN! Brynn Larkin's life is about to change when she finds herself being wooed by a drop-dead gorgeous surgeon....

The heroines in these next three books are destined for happiness—or are they? First, Susan Mallery concludes her enchanting series duet, BRIDES OF BRADLEY HOUSE, with a story about a hometown nanny who becomes infatuated with her very own *Dream Groom.* Then the rocky road to love continues with *The Long Way Home* by RITA Award-winning author Cheryl Reavis—a poignant tale about a street-smart gal who finds acceptance where she least expects it. And you won't want to miss the passionate reunion romance in *If I Only Had a... Husband* by Andrea Edwards. This book launches the fun-filled new series, THE BRIDAL CIRCLE, about four long-term friends who discover there's no place like home—to find romance!

Rounding off the month, we have *Accidental Parents* by Jane Toombs—an emotional story about an orphan who draws his new parents together. And a no-strings-attached arrangement goes awry when a newlywed couple becomes truly smitten in *Their Marriage Contract* by Val Daniels.

I hope you enjoy all our selections this month!

Sincerely,

Karen Taylor Richman
Senior Editor

Please address questions and book requests to:
Silhouette Reader Service
U.S.: 3010 Walden Ave., P.O. Box 1325, Buffalo, NY 14269
Canadian: P.O. Box 609, Fort Erie, Ont. L2A 5X3

VAL DANIELS

THEIR MARRIAGE CONTRACT

Published by Silhouette Books
America's Publisher of Contemporary Romance

Thanks for getting me through
whatever I need to get through:
Sharon Flannery, Candy Cole, Nancy Parra,
Gay Thornton, Marcia Blinzler, De Ann Sicard
and Carol Monk

 SILHOUETTE BOOKS

ISBN 0-373-24248-4

THEIR MARRIAGE CONTRACT

Copyright © 1999 by Vivian A. Thompson

This edition published by arrangement with Harlequin Books S.A.

Look us up on-line at: http://www.romance.net

Printed in U.S.A.

Books by Val Daniels

Silhouette Special Edition

Their Marriage Contract #1248

Silhouette Shadows

Between Dusk and Dawn #42

VAL DANIELS's

heartwarming, humorous stories have charmed readers
for nine years. According to one fan, "Reading a Val
Daniels book is like being wrapped in my grandmother's warm quilt." Her gift for touching readers'
hearts garnered her a Write Touch Reader's Award and
several places on Ingram's Most Requested Romance
list. With over three million copies of her Harlequin
Romance novels in print, Val hopes her readers will
enjoy her debut novel for Silhouette Special Edition. She
loves hearing from readers. Please write: P.O. Box 113,
Gardner, KS 66030.

Val lives in Kansas with her husband, two children and a
Murphy dog.

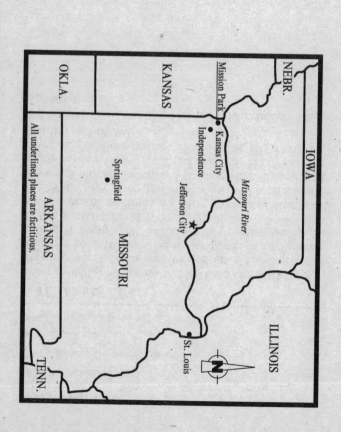

NEBR.

IOWA

KANSAS

Mission Park

Kansas City
Independence

Missouri River

Springfield

Jefferson City

MISSOURI

ILLINOIS

OKLA.

St. Louis

N

ARKANSAS

All underlined places are fictitious.

TENN.

Chapter One

He hated grocery shopping.

This particular store made him hate it more than usual. If this was anything to go by, Josh Maxwell had a sneaking suspicion he wasn't going to like much about the neighborhood he'd just moved into, either. It wasn't that he didn't like older things, he just preferred them more...up-to-date.

Narrow aisles—with cut-back boxes of canned goods stacked at random in the middle of them—didn't make things easier to find. That he could tell—the management didn't have any special rhyme or reason for the placement of their stock. He'd found the general necessities across from condiments. What did mustard and pickles have to do with flour and sugar?

Then he'd had to backtrack for spices. For some mysterious reason, he found them at the end of the refrigerated fruit- and vegetable-display cases.

"The store brand is cheaper and you get twice as much," a small gray-haired woman offered helpfully, stopping beside him. She took the container of chili powder right out of his hand and replaced it with an industrial-size canister with a no-nonsense label. "You won't be able to tell a teensy bit of difference, either," she assured him, reaching across his basket to get oregano for herself. Then she toddled off toward the bananas where she'd left her cart. "Most of the store brands are just as good or better than the national name brands," she told him as she passed again, looking smug in her self-appointed role as Good Samaritan.

I've got to get married.

He gritted his teeth and forced a grateful smile in her direction. As soon as she rounded the corner and was out of sight, he put the can she'd handed him back on the shelf. At least you could diplomatically ignore helpful old ladies, he thought as he dropped the more appropriately-sized container into the basket. The massive supply of vamps out shopping for husbands in his grocery store back in New Jersey had been hard to ignore or avoid.

Looking back at his list, he checked off the chili powder and noted with a sigh of relief that he had only two more items to get. Bread and milk shouldn't be that difficult to find.

He started his final sprint toward the farthest aisle—logically that was where they'd put milk and bread—and jolted to a stop as another shopping cart rammed into his. His teeth clenched at the impact.

A polite but chilly "Excuse me" died on his lips as he glanced up into the widest, prettiest hazel eyes he'd ever seen. They seemed to fill the woman's entire face. Her mouth had fallen open in an exaggerated "Oh," and the hand that rose to cover it only enhanced the surprised expression.

Her fingers were ringless, he noted with growing irritation. Yeah, sure. This had been an accident. He knew the tricks. He'd seen everything from women who were certain he couldn't pick a good banana by himself to miniskirted Amazons who needed help getting something off an upper shelf, despite being taller than he was.

At least this one had on a half-inch less makeup. A soft flush spread slowly over her flawless creamy complexion. Nice touch, he decided as he braced himself for the coy batting of eyelashes that was certain to come. She'd apologize and start some inane conversation about the price of frozen spinach versus fresh. At some point soon, she'd extend her hand delicately and introduce herself.

He wished those slick magazines would quit publishing those obnoxious articles about how to meet men.

But he was ready. He knew exactly what to say before he stalked off, leaving this manhunter gaping.

"You need to—"

"Sorry," the woman murmured and started past him.

—update your technique. Surprise trapped the words in his throat. He muttered his modified statement at her back. "—to...to watch where you're going."

With a weak apologetic smile, the woman turned and mouthed another "Sorry." She nodded dismissively and headed up the aisle he'd just left, leaving *him* gaping.

It was an accident, a voice in his head chided him. "Maybe," he answered, still watching her.

The woman bent to take something from the bottom shelf. His body responded automatically to the intriguing display. She did have a cute butt.

He forced himself to close his mouth before he started to salivate.

Without a backward glance, she put whatever she picked up into her cart and went on down the aisle.

Maybe they published different advice for the lovelorn in magazines in the Midwest. Maybe *better* advice. Because he certainly had the impulse to follow her. Find out who she was.

He shook his head, shaking off the thought, shaking off the distractions. Time to get back on track. He looked at his list. Bread. Milk.

And marriage.

The clarity of the thought made the word leap at him from the end of his list—as vivid on the white page as eggs and flour.

He *needed* to get married. It would solve most of his problems. The idea had been gnawing at the back of his mind for the past year. Now it moved forward. Front and center.

Marriage wouldn't solve most of his problems. It would solve *all* of them.

But who? He'd been ready for marriage and domesticity for a while. The "who" was the problem. It wouldn't be someone who picked him up in a grocery store.

He pulled a quart of milk from the dairy case and headed for the cash register. He caught himself glancing down the aisles he passed, hoping for another glimpse of *her*. She wasn't married—unless she just didn't bother to wear a ring.

He brushed thoughts of her aside impatiently. That was the other problem. He'd spent the last several of his thirty-six years expecting to run into the perfect candidate and fall in love. He'd done an imitation of falling in love with the perfect candidate once. Now it was time to get practical. Time to make a workable plan.

As the clerk began her antiquated method of ringing up

his groceries by hand, he had his nicest thought yet. If he got married, he'd never have to grocery-shop again.

The telephone was ringing when Josh walked in the door with both arms full of groceries. With only six hours' possession of the little house he'd rented behind him, he had to stop and listen to remember where he'd hooked up a phone.

He finally located it in the living room, behind a small box on the end table.

"Maxwell," he answered.

"You're in." He heard his sister's pleasantly surprised reaction on the other end of the line.

"Kinda, sorta." He looked around him at the stack of boxes he still had to unload. "How you doing, Janet?"

"That's what I called to ask you," she said cheerfully. "I was so glad when I called information and they gave me your number. That means you're settled?"

"Kinda, sorta," he said again. This time he looked toward the kitchen where he'd dumped three bags of food on the table. "Listen, Janet, can I call you back? I just got in from the store. I'll have frozen things melting all over if I don't put away the groceries."

"Get your cordless."

"Haven't found it yet." He glared at the boxes again. It would have been easier and quicker to have the movers unpack for him, but he liked knowing where his things were.

"Okay. Call me back. I'm dying to know how it's going. Do you like it there? Have you seen Marisa yet?"

"If I answer all that, my ice cream will melt. I'll talk to you later. Round ten tonight?"

"Remember I'm an hour later than you," she reminded him in that bossy sisterly way that drove him half-crazy.

"Your time," he confirmed, just to get her off the line. "I'll call before ten your time."

She hung up and he put his groceries away, rearranging items he'd already put in the cabinets as he did. By the time he finished, he was hungry—and no longer in the mood to dig through boxes to find pots and pans so he could cook. That had been the plan when he'd gone to the store. The plan had changed. He'd go out, he decided, instead, maybe to that little neighborhood café he'd passed two blocks from here. It had looked like the kind of place that might have something home-cooked on the menu.

Though there were still lights on and several cars in the parking lot, a big Closed sign filled the window of the neighborhood joint. Josh's stomach growled in protest as he glanced at his watch. Ten after eight.

"Probably just missed it," he muttered.

"Where to next? Back to fast-food alley." Josh shook himself. He'd been talking to himself a long time. But now he was starting to answer. That could be a problem, he thought wryly.

Marriage. It would solve that problem, too. He wouldn't *have* to talk to himself.

With a sigh he backed out of the potholed lot and drove toward the brightly lit main thoroughfare bisecting this part of the city.

Suburbs, he thought. I want to live in the suburbs. Compared to his high-rise apartment in the city, this was the suburbs. But his small rental house was still city center. He wanted to live on the outskirts in a new house with all the conveniences and trimmings. He wanted a yard large enough to putter in on pleasant evenings. He wanted to sit silently on a deck with his wife.

His gut tightened sharply from the sudden strong desire to possess and be a part of the image that settled in his mind. Or maybe it was simply hunger, he reasoned as stomach pangs assailed him. But he could see the picture as clearly as he could see the stoplight ahead. Two redwood chairs, side by side, floral cushions—she'd have chosen them—his hand resting easily over hers. The sky in the distance striped, painted by the vivid colors of the setting sun. Her golden brown hair ruffling in the breeze as she smi—

A car honked behind him, jolting him out of his reverie.

He glanced in the rearview mirror, half expecting to see the woman from the daydream—and the grocery store— smiling back at him. The tight jaw and red face of an irritated middle-aged man confronted him, instead.

Josh gave the car gas as the left-turn light blinked from green to amber.

Damn. He had to stop this nonsense.

Or did he?

Getting what he wanted had always been a matter of deciding what it was, precisely, and going after it. Maybe that was why he hadn't found someone to marry yet. He hadn't gone after it with the same intensity he usually went after something he wanted. He'd waited for it to happen. And the one time he thought it might happen had been a disaster.

Labeling his thoughts fanciful, he forced them aside and pulled into the parking lot of the twenty-four hour "breakfast, lunch or dinner" franchise.

The older woman who led him to a booth by one of the windows eyed him appreciatively as she handed him a menu. He glanced at her hand and wasn't surprised to see a wedding ring. Happily married. She wore the label like a sign. I'm content with what I have so I can appreciate an attractive male from a pleasant distance, her expression seemed to say as she smiled and turned to go back to the hostess station by the front door.

Okay. Admit it. You want what she has.

"You want what?" An attractive waitress had approached his table.

He'd been talking aloud to himself again. Josh straightened and cleared his throat. "I just wondered if there was a special tonight."

She opened his menu to the middle page and waved toward the plastic insert like a game-show babe opening a curtain to reveal a flashy prize. "This is our special promotion this month," she said. "Our homemade-bread bowls filled with all sorts of sinfully good things." She let her voice draw out the "sinfully" as she slowly straightened away from him. Twenty-one, maybe twenty-two, she was a nice-looking blue-eyed blonde who wore her long, carefully mussed curly hair in a ditzy ponytail on the side of her head. Her smile was flirtatious and inviting. "What can I get you to drink while you decide?"

"Coffee. Black," he added as she opened her mouth to ask. He didn't know if he was in the mood to flirt back, so he tacked on an indecisive smile as she backed away. It was encouragement enough. Her grin widened.

She's after a good tip, he told himself. But that wasn't all, he knew as her gaze held his just a second or so longer than necessary before she turned and flounced off. He was an eligible, attractive male—with a good job, he added to his score sheet—and everyone seemed to be looking for the same thing he was preoccupied with tonight.

She looked pleasant enough. But he wouldn't want her, he had to admit. He'd feel as if he was baby-sitting, for one thing. Shoot, he'd been well into puberty, probably thirteen or fourteen, before she was even born.

And that was the problem. He'd waited too long to start

thinking about marriage. The women he would truly be interested in keeping were already kept or young enough to make him feel he'd be parenting, instead of husbanding. He didn't like the slightly bitter taste in his mouth as the blonde came back to take his order.

She quickly lost interest when he only halfheartedly responded to her flirtatious teasing, which left him to eat in peace—if you could call it peace. His body demanded he respond to her, though his mind refused. There were times he regretted his genuine reluctance to indulge in casual sex.

His meal turned tasteless when he realized the turn his thoughts had taken. Was he seriously thinking of adding "wife" to his shopping list for the benefit of regular sex?

Leaving a better-than-average tip on the table, he went home to finish unpacking and to call his sister. Now that his stomach wasn't rumbling, he was in the mood to hear Janet's cheerful voice.

"So tell me about your house," she said as soon as she said hello. "Room enough for guests?"

"You coming to visit?"

"Not right away," Janet answered. "But I figure I have two reasons to make a trip to Kansas now. I never could quite justify it when it was just Marisa there."

"So it isn't me you want to see," he said with some humor.

"It isn't that I don't want to see you, big brother," she drawled, "but it's only been a week. It's been almost six years since I saw Marisa. Brad's never liked the idea of me coming to the Wild West to hang out with my wild friends from college." Janet laughed out loud. "If he only knew."

"Now he doesn't mind?"

"We've been married a long time, Josh."

"Six years isn't that long. You're saying your marriage is going stale, sis?"

"I'm saying—" she reverted to her lecture tone "—that this marriage thing sort of grows on you. The longer you're married, the more you learn to love and trust each other. Some of the early insecurities fade. It gets better," she added.

Josh had learned to tune out Janet's rhapsodizing over how wonderful married life was. This time, however, he found himself listening. He put the "learn to love and trust" part in a corner of his mind to think about later.

"Shoot," she said, interrupting his thoughts. "With you there to entertain him, I could even bring my husband with me."

"You couldn't before?"

"What would I have done with him?"

"Good question," Josh said wryly, remembering some of the things Janet and her friends had gotten up to when they were kids. Poor Brad.

"Brad wants to meet Marisa again. I think he knows how preposterous his early ideas were. Just because she's unmarried—"

The word had him sitting up straighter.

"—and has a kid," Janet went on, "he jumped to all sorts of stereotypical conclusions."

"What's wrong with her?" Josh heard himself asking. He tried to visualize the shadowy woman he'd met briefly at Janet's wedding.

"Nothing," Janet responded indignantly.

"That she isn't married, I mean," Josh clarified.

"I take it that means you haven't gotten in touch with her yet."

Josh wasn't even sure he'd kept the number Janet had scratched out for him last week when they'd gotten together at their parents' home in Pennsylvania right before his move. "I've been here two days, Janet," he said dryly. "One in a motel, the other moving in."

"Get a pen," she said. "I'll give you her number again."

"Getting bossier and bossier in your old age, sis," he said, scrambling for something to write on. Suddenly he was interested in the friend Janet had been raving about for years.

"It's the motherhood thing," she answered his accusation. "Brad says pregnancy is making me demanding. It's making me anxious to visit Marisa," she added irritably. "You never said if you had room for me, did you?"

"I'll have more room six or eight months from now when I find a lot and have a house built," he said. "But I could squeeze you in, I suppose. This house has two bedrooms."

Janet gave him Marisa's number.

"Exactly what is wrong with your friend that she never married?" he asked again.

"You know, there were times I wanted to do bodily harm to her parents," Janet said.

That didn't exactly answer his question. "Why?"

"She's such a sweetheart," Janet replied. "And don't get me wrong. Her parents were very supportive after she found out she was pregnant. But somehow, one glitch, one small life-changing glitch," she repeated, "and they were convinced—and subconsciously convinced her—that she no longer had any right to expect a normal life, a husband, home and 2.3 kids, or whatever the statistics are."

"What do you mean?"

"You know—" he could imagine Janet gnawing at her lip the way she did when she was considering something "—an out-of-wedlock pregnancy, disappointment in herself for not living up to her expectations. And somewhere deep in her heart, she quit believing she deserved to dream dreams of a husband and family.''

"You're saying there's nothing wrong with her.'' He had to make sure that he understood what Janet was saying.

"Nothing a good husband wouldn't fix.'' Janet chuckled.

Somewhere deep in Josh's mind, something clicked.

He'd never spent a more restless night. He wondered at one point if the mover had sneaked a new mattress onto his familiar bed frame in place of his comfortable one.

And he awoke passionately entwined with his pillow.

While he was taking a cold shower, he wondered if he was losing his mind. Definitely, he immediately confirmed when he realized he'd been dreaming of the total stranger who'd run into him at the grocery store. Visions of smooth chin-length golden-brown hair and wide hazel eyes still filled his mind.

At least the crazy thoughts kept him from getting uptight about his first day in his new job, he congratulated himself as he put on the pin-striped gray suit with a new tie.

He critically approved himself in the mirror, straightening his shoulders and sucking in his gut. There wasn't an appreciable difference after he tightened his stomach muscles. He kept expecting one. A lot of friends his age seemed to have expanding waists and receding hairlines. He took some pride in still wearing the same size clothes he wore when he graduated from law school. His dark hair was as thick as ever and laced with only a couple of gray hairs at one temple. And those, he thought wryly, he'd earned in the last year at his former law firm.

The one nice thing about his house and new neighborhood was the proximity to his new job at City Hall. He was there before nine for his appointment with the mayor, despite leaving at ten minutes to.

The sight of City Hall stirred him with anticipation. The law firm in New Jersey had been black marble and glass, an imposing twenty-story structure. This three-story building, made from bricks the color of wet sand, sprawled over almost a city block. It was dignified yet hospitable. The green space that filled the rest of the block was almost a park, complete with inviting benches placed at intervals.

Josh squinted up at the arched clock tower, into the morning sun, and savored the feel of the smog-free warm breeze in his hair. He sighed deeply. This part of his new life he was certain he was going to like.

"Josh. Josh Maxwell?"

He turned, frowning to readjust his eyes, and extended his hand to the red-suited mayor rushing toward him.

"I was afraid I was going to be late," Alana Shaw said breathlessly as her long scarlet-tipped fingers closed around his. "I'm so glad you made it. Did the move go all right? Are you settled?"

"Getting there," he said in answer to the last question. They started together toward the entrance.

"I meant to have someone meet you in the parking lot to show you your space," she said apologetically. "I hope you didn't have a problem finding a place to park."

She'd obviously forgotten where he moved from. Parking there hadn't been a problem; it had been nonexistent. "I found a spot easily," he told her. "Maybe someone can point out my reserved space later."

She cast him an agreeable smile as he held the door for her. A mosaic seal imbedded in the foyer wall between two elevators read Progress through Service.

"We'll settle you in your office and introduce you to your staff first," Alana said. "Then at eleven, we have a luncheon meeting scheduled with the city manager and the department heads. I thought maybe the best way to ease you into the job would be an informal session where each of them could tell you their immediate problems and major legal concerns for the future.''

''Sounds perfect.''

The mayor paused before the elevators and punched the button. The diamond wedding ring on her finger glinted in the sun streaming through the two-story bank of windows behind them.

Mayor Shaw—Alana, she insisted he call her—rushed him through the rest of the morning with barely enough time to catch his breath. As soon as the long, long lunch was over, she accompanied him back to his office. Instead of leaving, as he hoped she would so he could unpack the boxes stacked in one corner, she closed the door behind them and kicked off her medium-high heels. ''Ah,'' she sighed, making herself at home on the dark leather couch filling one wall of the large office, ''that's much better. You can change anything in here you like,'' she added with a wave at the room. ''I told you that, didn't I?''

Josh nodded.

''I believe the budget we approved was...about $35,000.''

Josh whistled. ''Can't imagine making that many changes.'' He glanced around the dark-paneled room. ''I may want to get rid of the curtains.''

''Drapes,'' she corrected.

''Get some blinds, instead. Let in some light,'' he said. ''Other than that...'' He shrugged.

She smiled, exposing laugh lines around her mouth that would be permanent features soon. ''We want you to be happy here, Josh. I was amazed at our luck in getting someone with so much experience and your background, especially for the salary we were able to offer. I want you to be happy with your decision.''

"Thank you." Josh settled on the edge of his oversize desk and crossed his arms.

The phone on his desk buzzed. He picked up the receiver, noting the prehistoric nature of the system only after he didn't get a response to his "Maxwell." He considered suggesting they use his decorating allowance to update the city's telephone equipment. It would be nice to have the state-of-the-art phones he was accustomed to at the law firm.

He pressed a blinking button. "Maxwell," he said again, and then extended the phone to his companion. "For you."

He went to open the top box on the stack in the corner as she answered. He tried not to listen as her tone turned softer and softer during the course of the call. He began putting his law books into the cases lining one entire wall.

"My husband," Alana said after she finally rang off.

"That's a relief." He chuckled. "I'd be concerned about the kind of things I'll have to handle if I thought you ended all your calls that way."

She laughed, belatedly flushing at the "Love you" she'd tacked on to her goodbye. "Sorry," she said. "He's off to Boston."

"Unexpectedly?"

She nodded and grinned at him. "Your reaction is a relief to me, too," she said.

He frowned and lifted another stack of books from the box.

"Two of the city-council members thought your single status was a big drawback."

"The interview eased their minds?" Josh asked.

She lifted a hand in a vague gesture. "In some ways, it made them more nervous. Besides being single, you're a very attractive man and have an impressive résumé. They speculated that you were running from something, probably to do with a woman. They felt you might be bringing problems with you.''

''Such as?''

''What if you're a womanizer? Or worse.''

His frown deepened.

''Hey. That's what *they* said.'' She held up her hands in self-defense. ''Donita Marsten couldn't figure out why you weren't married if you're as good as you look on your résumé.''

''So how does my comment make you feel better?''

She laughed again, resettling herself on the arm of the couch. ''Your concern about the way I end my phone calls is reassuring. At the very best, you have a healthy respect for marriage. At the very least, you have a high regard for propriety in the workplace.''

''That I do.'' He dropped his gaze to the last book in his hand. ''I can't wait to join the ranks of the happily married myself,'' he added quietly.

''You're getting married?''

His declaration startled him as much as it had surprised her. He had to get over his recent habit of talking to himself aloud. ''Maybe.''

Her eyebrows raised a notch. ''Someone from back East?''

He slid the book into the proper order beside its companion to avoid the growing gleam in Alana's eyes and cleared his throat. ''Actually, there's a friend of my family here,'' he went on, wondering why he was answering with specifics, instead of a yes or no. But he seemed incapable of stopping his mouth or his train of thought. ''My sister's roommate from college,'' he finished.

''Well,'' she said delightedly. ''I guess that further explains your interest in coming to this part of the country. Congratulations are in order?''

He held up his hands as if she was sticking him up, instead of extending a congratulatory shake. "Premature, I'm afraid."

"You haven't asked her yet," the mayor said with a knowing smile. She stood and slipped her feet back into her shoes.

"Still getting up the nerve," he admitted sheepishly.

"I guess I'll wish you luck, instead of congratulations," she said, opening the door. "I'll look forward to meeting her."

I'll look forward to meeting her, too.

Alana raised her hand in a see-you-later wave. "Let me know if you need anything."

"Thanks." He watched until the door closed, then reached into the inside breast pocket of his suit. He retrieved the small piece of paper he'd written Marisa Reynolds's number on. He guessed it was time to at least call his future bride.

Chapter Two

"You're my mom's date?"

Marisa Reynolds looked down at the watch lying beside the bathroom sink and groaned. Of course, Janet Maxwell's brother *had* to be as punctual as Janet had always been. It was six-thirty on the dot.

Marisa didn't have to see Ryan to picture him as he quizzed the man. His nine-year-old hands, hands that seemed too big for his scrawny body, were settled on the waist of his too-baggy jeans. His feet were planted wide, one knee slightly bent as he stood his ground just inside the front door.

She strained to hear Joshua Maxwell's reply. All she could decipher was a low, pleasant rumble. She'd told Ryan at least ten times that this wasn't exactly a date. She was just going out to dinner with her best friend's brother.

"She's not ready," she heard Ryan's still-childish voice tell him. "Ya might as well find somethin' to do for a while," he added after another brief rumble. "She takes hours."

I'm almost ready, Marisa wanted to protest. She was getting there. She leaned toward the mirror and brushed one last stroke of mascara on her lashes. Shoes, earrings, perfume, she mentally checked. She grabbed her watch and fumbled with the clasp for what seemed like forever.

Oh, Lord, please let Ryan at least ask him to sit down.

The bathroom doorknob came off in her hand. Taking a deep breath, she grabbed the screwdriver from the medicine chest and began the magic trick she knew far too well. Someday she really was going to get this fixed.

This guy's opinion of her, one way or another, wasn't all that important, she reminded herself as the latch popped open. She'd agreed to go out to dinner with him only because she felt obligated. Being nice to Janet's brother was a courtesy Marisa owed her closest friend. He was new in town, probably didn't know very many people. And when she'd met him at Janet's wedding, she'd probably made such a bad impression—or no impression at all—that anything she did tonight would be an improvement.

Hurrying into the bedroom, she slipped her feet into black flats as she grabbed her best perfume. Spritzing a bit behind each ear, she fumbled through her jewelry box with the other hand. The pearl studs were always buried at the bottom of their little section. She found them and put them on, paused another second before the mirror, but wasn't sure why. If she didn't look presentable by now, she didn't have time to do anything about it, anyway. With another glance at her watch to confirm that she was only…twelve minutes late, she headed down the hall.

Her pace picked up when she realized she hadn't heard a mumble from either Joshua or her son since she'd left the bathroom. She slowed when she got to the living-room door and saw the back of two heads—well, one dark head and two sprigs of Ryan's wheat-colored cowlick—over the top of the couch. They were sitting on the floor, two feet from the TV, playing Nintendo.

She didn't realize how uptight she'd been until her shoulders drooped as her tension eased. She smiled to herself. She might have been stressed-out, but Ryan looked as if he was in heaven. There was nothing he liked better than having a chance to beat an adult at one of his games.

Occasionally there were advantages to being late. And she should have known Joshua Maxwell couldn't be anything but a nice guy. After all, he *was* Janet's brother.

She wished she remembered him better, but that one trip to Pennsylvania was such a blur.

She started to make her presence known, but then paused. Ryan's eyes filled with admiration as he glanced up at the man beside him, then quickly back to the game.

Ryan's response was something she hadn't considered when Janet had said her brother was moving to the Kansas City area. If she and Joshua Maxwell became friendly, even a smidge as close as she and Janet were, Ryan might also benefit. Having a man around—a friend of his very own other than his friends' fathers—was something her son sorely needed. Since her parents' retirement to Arizona when Ryan was seven, he hadn't even had the companionship of his grandfather. He missed it.

Ryan looked tiny beside the man. Josh's solid body seemed to emphasize Ryan's boyish slenderness. She tucked the picture of them away in her memory. Since Ryan never seemed to stop growing, she'd take the memory out when she needed to keep him a child just a little longer.

Ryan put extra English into one of his shots and then whooped.

Josh straightened those broad shoulders. "You beat me, kid," he said.

"Wanna go again?"

Marisa let go a soft sigh. "You want me to find somethin' to do for a while?" she asked, mimicking Ryan's earlier tone. "I know for a fact this could take hours."

Ryan rolled his eyes, then looked up at his new hero, seeking confirmation that his mother was acting just like a dumb girl.

Joshua Maxwell set his controls on the floor and leaned over to ruffle Ryan's hair. Then he started to unfold. He stood up...and up. He had to be at least six foot two or three when he finally arrived at his full height. Marisa wondered why she hadn't remembered him being so tall.

She sidestepped the end of the couch and came toward him, her hand outstretched. "I'm so sorry to keep you waiting, Mr. Maxwell," she said. "Janet has told me so much about you over the years I feel like I know you, but I have to admit, I really don't remember much about our brief meeting at her wedding."

He stared at her for a moment, his mouth hanging slightly open as if he was stunned. Her hand hung in midair, and she was about to let it drop when he noticed and finally took it.

His hand was warm and firm. It felt...strangely pleasant as it tightened around hers. "And the one since then?" He let a wonderful smile grow.

She knew she frowned as she searched her mind for the occasion of another meeting. Surely she would have remembered. He looked a lot like Janet—the rich dark hair, the brown-black sparkling eyes, the tiny dimple just above one of the smile lines.

"You don't remember?"

She could swear he looked disappointed. "I'm afraid...no," she said bluntly.

"At the grocery store? A couple of days ago," he added as she continued to stare blankly. "We ran into each other?"

"I'm sorry." She shook her head.

"Literally! You ran into my cart," he said, sounding frustrated.

Some vague memory tickled her. "Oh? That was you?" she asked brightly, because obviously she was supposed to remember. "Oh, yes. Well, it's nice to meet you again on a friendlier basis," she assured him, and finally matched his smile. It wasn't hard. Besides being Janet's brother, he was a very attractive man, as attractive as she'd seen in a long, long while.

Ryan was still looking up at him, wholehearted approval in his gaze. "You've met my son?" she asked.

Josh smiled down at Ryan. "Not formally," he said.

"Ryan, this is Josh Maxwell. Josh, my son Ryan."

Josh extended his hand and Ryan took it, puffing up a little at the grown-up, one-guy-to-another treatment. "I will expect a rematch soon," Josh warned him.

"For sure," Ryan said. "But I'll beat you again." His tone had a confidence Marisa rarely saw. She felt a qualm of familiar protectiveness and hoped Josh wasn't just making polite conversation. Ryan believed everything adults told him, and he'd be extremely disappointed if the rematch didn't happen.

"We'll see," Josh challenged, then glanced at his watch.

"We'd probably better be going, Ryan." Marisa bent to kiss his cheek. "Evie's expecting you."

"Okay, Mom," Ryan said, scuffing the toe of his shoe into the faded green carpet, suddenly shy with his new friend. "See ya later."

"Soon," Josh promised. "Next time your mom and I do this, you'll have to come with us."

Ryan's expression brightened.

"Next time," Marisa rushed to add before Ryan could suggest that he could make it this time without any problem. "Now, off with you." She would have patted his rear but caught herself in time, remembering the way he'd inched away after her kiss a moment ago. "I'll lock the back door behind you."

When she returned from seeing her son off to the neighbor's, with whom she exchanged baby-sitting from time to time, Josh was standing exactly where she'd left him. He studied the small living room critically, probably thinking it was in desperate need of modernization. She resisted the urge to defend its condition.

"Well, shall we be going? I'm really sorry I'm running behind. I hope I haven't made us late for our reservation."

He smiled at her in a strange, indulgent way. "I figured we'd be pretty safe without them on a Monday night. Besides, I wanted to meet your son, so this turned out perfectly."

"Oh?" She was pleasantly surprised. That sounded like a good omen for her hopes for Ryan. "Janet must have told you more about us than I supposed."

"She talks about you from time to time," he said vaguely, following her into the foyer, where she hesitated beside the closet.

"It's supposed to rain. Do I need my umbrella?" she asked.

His hand settled briefly on her shoulder. "Afraid you'll melt?" he teased. "I don't know your weather here, but I think it'll hold off for a while. It's only heat lightning."

Her skin tingled pleasantly as his hand lingered at her back. He opened the inside front door for them.

His solicitous attitude had her analyzing this meeting again. Was it a "date"? It had been so long since she'd been on a date, she wasn't sure she'd recognize one if she saw it. After what he'd told Ryan, Josh obviously meant this occasion to be just the two of them—a couple.

She was glad he hadn't called it a date, though. That would be stressful for her. She'd feel obligated to get nervous. She'd just enjoy a rare evening out with her best friend's brother.

"Shall we go?" he asked near her ear, sending a shimmer of heat down her spine. It matched the small bolt of electric white that lit the dreary sky.

She smiled up at the handsome man beside her. The look he was giving her *seemed* more than friendly. She felt cherished and more feminine than she had since…since she couldn't remember when. She'd let herself believe he *wanted* to go out with her because he found her attractive and appealing, not just because she was Janet's friend.

The chivalrous man was "to die for," as her younger friends at work would describe him. Surely after…almost ten years, she realized with dismay, she deserved the ego trip of having a date. So she'd pretend it was a date.

Josh glanced over at Marisa as he stuck his key in the ignition and couldn't believe his eyes or his luck. *This* was the woman he was going to marry.

He'd thought of her as presentable, of course. Presentable but mousy was how he remembered her from the wedding. Her hair had been slicked back in some no-frills style. She'd had frail-looking dark circles under her eyes. She'd been a little plumper. And her shoulders had sagged, he was sure. She'd looked somber and not unattractive. But beautiful? He didn't remember her being sleek and elegant.

And she was already making him slightly crazy. That was surely a good sign.

As he'd held the door for her, the whiff of her subtle but tantalizing perfume had sent pleasant sensations other places besides his nose.

"Where are we going," she asked in a lyrical, quiet voice that wouldn't be hard to listen to on a daily basis.

"I thought we'd go to Neighbors."

She nodded and he immediately wished he'd chosen something a bit more romantic and cozy. At the time he'd thought the franchise bar and grill would be perfect. It would reflect the friendly, mutually beneficial marriage he planned to propose. "We could go somewhere different if you prefer," he offered. "Like I said, I didn't make reservations."

"Neighbors sounds great."

She wasn't going to be hard to please—one more point in her favor. But why were his palms sweating? And why did he suddenly *want* to please her?

"So-o-o," she said, "your sister said you moved here to take a job as Mission Park city attorney?"

"Yes." His throat was dry. He hadn't felt this awkward with a female since his first head-over-heels crush back in the sixth grade. "You talked to Janet lately?" That sounded a bit more normal.

He turned on his signal light, stopped in the middle lane and waited for the traffic to clear so he could turn into the parking lot of the restaurant.

"We talk at least once a week," she said.

"It's amazing that you've kept in touch." She had nice hands. They were folded primly in her lap. He caught a glimpse of her reflective smile as he whipped into a parking place near the front door.

"You don't keep track of the friends you made in college?"

He shrugged. "A few of them still send Christmas cards."

"I can't imagine what my life would be like without your sister," she said simply. "I envy you. She's the sister I never had."

"For several years after Janet moved back home, you were all she talked about." With a flash of clarity, he remembered being totally unimpressed at the wedding. But then, as best man, he hadn't had a lot of time—

"I'm sure I talked about her a lot, too. I think we had a mutual-admiration society going."

His hand tingled when he rested it at the small of her back as the hostess led them to a table a few moments later. He looked around at the brightly lit restaurant and was glad he'd requested the high-backed corner booth. It at least hinted at the necessary privacy, and they weren't too close to other diners.

The hostess handed them menus. He attributed his stomach's flip-flop to hunger and willed the butterflies to stop.

What did he have to be nervous about? If Marisa refused his offer, he'd be exactly where he was right now. Nothing in his life would change. That was the worst that would happen.

And *that,* he decided, was exactly what was making him jumpy. He was tired of his life as it was. Marriage—especially if it was to Marisa—made the life he'd always pictured himself having seem possible, and infinitely better than the bachelor's existence he was living now.

He'd been expecting the average-looking sisterly friend he remembered—not a woman who could launch fantasies in the middle of the canned-goods aisle in the grocery store. He hadn't expected to care this much about her answer one way or another. Before he saw her again, he'd reasoned that if Marisa Reynolds wasn't interested, he'd find someone who was.

He realized he'd been staring at her, probably gaping, lost in space with his thoughts. Marisa had used the time to study her menu. She looked up at him, her huge eyes framed by her golden brown bangs.

"You know what you're going to have?"

"Yeah."

She set her menu aside and he followed suit. He'd have whatever she was having.

"Janet hasn't said much about you the past couple of years," Marisa admitted. "But the last I remember, you'd been made partner at some big law firm?"

He nodded as the waitress appeared to take their order. When Marisa asked for a grilled-chicken salad, he inwardly groaned and ordered a basic burger and fries. This wasn't going the way he'd planned at all.

Marisa's expressive face indicated a determined interest as she returned to the subject of his career. "I was really surprised to hear you were leaving."

"Got too good an offer to refuse," he said.

"This new job?"

"An offer for a buyout," he corrected. "Then this job came along and I realized I was ready for something new."

"You didn't like what you were doing?"

"It was getting boring." Almost as boring as he was. He wanted to kick himself.

"But you were a partner? Right?"

"There were people waiting in line to buy me out," he said wryly. "And I was sick of corporate law."

"Won't this city-attorney thing be similar?"

"Some. But the environment will be different." He

shrugged and spread his hands. "I'm ready for a change. Lots of changes," he added, grinning inanely.

She fiddled with her water glass and didn't take the bait. "You must do a lot of cooking."

He knew his stupid grin turned to a frown. He'd given her the opening to ask what kinds of changes he wanted to make and she asked about cooking?

"You ordered a hamburger," she said. "I just thought…you must not eat all your meals in restaurants. I've noticed that bachelors who eat out most of the time always seem to shy away from hamburgers."

"You go out a lot, then?" For some reason, the thought that she might have a steady boyfriend hadn't occurred to him.

She laughed. "Well, no. That did sound like I'd made myself an authority on the subject, didn't it? I have lunch with several people I work with. It's my one treat," she added with a touch of guilt. "I *hate* taking sack lunches. Anyway, I've noticed the men who live alone never want to go to any of the hamburger joints."

"Oh." Did that answer his question? He was certain he was still frowning. "I eat out more than I'd prefer," he told her honestly. "But I enjoy puttering around the kitchen when I have the time."

Her nod of approval relaxed him slightly.

"I'm trying to make Ryan self-sufficient in the kitchen," she commented. "I think it's important."

"Me, too." Darn. He was sick of this hesitant, impersonal conversation. And he had the paranoid feeling everyone was leaning toward their table, listening. He glanced around them. No one looked the least bit interested. He gazed back at her. She was studying their surroundings and didn't look very interested, either, come to think of it.

"I'm surprised we didn't meet at Janet's graduation. You were in the same class, weren't you?"

Marisa stared at her hands and rubbed at the pale pink polish on one delicate-looking fingernail. "I couldn't justify staying for the actual graduation ceremony. Mom and Dad had shouldered my responsibilities long enough. I packed up and left for home the day of my last test." She winced and cleared her throat softly. "You know my situation with Ryan?"

"That must have been a difficult time."

Her quiet smile turned reminiscent. "I wouldn't change a thing." She shook her head as if banishing the memories. The gentle hazel eyes focused on him again as she tilted her head to one side. "But I assure you, you don't want to hear any of that past history."

"Oh, I don't know. Any kind of history fascinates me." The admiration in his tone was genuine. "Especially stories about people overcoming odds. Janet said you got pregnant in high school?"

"The end of my senior year," she admitted with a grimace. "Not too smart, huh? But like I said, I wouldn't change a thing. I can't imagine life without Ryan."

"He's a bright kid."

She glowed. Finally! A subject worth pursuing.

"How did you manage," he asked as the waitress brought their meals.

"You mean with Ryan?"

He nodded.

"You really don't want to hear all this," Marisa said when everything was set on the table. "Do you?"

Damn. How could that look be so innocent and come-hither at the same time? "I wouldn't have asked if I didn't."

"Well—" she squirmed, then forked a piece of chicken

from her salad ''—I would never have made it without my parents and a lot of help from friends. Like Janet.''

''Yes?''

''And Ryan even cooperated,'' she said, then added, ''You have to promise to stop me if I bore you.''

''Deal.'' He had the feeling he could watch her animated face for a long time without getting bored. ''How did Ryan cooperate?'' He took another bite of his tasteless hamburger.

''He had the good sense to be born during semester break my first year at the junior college here. I didn't even have to miss any classes.''

''You and Ryan stayed with your parents?''

She nodded. ''Like I said, I couldn't have made it without them.''

''Then Ryan stayed with them when you went off to K-State?''

''*That* was tough. He was two years old and adorable. I hated leaving him.''

''Why didn't you get an apartment and take him with you? You wouldn't have been the first young mother going to school. Or you could have gone to the other state school? Isn't it closer? Within driving distance?''

She grinned. He'd obviously been doing his homework on the area. ''You mean Kansas University? A lot of people would consider that blasphemy.'' Her soft chuckle brightened her eyes, turning them almost green. ''If I hadn't gone to K-State, I couldn't have afforded to go at all.''

''Why?''

''Getting my degree was a joint effort. Mom and Dad took care of Ryan, physically and financially.'' She grimaced as if she hadn't liked accepting even that. ''My room and board was covered by working on the dorm staff. I had a scholarship that paid part of my tuition, Mom and Dad paid some and I paid the rest with what I managed to save.''

"Working another job?"

"No. I worked part-time my junior and senior years of high school and during those first two years of college at JUCO.''

"But there are lots of government programs,'' he said.

"I thought those kinds of things should be there for the people who really needed them.'' She was shaking her head.

"You didn't?''

"Lots of people who find themselves in my predicament don't have the kind of support I had.'' She lifted a slender shoulder. "I consider myself very, very lucky.''

He considered her perfect. Well, almost perfect, he amended, remembering his slight irritation when she hadn't been ready at the appointed time. He hoped she was usually more prompt. But he'd been sincere about wanting to meet Ryan. That had been a must on his list before he could ask her to marry him. If the boy had been some unmanageable, wild child...

"What about Ryan's father? Did he help?''

Marisa leaned back in her seat and folded one arm protectively across her waist. "He was eighteen. And definitely not interested in being anyone's father.''

"But you were what? Seventeen? Surely—''

"Seventeen when I found out I was pregnant. Eighteen when Ryan was born. His father was more interested in convincing everyone Ryan could be the son of at least two dozen others. It wasn't worth it.''

"But—''

She placed her fork firmly on the edge of her plate and that arm joined her other at her waist. "If we had insisted he accept financial responsibilities, Ryan and I would be stuck with putting up with him even now. It wasn't worth it," she said again.

"Oh." He wasn't about to suggest that Ryan might *like* putting up with the man who was his father. However true it might be, not having some man around playing some territorial game was one less worry for him once they got married. The more she talked, the more he realized she was ideal.

He leaned forward, pushing his plate to the side. "I can see why my sister admires you so much. Very few girls in your position would have managed as well."

She loosened up again. Her shoulders relaxed; the tense line of her jaw eased. The positive stroke worked wonders.

"Thank you."

He breathed a sigh of relief when she picked up her fork and stabbed another piece of lettuce.

"What do you do now?" he asked.

"You mean for a job?"

He nodded. Janet had mentioned a local chain of drugstores when she'd given him both Marisa's home and work phone numbers.

"I work at Fine Drugs." Her melodious laugh warmed the atmosphere between them. "It's crazy. I got my degree, then came back and kept the job I had part-time in high school and college."

"Surely not the same job."

"Well, no." She glanced up at him. "I'm in charge of the small accounting department now. When I started in high school, I stocked shelves and eventually convinced Mr. Finegold that I could be trusted to clerk."

"So you've done—"

"Enough about me." She held up a hand. "Let's talk about you. How do you like our fair city so far?" Her enthusiastic expression said *she* liked it very much.

"When they told me Mission Park was a suburb of Kansas City—on the Kansas side—I have to admit I expected at least a few cows and scattered wheat fields. When I visited to interview, I was amazed that it's really part of the city."

"Only better," she said.

"Only better," he agreed.

"We're only fifteen minutes from wheat fields and cows," she said.

"I saw some coming in from the airport."

"But that's the Missouri side," she said.

"Oh."

"Are you missing New Jersey?" She didn't wait for his answer. "I know the Midwest is a lot different, but I hope you'll give us a chance. Most people find it very much to their liking once they've been here awhile."

"You forget. Where Janet and I grew up was pretty rural. I was ready to get back to a little less bustle and madness."

"And that's why you gave up your partnership at the law firm there?"

"I was ready for some changes." Dammit, they were back to square one, talking all around, over and under what he'd really come to say. Surely he'd given her enough time, even if she wouldn't pick up on the lead he kept handing her.

"I would have thought—"

"I'm ready for lots of changes," he said, interrupting. "And not just living in this part of the country."

She raised her eyebrows, not understanding.

"I plan to get married," he told her.

Her smile wavered, then brightened. "That's wonderful, Josh. Congratulations. Someone from—"

"Actually, I'm hoping *you* will do me the honor."

Marisa's half-open mouth froze in that position. Her fork hovered over her plate.

"So will you marry me, Marisa?"

Chapter Three

Had she just imagined that Josh Maxwell asked her to marry him? Somehow her mind couldn't get past some peculiar warp in her brain, a warp that had twisted his words. Maybe she was on the verge of going crazy. Or maybe there was something wrong with her ears.

Will you marry me, Marisa? That was what she thought she'd heard.

Her fork clattered to her plate, finally breaking her stunned silence. "I…I'm…sorry. What did you say?"

"I asked if you would marry me, Marisa." Josh's calm tone reflected his cool, thoughtful demeanor, contrasting the frantic, chaotic thoughts running around inside her own head.

"I thought that was what you said," she managed in a shaky whisper. She cleared her throat and glanced at the people surrounding them in the well-lit, busy restaurant. None of them appeared to have noticed anything strange about her companion. In fact, the only glances directed their way had been admiring ones. She looked back at Josh. And who could blame them? He looked…normal. Better than normal, she amended. He looked fantastic.

Her lips were suddenly so dry she wasn't certain she'd be able to talk again.

His warm hand covered hers, slowly lowering it to the table. Until then, she hadn't realized it was still hanging in midair.

"So will you marry me?" he asked again, slowly this time, enunciating every word.

She stared at him, felt her eyelids lower, then raise, felt the racing of her pulse as his thumb stroked the back of her wrist in a hypnotizing, soothing motion.

"I've obviously taken you by surprise, but—"

"Why?"

He grinned slowly. "Why do I want to get married?"

"Yes. No. You…" She squeezed the words out between lips as numb as her hand had been before he'd taken control of it. Now his fingers were sending tiny cascades of sensation up her arm. It was like tickles, only better. "You don't even know—"

"It's time," he said in a low, measured voice. "I'm thirty-six years old—too old to believe that the right woman is going to suddenly appear and fall madly in love with me. But I want to get married."

She gingerly removed her hand from his and folded her hands together in her lap. The action helped her regain her composure. "You don't want to fall madly in love yourself?"

"We all want love," he answered.

"But…but…"

His mouth pursed pensively. "I believe in love. I've just quit believing I have to wait for it to drop in my lap." He seemed to choose each word carefully. "I believe you can grow it."

"Grow it?"

"That's what I plan for us to do." He nodded. "Don't you think that's possible?"

"I...I..."

"How do you feel about my sister?"

Marisa saw his point. She'd arrived at college feeling like a fish out of water. Janet had been as intent on fulfilling her dreams of becoming a veterinarian as Marisa had been on getting a degree as quickly as possible. They'd been so different, yet so alike. Soul mates. She loved Janet. "That's not the same thing."

"Why isn't it the same thing? Do you believe every marriage is a match made in heaven? That two people see each other and instantly know they're fated to spend the rest of their lives together?"

"No, but—"

"If you grew to love my sister, don't you think you could grow to love me?"

"It's not the same th—"

"I handled a lot of divorces in my first few years practicing law, Marisa. I could give you one example after another of fairy-tale romances gone awry. And those fairy-tale romances created the divorces that were always the most bitter."

"But you don't even know me."

"I know the kind of person you are. You forget, Janet is one of your biggest fans. She gave me the idea."

"You mean to marry me?" Marisa noted the shrill rise in her voice and took a deep breath.

"The decision to get married was mine," he said as if the decision was the most practical thing in the world. "Janet brought you to my attention as the perfect candidate."

Could Janet still be considered a friend? Marisa wondered. She had the urge to laugh hysterically. What kind of friend would do *this* to you?

"When she found out I was moving out here," he went on, "she reminded me you still lived in the area and insisted I look you up."

"That's all?"

He nodded. "Since I was contemplating marriage, anyway, I remembered some of the things she said about you over the years, then I asked a few questions. The idea clicked into place."

Her friendship was safe. *Josh* was the one who was crazy. Marisa breathed a sigh of relief and giggled nervously.

"What's the matter?"

She shook her head. If she tried to answer, she *might* become hysterical. His attractive square jaw hardened. A muscle twisted there when he looked at her as if *she* was the one who might be a couple of ounces shy of a pound. His eyes narrowed as if it had just occurred to him that he really didn't know her in the least. *She* might be crazy.

She cleared her throat. "You actually decided to get married without having a specific woman in mind?"

"I've been thinking about it for quite a while."

He looked so sincere, so serious, that she could no longer find the humor in his suggestion.

"But why?"

He spread his hands. Nice hands, she noticed—strong, solid, dependable-looking hands.

"My age," he said, ticking off one of the long graceful fingers. "Have you noticed that potential dates seem younger and younger? Sometimes asking an eligible woman out makes me feel like I'm volunteering to baby-sit."

His social life was apparently more active than hers. But she couldn't contradict him. It had been a long, long time since she'd noticed anyone her age she'd even consider going out with. Then again, since she hadn't been looking, maybe she just hadn't noticed. But Josh wasn't *that* old. He'd said thirty-six.

"I'm ready to settle down."

She watched, fascinated as he tapped another finger. It was almost as if he'd memorized a list. She roused herself from her daze. "But, Josh, you could have anyone you wanted."

"And that's part of the problem," he said passionately. "I'm tired of the chase." He looked her straight in the eye. "Good Lord, do you know what I thought when you ran into my cart at the grocery store?"

He didn't wait for her response, which was probably best since she'd been about to confess she didn't actually remember the experience.

"I thought you were trying to pick me up. I thought you were using that worn-out, cheap advice women picked up from some magazine a few years ago."

Obviously he wasn't as tired of chasing as he was of running. He must have experienced lots of females on the prowl. "But how would I have known you weren't already married?" she asked illogically.

"I haven't noticed that it matters," he said wryly.

She couldn't help her slight grin. Oh, the curse of being a drop-dead gorgeous single man. Success and self-confidence seemed to ooze from his pores. She wondered how she could have forgotten to notice such things. There probably wasn't a woman on earth who wouldn't consider him a catch.

He glanced at her and grinned. "That sounded pretty conceited, didn't it? I guess that isn't fair since I've never worn a wedding ring. Maybe women would react differently.''

''It's probably fair,'' Marisa admitted. ''I've seen some pretty aggressive techniques at the drugstore myself.'' She shrugged. ''Hey. Like the old saying goes—if you've got it, flaunt it.'' Darn. She couldn't help but like him. There was some boyish, genuine quality about his sheepish expression that reminded her of Ryan. ''Maybe you ought to buy one,'' she added.

His brows gathered over the bridge of his nose.

''A wedding ring,'' she explained.

His scowl didn't ease as he rubbed his neck. ''That wouldn't strike you as dishonest?'' He eyed her skeptically, then seemed to deflate. ''I suppose that's the polite way to say you're not interested?''

She groaned inwardly. Why did he have to ask it *that* way and talk about honesty in the same breath? ''I...you...it wouldn't work.'' She waved her hand helplessly.

''Listen. I've had time to think about this. Let me make my case and then *you* think about it. You don't have to answer me tonight.'' One corner of his mouth turned down, as if he really didn't like making that concession but knew he must.

''Okay.'' She folded her arms. ''Make your case.''

''As I see it, I'm ready to get married. It would make life infinitely more pleasant.''

She stiffened her back. *Now* he'd finally gotten to his real motive. A wife would make his life infinitely more pleasant? ''Oh?''

''No more meals alone.'' He shrugged as soon as he said it. ''Well, I guess that doesn't apply to you, but wouldn't you like to have someone to talk to at the end of the day without having to make a date and arrangements?'' He shook his head and ran an impatient hand through his hair. "I guess that doesn't apply to you, either."

She nodded sympathetically and relaxed a bit. He hadn't been suggesting that he needed someone to do wifely chores. "Ryan does make a difference." That brought another thought. "It doesn't bother you? That I have a son?"

"I like the idea. That's another of the reasons I want to get married. If I want a family—and I do—it's time. If I wait much longer, I'm going to be too old to play with my kids."

He talked as though he was afraid he'd start creaking at any moment.

"Having a kid to start with seems like it would be good practice for having more," he went on.

Boy, was he a babe in the woods if he thought of someone Ryan's age as practice—

The implication of his words suddenly sank in. Marisa felt her face grow hot and quickly looked away from him.

"I guess I didn't make that clear, either," he said softly. "I intend to have a marriage in every sense of the word."

"You mean..." she stammered. "I thought...you mean...you want a *real* marriage? I thought you wanted a marriage...of convenience."

His low chuckle brought her gaze back to his face. "You don't think that sex in a marital situation is convenient? It sounds a hell of a lot more convenient to me than any of the...liaisons I've enjoyed thus far." He reached across the table and lifted her chin. "You blush very appealingly. Makes me want to find out how far it has spread."

She could feel the heat of it spreading rapidly over every inch of her body. She leaned away from him, distressed to be reminded of the uncomfortable longings she'd managed to make herself ignore and, for the most part, forget.

He dropped his arm to the table and traced the edges of

his napkin with one long, sensuous finger. "I don't plan to rush you, Marisa. I'd give you plenty of time, all the time you need."

She gulped.

"I think you'd eventually see the physical side of marriage to me as a positive. A bonus," he said with the self-confidence she was finding more and more attractive—and daunting. "There would be other benefits for you, too."

"Like?" she managed to ask without sounding as breathless as she felt. She couldn't seem to get air into her lungs except in shallow little gasps. She wanted him to name the other benefits quickly, to blot out the erotic images filtering into her mind.

"Some of them are obvious." He started ticking off fingers again. "Financial, of course," he said softly, as if concerned he might insult her. "And raising a child by yourself—a boy, at that—can't be easy."

She found herself automatically nodding in agreement and her heart settled back to its normal pace.

"I consider myself an intelligent conversationalist. Most people consider me interesting company."

He was definitely interesting company.

"You'd find me handy to have around," he went on. "I've always liked working on my own cars and fixing household-type things." He shrugged. "That's probably a byproduct of growing up with Mr. Fix-it, but you've met my father. Give him a little duct tape and WD-40 and he can fix anything."

And he never stopped. When she'd gone to Janet's wedding, Mr. Maxwell had only quit working long enough to give Janet away. Even the two times he'd visited them at college, he'd found things around the dorm to do, including building them a loft for their room. She found herself nodding again and willed herself to quit it. If she wasn't careful, she'd find herself nodding right into accepting his irrational proposal.

"And haven't you ever wanted anything for yourself?" he asked.

"What do you mean?"

"You must have had dreams. Like you said, you didn't get a college degree to work at a drugstore. Marriage to me would give you a few choices. We could live comfortably whether you worked or not. Maybe you could pursue some dreams of your own."

She'd effectively killed her dreams eons ago by impetuously following her heart, instead of her head. Now, she probably couldn't even remember them.

"So what do *you* get out of this," she asked.

"The kind of life I want," he said without hesitation.

"You don't even know me," she said again. "Why me? It's all very flattering but…" She let her shoulders drop to indicate that an open-ended "but" was the best she could do.

"I know much of what I need to know," he contradicted. "I know you're flexible, yet persistent. You obviously made the best of things after motherhood came a little early."

She liked him all over again. That was the most diplomatic way anyone had ever chosen to refer to her unplanned teenage pregnancy—her mistake, as everyone had called it at the time. She'd never been able to think of it that way. Ryan was the best thing that had ever happened to her, even if he had forced her to rearrange the plans she'd made for her life.

"You're responsible and dependable," he went on. "You've held a job with the same company for years. I know that your parents were both teachers and that you originally wanted to be a teacher, too. Your background is similar to mine—traditional family, middle-income.''

''And that makes me good wife material?''

''It means I know more or less what to expect. And you threw in something I didn't expect—a bonus.''

She frowned.

''I didn't expect beauty.'' He said this almost reverently.

She dipped her head and knew she was blushing again. She ought to suggest he get his vision checked, but the way he'd looked at her made her *feel* beautiful.

''It never occurred to me that I would be so attracted to you,'' he said softly. ''More than ever, I'd like to marry you, Marisa Reynolds. And unless you have other plans, I know we could have a wonderful life together.''

She closed her eyes. His insanity must be contagious. For a minute she believed in fairy tales.

She looked at him again and shook her head. How could he possibly think she'd take his suggestion seriously? ''Oh, Josh. You must know this whole idea is…is crazy. It's ridiculous.''

''Why?''

''If you don't intend to rush into…other things, why rush into marriage, Josh? We could just—'' she shrugged, trying to give her heart time to calm down ''—see each other and find out what happens.''

He exhaled heavily. ''That's what I've been trying to tell you. For me, this isn't rushing. All my life I've pictured myself as a successful, stable, happily married family man. Like my father and my grandfather and who knows how many Maxwells before me. I thought I'd do things the conventional way.'' He frowned in frustration. ''I counted on it. And that's been my mistake. I've waited for it to happen, instead of deciding it was going to. I've always been able to get whatever I really wanted. I want this. And I've never failed.''

The determination in his voice made the solid booth under her feel as if it was quaking. She'd hate to be in the way of him getting something he wanted. Or giving him the bad news that he'd failed. ''But you can't—''

''So what I have to do,'' he continued as if she hadn't spoken, ''is go about getting married like I would anything else. Set a goal—marriage. Position myself to achieve it— I'm here with you and we're talking about it, aren't we?''

She nodded.

''And go after it,'' he finished.

The look he gave her sent tremors down her spine. The feeling was a cross between terror and a startling sense of anticipation. He was going after her.

Their waitress came to fill Josh's coffee cup. ''Can I get you anything else? Oh.'' She looked at Marisa with concern. ''Wasn't the salad all right?''

''It was fine. I…wasn't hungry, I guess.''

Josh urged her to have dessert. When the waitress finally left, taking with her the plates that had been pushed aside, he looked at Marisa apologetically.

''I ruined your appetite.''

She grinned. ''I think you just stunned it. I'm sure it will return.''

He shared her smile. ''I screwed up. I tend to expect everyone else to be willing to go along for the ride once I decide on a course of action. I sometimes forget I'm too intense.''

''I'll bet that makes you very good at what you do,'' she said.

He reinforced his previous statement by not even addressing her comment. ''Just promise me, Marisa,'' he said, ''that you'll think about my proposal. I'm not accepting your previous answer right now. You haven't had a chance to think about it the way I have."

She opened her mouth and he held up a hand. "Please?"

"Okay." She nodded. "I'll think about it, but I don't—"

This time he held up one finger. "You're not thinking about it."

"Okay." She clamped her mouth around the word, then leaned forward. "Does Janet know you planned to do this?"

He laughed. "I don't tell Janet much about my personal life. She tends to use it against me." He reached for his wallet and put some money on the small tray the waitress had left. "That's a benefit I hadn't thought of," he said as they stood.

She looked up at him with a question in her eyes.

"I don't tell her much because—" his gaze landed on Marisa's lips "—she tends to think I have lousy taste in women. I'm beginning to think she's right," he added in an aside. "But we both know she already approves of you."

"She'd be my sister-in-law," Marisa said, leading the way out of the restaurant. "That's a nice idea."

"I thought you might like it," he said, somewhat pleased with himself at the additional carrot he'd dangled. The amused glance they exchanged before they stepped out into the night told her they both admitted that was what he was doing.

His hand at the center of her back made her feel safe, protected. It had been a long time since she'd gone anywhere and not had to be the one in control.

She enjoyed daydreaming on their silent drive home.

"Do we need to pick up Ryan?" he asked as he neared her street.

"I usually just run across the backyard to get him."

The stress-free atmosphere she realized he'd cultivated in the past half hour dissipated as he pulled up outside the house. She chewed at her lip and hoped he didn't expect her to invite him in. Tomorrow was a workday and Ryan—

"I won't walk you in," he said, removing the tension that had started to build again. He turned, stretching his arm across the back of the seat until his hand dangled near her shoulder.

That wasn't what she expected. She expected him to resume the conversation they'd temporarily tabled at the restaurant.

"I don't want to crowd you, and I suspect that's how you'd feel if I came in."

It was exactly what she'd been thinking. She studied him in the dim light of the car. "Thank you. For everything. I really enjoyed the dinner and—"

"Since you didn't eat," he said, "I'll take that to mean the company was the highlight."

She laughed, surprised to realize she *had* enjoyed his company—wacko conversation and all. She'd smiled and laughed a lot this evening.

She reached for the door handle. "Thanks again, Josh. I did enjoy meeting you again. You're nothing like your sister," she added.

"And *that* I'll take as a compliment." His hand lightly touched her shoulder. He leaned closer. His breath was minty-sweet from one of the peppermints the waitress had left them. It warmed her cheek and sent a wave of anticipation through her. "Before you go off to ponder my suggestion, we may as well settle one more point of curiosity, don't you think?"

His lips closed gently over hers, then hovered a whisper away before he covered them tentatively again. She opened her mouth slightly, automatically under his, and he sipped, tasted, then sighed deeply as he pulled away. She tightened her grasp on the edge of the seat, afraid she might float away without something solid to hold on to.

"Mmm." The sound rumbled from his chest rather than from those tantalizing lips. It resonated to her knees and she felt almost too weak to open the door.

"I'll wait till you get in," he said quietly as he leaned across to open the door for her. The overhead light came on, spotlighting him. He was smiling. His eyelids drooped lazily over those startlingly warm brown eyes.

"Thanks." The word came out almost soundlessly. But he heard and nodded.

When she was inside, she heard his car drive away as she leaned wearily against the closed door and groaned.

She fingered her still-trembling lips. Oh, God, insanity *must* be contagious. Marrying Josh Maxwell, a man she barely knew—a man she knew to be crazy, she amended—suddenly seemed like a terrific idea.

She didn't sleep well.

At work, the day passed in a blur. She was thankful she'd arranged to leave early to take Ryan to school for preenrollment for the fall semester.

Ryan dragged his feet as they left the long lines in the school cafeteria and started home.

"What's the matter?" she asked, digging in her heavy purse for her car keys.

"I got The Bitch."

"Ryan!" Her son's pronouncement startled her so much she stumbled over nothing.

"That's what everybody calls her. Mrs. Brack," he clarified, lifting his chin slightly.

"Everyone but you," Marisa told his back as he went to

the passenger side. She unlocked her door, then reached across from inside to let him in. "*We* don't talk that way."

"You do some of the time," Ryan muttered belligerently, and slumped into the passenger seat.

Marisa started the car, scowling as she tried to remember using that language. She just didn't. Maybe one of her friends had said it in a conversation, and Ryan had overheard.

She shook her head irritably. He'd gotten her off the subject. "If you think you've heard me say something like that, I'm certain you were mistaken, but I'll watch myself very carefully," she told him, negotiating out of the pothole-riddled parking lot. "But why don't you like Mrs. Brack?"

"She's mean. And she hates boys."

"Oh. You know that for a fact. You've had her so many times."

He glanced over at her sheepishly. "Everybody says so."

"Ryan, you cannot listen to everyone else. You have to form your own opinion."

He sighed wearily and slid deeper in the seat. "I know."

"You have to give Mrs. Brack a chance, just like she has to give you one. You don't want her to expect the worst of you just because you're a boy, do you?"

"No."

"So is it fair to expect the worst of her just because everyone says she's…says she isn't very nice?"

"No."

"Come on." She nudged him. "Cheer up. Who did Brian get?"

"He hasn't enrolled yet. He'll probably get Miss Jackson. He's always lucky."

Brian lived a charmed life, according to her son. "Aren't

you glad he's your best friend, then? Since he shares his luck with you?'' Marisa had to smile.

Whatever Ryan mumbled was lost in the noise of rush-hour traffic. She sobered as Ryan reached and turned up the volume on the radio. Brian's father was one reason Ryan believed in Brian's luck. Very few Saturdays went by that Bob Hanson wasn't out playing catch with his two sons, or swimming, or taking them to a baseball game. Ryan was almost always included. He didn't know how lucky he was.

She reached across to ruffle his hair, hesitated, then did it, anyway. Shoot, she'd compromise. She wouldn't touch him when other people were around. She refused to give up touching him altogether.

She grinned as he did his ''Aw, Mom,'' bit and hunkered into the far corner.

''How 'bout if we get a big bag of greasy tacos to take home for dinner?''

That brought him up in his seat and brought back his smile. ''Cool.''

''Thought you'd like the idea.'' She turned on her signal to change lanes as her mind changed gears, going back to the subject she hadn't been able to get very far from today. Braking for the red light ahead, she glanced at her growing son again. She wondered if his ''cool'' response to everything would apply if she said, *How 'bout if I marry Mr. Maxwell and we bring him home to play father to you?*

She grimaced and released a frustrated sigh. Why was she even thinking about it? It was a nutty idea. Or was it? At least Josh expected her to think about it from a practical perspective. He hadn't asked her to make an emotional decision. Even the kiss had been a common-sense, curiosity check on their physical reaction to each other. She gnawed at her lower lip and wriggled restlessly. He definitely appealed to *her*.

The drive-through line at the Mexican restaurant was long. Marisa pulled into one of the parking slots.

"Are we eating here?" Ryan asked.

"Look at the line. I thought I'd let you run in and get them," she said, pulling a five from her wallet. "Get half a dozen. I'll wait here."

"Cool."

He got out, then leaned back in. "Shall I get pop?"

"Nah." She shook her head. "We have some at home." She watched him hurry importantly to the front door.

She'd tried hard not to do the you're-the-little-man-of-the-house thing she'd seen other single mothers do, but she was trying to give Ryan more and more responsibility. Would it be such a bad idea to give him a father now? He would soon be the age when she wouldn't be able to teach him some things, things she didn't understand herself. Man things.

She caught herself smiling again. What kind of man things would Josh Maxwell teach her son? To propose to an almost total stranger when you decided it was the right time in your life to get married.

Ryan had liked Josh. "Liked" could be too mild a word. The way her son had looked up at him—

She gave a start as Ryan opened the passenger door and handed in the white, already grease-spotted bag.

"What happened, Mom?"

Marisa frowned at him as he closed the door.

"You were grinning like something funny happened," Ryan said.

"Oh. Um, I was just thinking."

He shrugged, turned up the radio again and fastened his seat belt.

Yeah, Ryan, something funny happened. Josh Maxwell asked me to marry him. What do you think?

She wanted to tell him. Get another opinion. Have someone reconfirm for her that Josh Maxwell was nuts for asking and that she'd be nuts to accept.

She wanted to call Janet. But by the time she'd picked up Ryan at Evie and Bob Hanson's the previous night and supervised the nightly rituals to get Ryan to bed, it was too late. By this morning, she'd realized it wouldn't be fair to Josh to confide in his sister. If he wanted Janet to know, he would have told her.

The phone was ringing when they walked in the door. Ryan hurried to answer it as she opened a can of green beans, dumped them in a bowl and set them heating in the microwave.

When his conversation degenerated into "Cool" and "Bummer," Marisa started setting the table.

"Yeah, I got The Bi—" Ryan's gaze caught hers "—Mrs. Brack." Marisa hid her smile. The friend at the other end of the line—Brian, she assumed—obviously was assigned the poor, unfortunate woman, too. It seemed to cheer her son immeasurably.

Getting the green beans from the microwave, Marisa sat down at the table to wait. *She* would have made a great teacher, she thought. Somehow, she just knew her students wouldn't be talking about her the way they were talking about the mysterious Mrs. Brack. Marisa would have been a Miss Jackson, someone students looked forward to getting.

Marisa started to take a sip of the soda she'd poured for them, then paused in the act.

Josh had said marrying him would give her a chance to pursue her dreams. Teaching had been the dream she'd had all her life—before Ryan. She'd wanted to follow in her father and mother's footsteps.

She glanced at her son, the son she loved so much. She loved the way his fair hair flopped as he nodded his head. She loved the way he could smile only seconds after learning of one of life's disasters—like finding out he'd been assigned the ogre, Mrs. Brack. But his very presence in her life had made her dreams impossible.

Marisa's father had been the first to point out that no one would hire an unwed mother to teach their children, especially their teenagers. She'd wanted to teach speech and drama in high school.

By the time Ryan was born, she accepted the truth of her father and mother's declarations. She knew no one would hire her as a teacher.

But if she was married…

An earthquake seemed to start in her soul. Her hand covered her mouth, and everything around her became surreal. She'd never allowed herself to think of the distant future.

The other day, she'd overheard Ryan say, "When I go to college…" to Brian. College and the future had seemed so far away. But nine years would pass in a flash, the way the past nine years had.

What would she do then? Would she be like Josh Maxwell, longing to have someone there at the end of the day? Would she be eating alone?

She could hear Ryan ending his conversation. She knew the food on the table was getting cold. She heard a step on the creaky old porch and expected the doorbell to peal a moment later. It all seemed like a dream. The future loomed larger than reality. What was she going to do with it?

She was twenty-eight years old. She hadn't thought of teaching in years. She'd put that dream away with the rest of her childish things. But surely it wasn't too late to pursue it. If she was married—

"Mom?" She heard the click as Ryan hung up the phone. "Aren't you going to see who's at the door?"

Marisa gave a start.

"Never mind," he called wearily. "I'll get it."

Marisa roused herself to follow Ryan to the wide arch separating the living room from the kitchen.

She couldn't see who was there. Ryan opened the door, leaving the storm door between himself and the visitor latched the way she'd taught him.

She glanced at the drive, then to the street in front of the house. She saw the car she'd ridden in the night before, just as she heard Josh's voice.

"Ryan, my man, ready for that rematch?" he asked.

"Gosh, Mr. Maxwell, I'm ready whenever you are." Ryan opened the door. "Come in."

Chapter Four

She stood by the TV, between the living room and the kitchen. Her mouth hung open in surprise. She looked frazzled...

...and good! Even frazzled, she looked appealing.

No. Josh cleared his throat. He couldn't let himself be distracted by her beauty like he'd been the previous evening. He had to stick exactly to his plan.

Last night he'd planned what he was going to say, even made lists of the pros and cons. But he hadn't actually thought out his approach, formed a strategy.

He'd blown it. He wasn't going to do that again. The plan for tonight was to focus on the kid. Let Marisa see the logic of providing her son with a father. A good father, he added. He knew he'd be a great one.

Forcing a casual smile, he looked back down at Ryan. "We'd better ask your mom if it's okay."

Ryan look hopefully at Marisa.

Josh noted the way she smoothed her golden-brown hair. Good sign. The light circles under her eyes were probably another good sign, he thought smugly. Thinking about his proposal had kept her awake last night.

"We were just getting ready to eat," she said apologetically. "I'd ask you to join us, but—"

"We've got six tacos, Mom. That's two for everyone."

Her gaze went from Ryan to Josh and back again. "I don't mind if you don't, Ryan. But it's been a while since you thought two tacos were enough."

Ryan rolled his eyes. "You made some other stuff," he said.

"And I'll provide dessert after our rematch," Josh offered. "I'll take everyone for ice cream later."

Ryan's smile grew even wider. "Cool."

"Go wash your hands," Marisa told him, and he ran from the room. "You may be sorry," she warned Josh, avoiding his eyes. "I was trying to rescue you from Ryan's enthusiasm. We picked up tacos on our way home. They're small. And they've been sitting on the table getting cold for the past ten minutes."

"I should have called," he apologized. "I didn't mean to interrupt your dinner. I intended to go on home if Ryan was busy. But I did promise... I didn't want to disappoint him."

Her smile softened. She met his eyes.

"I didn't come to pressure you," he added for good measure as he heard Ryan clattering down the hall, returning.

"Then I'm glad you came." Some of the tension left her face. "Come on." Turning her back, she led the way to the kitchen. "I'll set another place at the table."

He used the opportunity to verify that her butt was as cute as he'd thought it was in the grocery store. Her legs weren't bad, either, he noted as he took the seat she indicated. But it was her wide-eyed innocence that fascinated him, he decided. He was pleased with himself all over again for choosing her—and more determined than ever to get her to agree to become his wife.

Marisa was quiet during the meal, carefully studying him when she didn't think he would see, lost in her own thoughts. Josh directed his energies to courting Ryan with guy-talk.

"You played for Ohio State in college?" Ryan's eyes filled with awe. "Mom? Did you hear that?"

"Till my senior year when I blew my knee out. That pretty much ended my idea of making a career of it."

Ryan's jaw dropped in stunned appreciation. "You were going to go pro?"

"Who knows if it would have worked out?" He lifted a shoulder. "But everyone thought I'd at least be picked in the draft."

Ryan turned grim. "Everyone says I'm too small to play football."

Josh shot Marisa a look to see if she was part of "everyone." It wouldn't do to encourage the boy if she was one of those mothers who didn't want her kid playing football, for whatever reason.

Either the conversation didn't bother her or she hadn't been listening. He took one of Ryan's hands, examining it. "If you grow into these, I'd say there's a good chance you won't be small forever. And size isn't everything." Josh smiled at him. "You going to play this fall?"

"They only have city league for my age," Ryan grumbled.

"But that's great experience." Josh glanced at Marisa again to see if he was stepping on any toes. "Maybe I can give you a few pointers."

She smiled—at Ryan.

"Gosh. Would you?"

"Sure," he agreed, hoping for an affectionate smile of his own. Instead, Marisa stiffened. Maybe it was time to change the subject. "Are you ready for school?" Josh asked.

Ryan made a horrible face and launched into a detailed, enthusiastic description of the joys of summer.

Josh listened, liking the kid more and more. He was well behaved. Nice manners. Well, they seemed nice for a kid his age. Josh couldn't quite remember what he'd been like at nine, but several of Ryan's comments brought the memories closer.

"We're going to catch lightning bugs tonight," Ryan said. "We're going to make a lantern if we can catch enough. We already have some."

The boy had a few rough edges, but those would smooth out when he was a little older, more sure of himself. Having a man around would help build his confidence, Josh thought. He hoped Marisa saw the same things.

As if on cue, she rose and reached for Josh's plate. "It's your turn to clear the table," Marisa told Ryan, "but I'll let you off the hook tonight since you have such an important rematch."

Ryan whooped and was out of his chair, heading toward the TV. "I owe you, Mom."

"I know." She grinned affectionately at her son's back, and Josh felt another momentary tug of jealousy. Especially when her expression dimmed and became wary when she looked at him.

"I really can't tell you how much this means to him. And football pointers..." She let the quietly spoken words drift, unfinished.

"You don't mind, then?"

Her smile returned, only this one was just for him.

He felt his own smile turn up a notch or two and hoped it was the one women found charming. He was afraid it was too tense.

"Sometimes I worry that…" She paused, searching for words. "Sometimes, people make promises lightly." Again she paused. "Since you're here tonight to keep your promise about the Nintendo game…well, I guess I don't have to worry that you'll keep this promise, too. I just hate it when he's disappointed."

"I thought maybe you were troubled by the football," he admitted. "Some mothers don't want their sons anywhere near the game."

She grinned, shaking her head. "He loves it—thanks to my father. Since Ryan's determined to play, I like the idea of him having a little more help than I can give him. The more he knows, the less likely he is to get hurt. Right?"

"Right." Damn. He wanted to kiss her. Her lips were parted in a tantalizing way. She kept surprising him and unintentionally seducing him and—

"You ready, Mr. Maxwell?" Ryan called.

"I'm ready," Josh answered over his shoulder.

"Thanks," Marisa said softly. "I really do appreciate it."

"Then we're even." He lifted one shoulder. "Thanks for letting me share your tacos. It's been a long time since I've been a stranger in a strange place. I wasn't looking forward to an evening alone." Without waiting for her response, he swiveled and sauntered into the living room where Ryan had set up the game.

He felt Marisa's gaze on him. It took all his willpower not to look and see if he was imagining it.

Marisa stayed out of the way while Ryan and Josh played their challenge match. She changed from her work clothes into a nice pair of shorts, started a load of laundry, then took refuge in the "guest room," which had gradually become her office since they so rarely had guests.

From time to time Ryan hollered excitedly. When Josh responded or said something himself, his deep voice reminded her of the low, heavy counter-beat of bass on the stereo.

Almost without thought, she pulled her old college catalog from the bookcase and thumbed through it. She sank into the easy chair next to the small desk, wondered what she'd have to do to finish her teaching degree. How long would it take?

She'd have to do her student teaching for certain.

A quiet thump startled her. She looked up to find Josh watching her from the open door, his fist poised to knock again if she hadn't heard. Her face warmed as she hurriedly closed the catalog, which at some point she'd cradled against her chest while she drifted off into some dreamworld.

"Ryan thought you'd be in here. I was dispatched to find you so we can make our ice-cream run. He went to his friend's to crow about his latest victory."

"Would you mind if I went back to school?" she asked.

Josh blinked. A crease appeared between his brows, then disappeared just as quickly. A devastating smile started at one corner of his lips, then spread until it lit his entire face. "Tonight?"

Her flush deepened, but she managed to answer his grin. "No. Not tonight." She carefully placed the catalog back in the bookcase beside her chair. "I mean...I just thought if..."

"I assume you mean when we get married?" He took a step into the room.

"Yes, that's what I mean." As soon as she said it, she realized he'd said *when,* not *if.*

"If that's what you want to do, I think it's a great idea."

"I've always wanted to teach," she said. "But it wasn't practical when... I'd need to go back a semester or two. I'd have to do my student teaching."

His grin widened even more. Somehow, during the course of the conversation, he'd moved across the room and now stood dauntingly close to her chair. "Are you saying you've decided?"

Her mouth felt drier than two-day-old toast. "I'm thinking about it." She concentrated on removing the leg she'd folded from beneath the other knee.

He held out a hand to help her up. "Anything I can do to influence the decision?"

She put her hand in his and he tugged, bringing her face-to-face with him. They were inches apart and her breath caught in her throat. "You just did."

His eyebrows raised. His low chuckle sounded very pleased. The pleasant sound helped confirm that marrying him wasn't such a bad idea. "That's a yes?"

Less than twenty-four hours ago, she'd thought he was crazy. With a great deal of effort, she reined in her impulses. She licked her lips. "It's an 'I'm seriously thinking about it.' But I need to do more. I need more time to—"

"Mom?" Ryan's voice interrupted.

Josh squeezed the fingers he still held and turned toward the door just as Ryan appeared.

She quickly disengaged her fingers from Josh's, but not before Ryan's eyes practically popped out of his head.

If he wasn't flushed from his excitement to begin with, he would have blushed now. She blessed him as he looked from one to the other of them but didn't comment. He managed a squeaky "We ready to go?"

"*We* are. You aren't," Marisa said in her most official Mom voice. "What have you been doing?"

Ryan glanced down at himself and grimaced. "Brian tackled me." He brushed dried grass clippings off himself and all over the floor.

"In the bathroom," she ordered, her thumb pointing the way as if he didn't know it. "Wash up. And comb your hair," she called out for good measure as he hurried to comply. "I'm sorry," she said to Josh.

He smiled. "I have a feeling this might be an adventure."

She didn't think he was referring to going for ice cream. "Living with a boy his age is definitely that," she confirmed. "Are you sure *you* aren't having second thoughts?"

Josh's dark gaze caught hers and held. He knew she wasn't talking about ice cream, either. "None." He reached purposefully for her hand and laced his fingers through hers. "We may as well keep giving him the impression he had a minute ago," he said dryly, lifting their entwined hands, turning them one way, then the other.

The contrast between his tanned one with its sprinkling of dark hair and her pale, smooth one was somehow erotic. Her pulse quickened. "In the long run, letting him think something might be developing between us will make it easier to explain if—" he emphasized the *if* "—you decide to marry me." He gave her hand a reassuring squeeze.

The warm sensations running from his hand to hers spread upward and outward, making Marisa wonder if the central air-conditioning was doing its job. Once again her lungs were fighting to pull air into them, and they weren't doing a very good job. "Let's wait on the porch." Her words sounded as breathless as she felt.

Josh nodded at the suggestion.

"We'll wait for you outside, Ryan," she called toward the bathroom as they started down the hall.

"'kay, Mom. Be there in a minute."

Opening the screen door gave her an excuse to untangle her hand from Josh's. She sucked in the fresh air that was, at last, starting to cool.

The August heat had taken a toll on the yards around the neighborhood. Except for a couple of lawns that were watered regularly, the green grass was marred by coarse, brown edges.

With a broad gesture, Marisa invited him to sit on the step. "Every spring, I promise myself to get a porch swing," she said. "But I never get around to it."

He waited for her to sit before he eased down beside her. "Having a man around to do things like that might be handy."

"I could do it," she said.

"But you haven't," he reminded her.

Having a man around… She and Ryan were fine without one. But every word this man uttered made her question that assumption.

She was thankful when Ryan burst through the front door, letting the screen door slam behind him.

"We gonna walk?" He leaped from the edge of the porch to the ground.

Josh looked at her and shrugged. "Where's the nearest ice-cream joint?"

"We go to Express Stop," Ryan answered for her.

"But we don't have to," Marisa said. "It's about three blocks. But they don't have a wide selection. Just three basic choices and a flavor of the month."

"As long as one of them is chocolate." Josh rose and smoothed the wrinkles out of his dark slacks. "That's what I usually end up with, anyway."

"Me, too," Marisa admitted as he glanced pointedly at her son, then offered her his hand again.

"Me, three," Ryan said, chortling, hyped as much by the hand-holding thing as he was by his joke, she suspected. He took off across the yard and she breathed a sigh of relief that he'd kept his mouth shut about it.

They strolled, hand in hand, behind the boy, catching up from time to time as Ryan paused to examine something or flip clumsy cartwheels across the neighbors' lawns.

This must be how it feels to have a husband, Marisa thought, glancing over at the man beside her.

All her adult life, she'd watched her friends and neighbors walking, playing, sharing their children with a spouse. Except for an occasional lonely twinge, she hadn't been envious. Ryan was her family. She'd accepted the fate she'd chosen, even if the choice had been unintentional.

"You and Ryan must do this a lot," Josh said, interrupting her thoughts.

She frowned. "Oh, you mean going for ice cream?"

He nodded.

"We usually go about twice a week in the summer. It gets Ryan away from the TV and Nintendo and both of us out of the house."

"And I thought I was suggesting something novel."

"This is novel. We usually ride our bikes, get some exercise first, so we can justify the treat."

"This is exercise," he said with a grin, adding, "Maybe I'll have to get a bicycle." He studied her legs and she immediately tripped over her own feet.

Putting an arm around her waist to steady her, he laughed. "I'll have to make a note to get the city to fix that. Defending lawsuits because of cracks in the sidewalk doesn't sound like a pleasant way to start my new job."

She could stand having a man around who made excuses

for her clumsiness. He made her feel uncomfortably impatient for more of his touch when he dropped his arm and reached for her hand again.

She stopped suddenly, turning to him. "Josh, I—"

He pressed a finger lightly against her lips. "I didn't come tonight to pressure you. Think about this as long as you need to."

How did he do that? How did he read her mind? Maybe he was having second thoughts. She searched his expression and didn't find the slightest hint of hesitation there.

"Mom? Are you guys coming?" Ryan called from the corner. Even from a quarter of a block away, Marisa heard his exasperated sigh.

"Later," Josh said quietly. "I don't want to rush you." His gaze lingered on her mouth and he swept a gentle finger along the curve of her lower lip suggestively. "At least not about your decision," he added, hinting that in other matters, he wouldn't mind rushing her at all.

"We're coming, Ryan," he called, not taking his eyes from her. "Later," he promised again then released her. He caught her hand and whistled quietly as he led her to where a frustrated Ryan waited at the corner.

Marisa was sitting at the kitchen table when Ryan finished his shower and joined her. "What're you doing?"

"Paying bills," she answered absently, then made the mistake of looking up to see what was dripping. "Ryan. Go get your towel." His wet hair was dripping all over her and the checks she'd already written. "And bring a comb," she called as he ran to do as he was bid.

She blotted the drops of water off the checks with a paper towel and wondered if she dared add yet another item to the list of things she had to constantly remind him of.

"Come here," she said unnecessarily as he returned with

the towel. She wrapped the towel around his wet head. "I'm delighted that you're finally washing your hair without being specifically told," she said as she rubbed his hair. "Would it be too much to ask you to dry it, too?"

"You do it better," he mumbled.

"Oh, I do, huh?" She gently massaged his head and smiled.

"Uh-huh."

She draped the damp towel over the chair beside her and held out her hand for the comb. She turned him to face her and met the blue eyes fixed on her face. "Do you like him, Mom?"

"Who?" She knew as soon as she said it that the question didn't ring true. "Mr. Maxwell, you mean?"

Obviously her son didn't think so, either. He rolled his eyes. "He said we could call him Josh," Ryan reminded her. "Do you like him?"

She nodded. "He seems to be a very nice man."

Ryan gazed at her skeptically, and she felt her face grow warm under his scrutiny. "You were holdin' hands," he reminded her.

"I...yes," she admitted. Honesty had always been the right policy with her son. Even before he could talk, he'd been able to fix her with a look that cut through any pretension.

"Are you ever gonna get married?" Ryan stunned her by abruptly honing in on the real subject.

"I...I..." She changed tactics. "Do you want me to?"

His thin shoulders lifted. "I dunno. Maybe. Sometimes."

"What brought this subject up?"

"Him. Holding your hand."

Marisa set the comb aside and gently touched Ryan's cheek. Breathing in his soapy clean scent, she suddenly missed the sweet little-boy smell of him that had somehow diminished in the past few years.

"You've never held anyone's hand before," Ryan said. "Besides mine and Grandma or Grandpa's," he added as if he had to set the record straight.

"I've never had anyone else's hand to hold," she pointed out.

"Yeah. Why?" His face furrowed in a uniquely Ryan scowl.

She ruffled his still-damp hair and then picked up the comb again to repair the damage. "Who would you suggest I hold hands with?" she asked lightly.

"You're awful pretty, Mom."

She smiled. How did "awful" and "pretty" ever get connected in the same sentence? She'd never understood that peculiar yet common phrase. "You're prejudiced."

"My friends think so, too."

"Oh?" She raised her eyebrows. "Since when have you and your friends been discussing pretty women?"

She was almost relieved when he looked disgusted. "We were just talking about you," he said. "Brian said you were pretty, and Jeff and Buddy said so, too."

"Well, I'll have to thank th—"

"Lots of guys look at you like Josh does," Ryan interrupted, obviously refusing to be led too far from the subject.

"Like what?"

Ryan backed away half a step, and Marisa realized maybe her question had been a little intense. "Like what?" she asked again, much more casually.

Ryan shrugged. "Like he really likes looking at you," he said, ending on a note that suggested he certainly didn't understand it.

"Oh."

"Don'tcha wanna get married sometime?"

Marisa sighed heavily. "A long time ago I used to think about it lots," she admitted. She rested a hand on his shoulder. "Then I had you and I didn't need anyone else, so I didn't need to think about it anymore."

Ryan's expressive face turned pensive.

"You didn't really answer *my* question," she said.

"What?"

"You didn't say if you *wanted* me to get married."

"Oh."

"Do you think it would be nice to have a father?"

Ryan frowned. "But if you got married, he...wouldn't really be my father, would he? Not like Brian's dad."

"Well, not exactly," Marisa admitted, understanding his confusion. She'd always honestly answered his questions about the birds and bees. He knew the biological facts, whether or not he fully understood them. "But," she added brightly, "I wouldn't marry anyone I couldn't trust to be as much a father to you as he was a husband to me."

Ryan just looked confused. And weary of the whole subject. He probably regretted bringing it up. "Josh would be a good father, wouldn't he?" he surprised her by asking.

From everything she'd seen, Josh would probably be excellent. "I think he probably would," she admitted.

As if her confirmation was all he needed, Ryan nodded. "I bet he would."

"And now you, my sweet Ryan—" she kissed his forehead and he made a pretense of shrinking away "—had better get to bed."

She wasn't sure if his "Aw, Mom," was for the kiss or for the idea of going to bed. The kiss he absently wiped away.

"You'd have to kiss him, wouldn't you?" Ryan looked worried.

"Who?"

"Josh. If you married him."

His remark took her breath away. Ryan's matter-of-fact way of cramming the two subjects they'd been discussing together always amazed her. And she'd already been having trouble concentrating on paying the bills because she'd been—irrationally—irritated when Josh didn't even hint that he'd like to kiss her when he left after the ice cream.

She stammered for a moment while Ryan eyed her with interest. "If I married anyone," she finally managed, then amended it immediately, "I wouldn't marry anyone if I didn't *want* to kiss him."

The face Ryan made told her exactly what he thought of that idea. "Why would you want to kiss anyone?"

"Well—"

"Unless they paid you," he added.

"What do you mean?"

For a second he looked as if he would gag. "Debi Darcy said she'd pay me a dollar to kiss her."

Marisa had to work hard not to smile. "So did you?"

"I'm thinkin' about it," he said a little belligerently.

"Then you probably shouldn't do it," Marisa said quietly as several things clicked in her mind.

He frowned.

"If you don't want to kiss someone unless you're paid," she continued, "you probably shouldn't do it at all. Like marrying someone. If you don't *want* to marry someone because you like them and want to be with them, you definitely shouldn't marry them for any sort of gain."

The look Ryan gave her changed from confusion to total bewilderment.

"And it's far past time for you to get to bed," Marisa said, pulling him tightly against her. "We have to get up a little early to pack your lunch for your field trip,'' she reminded him.

''Oh, yeah.'' He pushed away and was ready to escape to his room.

''Can I at least have a kiss?'' She pointed to her cheek.

He instantly complied and she heaved an exaggerated sigh of relief. ''Whew!'' She wiped her brow as he looked at her questioningly. ''I was afraid I was going to have to get my purse out now that your kisses are so valuable.''

''Aw, Mom.'' He grinned and started to shuffle away.

''Hey. When you start making the really big dough for passing those out, maybe you can pay some of the bills around here,'' she called to his departing back.

She heard the grin in his second ''Aw, Mom.''

And she had her logical answer for Josh.

Chapter Five

Josh hoped his new strategy was working. Before he did the sales pitch the other night, he should have considered how women's minds seemed to work. He should have wooed Marisa, instead of being impatient and honest.

The games with Ryan the other night, the ice cream, not kissing her good-night—*that* had all been a stroke of brilliance on his part. He thought. He hoped. He could still picture the look of bafflement on her face as he'd taken his leave when they'd returned home after getting ice cream. He'd said he should be going and she'd checked to see what Ryan was doing, then automatically turned her face up toward his. And he hadn't taken the bait. Or seen her for a couple of days.

He smiled as he pulled up in front of her house. Who would have guessed the magnetic pull between them would have been so good? He wondered briefly if it was luck or if it was a mind-set he'd created once he'd decided to marry her.

Stepping out of the car, he ran a finger around his stifling collar, straightened his tie and tugged his starched white cuffs into place. After smoothing the creases in his slacks, he buttoned his suit coat and willed the evidence of his thoughts of her to go away. He shouldn't seem too hungry to see her now.

His foot hit the first step of the porch, and Ryan opened the front door. "Mom will be ready in a minute," he muttered. He wandered out and kicked a nonexistent stone from the edge of the porch.

"What's the matter, pal?" Josh dropped a companionable hand on the boy's shoulder.

"Nothin'." Ryan shrugged his hand away.

Josh swallowed a sigh. This was a complication they didn't need if they were to make it to the mayor's reception in time, he thought, glancing at his watch.

"That's an awfully long face for nothing."

Ryan ignored him.

Josh sounded like his father, he realized, but he couldn't think of anything else to say.

He was relieved when Marisa came out. Relieved and hot and bothered all over again. She looked... He couldn't think of an adequate description. She'd chosen a dress of some lightweight material with a flared skirt that ignited his imagination. With every high-heeled step, the hem swayed and played a subtle peekaboo, taunting him with the mouth-watering prospect of seeing more of her shapely legs. A waist-length jacket lent a businesslike touch to the scooped neckline that flirted with showing cleavage.

Her hair gleamed like fine polished brass above the beige collar and circled her face like a halo. Her eyes glowed with anticipation. "I feel so important," she said nervously.

"I've never been to one of the mayor's highly publicized receptions. And I'm going with the guest of honor."

He smiled ruefully. "Like I said last night, it's just one of those official things to introduce me to community leaders I need to know."

"And like *I* said, I've never been one of the people anyone needs to know." She wrinkled her nose. "Do you think this is appropriate?" She turned in a circle, giving him a tantalizing longer look at her thighs, instead of the slight glimpse he'd had a minute ago.

"Perfect. Not a soul will look at me." The huskiness in his voice startled him. He cleared his throat, then checked the time. "And we'd probably better be going, or the guest of honor and his date will be late."

"See, I told you," Ryan murmured belligerently from the perch he'd taken on the side of the porch.

Marisa looked at him warningly. "We've already discussed this, Ryan," she said. "Now, you'd better get going. Evie promised to hold supper for you. You wouldn't want them all to starve, waiting." She leaned over to kiss him, then changed her mind and placed a lingering pat on the back of his neck. "See you later." She glanced at Josh, a question in her eyes.

"About midnight," he said.

"Around midnight," she repeated to her son. "If it looks like it'll be any later than that, tell Evie I'll call her."

Ryan sighed heavily, hopped down and, his shoulders slumped, shuffled toward the backyard.

"Shall we go?" Josh asked when she seemed lost in thought.

She turned abruptly and gave him one of her dazzling smiles. "Let's."

"What's wrong with Ryan?" He took her arm possessively as they started down the steps. The long sleeves of her jacket disappointed him. His fingertips tingled with the desire to see whether her smooth skin was as silky and warm as he remembered.

"You told him he could go with us the next time we went out. He's upset."

"I should have thought of that."

"This is business. He knows it," Marisa said. "But when you're his age, I don't think understanding something—which he does—is the same thing as accepting it. He'll get over it," she added dryly. She grinned up at him as he held the car door for her. "You certainly didn't help things by calling me your date."

"Ah." Josh's eyes lit with understanding. "That's what his 'See, I told you' was all about. You told him it wasn't a date?"

She waited for him to get settled in the driver's seat before answering. "I told him there was a big difference between a date and accompanying someone to a business engagement. Nine-year-olds take things very literally. But it won't take you too long to discover that yourself."

Josh started the car. His hand hesitated over the keys in the ignition, then fell to his side as he turned to her. "That sounds like an answer," he said, almost surprised to find he could talk. His heart had jumped to his throat. "You've made a decision?" He felt the urge to run his damp palms down the legs of his slacks.

Marisa's frown slowly grew into a weak smile. "I think I have."

"And?" He held his breath.

For some inexplicable reason, her nervous giggle made his own nerves settle. "Silly question, huh?" He faced her, one arm behind her on the back of the seat. "Your statement sounds like you expect me to be around a certain nine-year-old long enough to discover the way his mind works."

"I think I do." Her voice and her words were hesitant.

"But?"

"What *do* you expect of me?"

The words rolled out impulsively. He pondered the question, certain he had to get the answer right. "Companionship," he started. "A...friendly partnership? All the things I told you the other night." His impatience got the best of him. "All the things a man expects from a wife."

"Except love?" she asked in a low tone, glancing up finally, pinning him with her innocent gaze.

"I'll settle for a healthy dose of like," he said. "We can build on that, don't you think?"

She nodded shyly.

"I wouldn't mind hearing an answer," he added softly. "Just to make sure I haven't jumped to any erroneous conclusions."

That brought her startled eyes to his, then she stared down at the hands she'd folded together in her lap. He watched her breasts rise and fall as she took a deep breath. "I've decided I will marry you, Josh." Her voice was a mere whisper.

"Good." His heart hopped around inside his chest. He didn't want to overreact and scare her off. "Good," he said again. He had to do something to express his pleasure. Gently picking up her hands from her lap, he kissed the lightly polished fingertips of one hand, then the other. Her hands were as silky smooth as they looked. His body shook with the effort to keep his own relieved sigh inaudible.

After one more heartfelt "Good," he glanced at his watch. "And we're going to be late." Putting the car into gear, he drove smoothly away from the curb.

He glanced her way again, only to find her concentration once again locked on her folded hands. "At least we're late for a very good reason. Something important."

A slight smile loosened the corner of her compressed lips. "And we'll discuss the details later?" she asked.

"Later." The word was filled with promise. He caught himself whistling along with the CD. Everything was working out just like he'd planned. Better, he amended. Yes, things were going to be even better than he'd planned.

And they could announce their impending marriage tonight.

"We can announce it tonight!"

"No." Marisa looked horrified.

"No? You aren't sure?"

She shook her head, then nodded almost immediately. "I am," she protested. "But we can't announce it until we tell Ryan and my parents. And yours," she added. "And Janet."

"I see what you mean. It wouldn't be good for them to hear it secondhand."

"Or until we discuss the details," she said. "I won't feel really good about the decision until we work out some of the details."

"Lousy idea," he quickly concurred. "Announcing it tonight," he added when she looked up at him. His comment replaced the concern on her face with a smile. Just what he'd hoped for. He turned his attention back to the road.

One lousy kiss on the hand? That was his way of showing his pleasure that she'd agreed to marry him?

Marisa felt irritated. And let down. And really, really stupid. Hadn't one of her biggest worries been about what he might expect from her? So now she was upset with a lukewarm kiss on the hand, instead of…?

She pressed her fingers against her lips, willing them to quit tingling. One silly little kiss he'd given her that first night, and now she seemed addicted to the idea of feeling his mouth on hers just one more time. She wanted to know exactly what he'd done to her thought processes. After everything she'd told herself about thinking about his proposal logically, his kiss had been the deciding factor. After what she'd told Ryan, how could it not be? But that was a practical consideration, she told herself for the umpteenth time. It wouldn't be practical to marry someone who didn't appeal to you.

She'd needed him to kiss her again for reassurance.

He pulled up outside the hotel where the reception was taking place and waited for a valet to come park his car. When no one came immediately, he touched her shoulder lightly, yanking her from the daze she was in.

The look he gave her was indulgent. "Second thoughts?"

"You didn't even kiss me."

He looked dumbfounded.

"To seal the bargain," she stammered. If the heat in her face was anything to go by, she was certain her skin was flaming red.

His soft laugh was husky, triumphant. His arms enfolded her, bringing her to his chest. "The trouble is—" he dipped his head and grazed the spot right below her ear with a whisper "—I'm afraid to, sweet Marisa. I'm afraid I won't want to stop."

As if to contradict himself, he pressed his lips tenderly against hers. It took Marisa a second to realize the heat that rushed over her came from someone opening the door of the car. At least part of it did. The other she'd think about later.

But he'd definitely reconfirmed what she'd decided last night. She wanted him to kiss her. She liked being with him, an ingredient she couldn't marry him without. She wasn't sure it was enough for a marriage, but it was a start.

Josh opened his own door and hurried around to give the red-coated young man who'd opened hers his keys.

"I have no desire whatsoever to go to this reception," he said as he squeezed into the same section of revolving door. "I can think of lots I'd rather do," he added as they came to an abrupt stop in the marble-lined lobby on the other side.

His arm draped around her waist and pulled her to his side. They stopped beside the concierge desk to find out what room the reception was in. He didn't release her even as they started down the stairs the man at the desk had directed them to.

Marisa glanced up at Josh when they reached the bottom, waiting for him to indicate which way they should go. His gaze fell to her mouth again. She felt his warmth block out the chill of the hotel's air-conditioning. And she hoped he was going to kiss her again.

Until she heard someone call his name. "Oh, there you are, Josh." An attractive woman started toward them. As she drew closer, Marisa recognized the mayor. She was older than she looked on TV, Marisa noted as Josh introduced them.

"Josh's fiancée?" Alana asked as she shook Marisa's hand.

Marisa's gaze jolted to Josh.

"Not officially," Josh corrected smoothly. "Yet," he added with a growing smile.

"Oh? Have I let the cat out of the bag?" She smiled at Marisa but didn't look the least apologetic. "You still haven't asked her?"

"She's said yes," Josh answered with a cocky arrogance

Marisa found appealing. "But we haven't told our families. Or anyone else," he added.

The mayor looked even more pleased. "Then I get to be the first to congratulate you? I love being on the cutting edge of the most important news," she said. "This is so exciting." She ushered them toward a room down the wide hall. Without allowing them a chance to catch their breath, she pushed them inside. "I guess we can officially start the festivities."

The mayor dragged them to the front of the room toward a microphone set up beside a small dance floor. Marisa's stomach clenched as Alana introduced Josh as the new city attorney. With a sinking feeling in the pit of her stomach, Marisa knew what was coming before the woman introduced her—as Josh's fiancée.

Josh looked at her with a plea for understanding, then said a few words to the assembled guests. Marisa was impressed with the easy way he took the microphone and managed to compliment and flatter them all with his first impressions of their small city. Then Alana swept him away.

The rest of the evening rushed by as the chairman of the city council took charge of Marisa and presented her to the movers and shakers of the community. Josh finally rescued her and swung her onto the small dance floor.

"I'm sorry," he said breathlessly. "That isn't what I intended. Or promised," he added as if that was important to him.

"If I've learned anything," Marisa said, "it's that everything in life can't be planned."

The surprised look on Josh's face quickly evolved to one of relief. He drew her closer. "I want you to know I do intend to keep my promises to you," he said close to her ear.

"I don't know anything you could have done differently," she said. She was glad she'd had a chance to think about the premature announcement, because at first, she had been upset. Now she found Josh's obvious approval gratifying. "Of course, I'll have to tell Ryan tonight when we get home," she added. "But since neither of our parents live in the area, we'll still have time to break the news to them in the next couple of days." Tomorrow, Marisa mentally amended, when a flashbulb went off near them. Her father and mother's friends here would read the paper in the morning and fall all over themselves to call her parents in Arizona and check the accuracy of any statement that described her as the new city attorney's fiancée. The local newspaper always covered the mayor's parties, usually on the society page.

"Then you're not upset?"

"No." She shook her head.

With a relieved sigh, Josh lightly pressed his cheek to hers.

It had been far too long since she'd danced. She realized with a start exactly how long. Since high school. Prom night. That was the last time.

His hard body next to hers didn't resurrect any memories, though, she thought with a secret smile. The guys she'd danced with back then had been babies compared to this man. His shoulders felt rock solid, strong. And those boys certainly hadn't affected her like Josh was doing now. She could almost feel the roughness in the texture of his cheek, although it was an inch or two away. Even his cologne was a more sophisticated blend than the stuff her boyfriends had worn back then. Its scent was clean, subtle. Masculine.

He pulled her closer and her breasts brushed his chest with every step. They suddenly felt tender, sensitive. She wasn't sure she'd continue to breathe if the elevator music that the small three-piece ensemble played didn't end soon.

"How'd the mayor know?" She hoped to distract herself from the disconcerting sensations.

"My first day, she mentioned that a few members of the city council had been reluctant to hire me because I wasn't married. I told her I planned to be soon."

Marisa drew away far enough to look up into his face. "You didn't even know—" She broke off abruptly. When he'd proposed, he'd made it clear that if she wasn't interested, he would find someone who was.

"Was that the reason? The city wanted you married?"

He frowned. "It was one item—a small one—on my growing list," he admitted. "But I'd decided before then. It was a matter of finding the 'who.'" His eyes sparkled in the dim light before he pulled her back against him. "I'm glad it was you," he whispered close to her ear.

A shiver ran through her. She was glad it was her, too— and suddenly a little frightened.

The midsummer heat seemed to evaporate as they started the twenty-minute drive home later. Marisa couldn't quit shivering.

She eyed Josh surreptitiously from beneath her lashes. He reached over and laced his fingers through hers. "Your hand is cold," he commented.

"I think I'm nervous," she admitted.

"About?"

"Everything. Mostly telling Ryan, I guess, since that's the next thing I have to do."

"You think he's going to have a problem with it?"

"No," she told him honestly. "But you never know."

"He'll have some adjustments to make."

"We all will." She wished it wasn't so dark in the car

so she could see his expression. His grip tightened. "It's going to be very strange. For me and Ryan."

"You aren't sorry, are you?" His voice sounded tight.

"I like the idea," she said, "but I'm also trying to deal with reality. I know it isn't going to be as simple as you make it sound."

He lifted her fingertips to his lips. His breath warmed them for a second as he placed a kiss there. "Tomorrow's Saturday. Why don't I pick you both up first thing in the morning? We'll go out to breakfast and tell him together," he offered.

Marisa had to think about that for a moment. How did she want to break the news to Ryan? He gazed at Josh with unadulterated hero worship in his eyes. Except tonight…

"He would think breakfast in the morning was a real treat," she said. "It would make up for tonight."

She saw Josh nod in the dim light and knew he'd thought of that. That intuition was probably partly responsible for the suggestion.

"But we have to have answers to his questions," she added. "He'll have a lot of them."

"The details," he reiterated as he pulled up in front of her house.

She sighed.

"Shall we get Ryan first? Get him to bed?"

She shook her head, then realized he probably couldn't see. "When I called to tell Evie we weren't going to make it by midnight, she suggested she put him to bed with her kids. I'll pick him up first thing in the morning." She heard Josh's sharp intake of air and realized the implications.

She stared at her dark house and was suddenly reluctant to invite him in. She jumped when his finger grazed her cheek. He absently hooked a strand of hair behind her ear. "So what details did you want to discuss?" he asked softly.

"Would you...would you like to come in?"

"Not really," he replied. "Knowing we have the house to ourselves would be distracting," he explained when she didn't say anything. "At least for me."

She nodded, surprised again by his understanding. And grateful.

"Doesn't this seem a little more...likely?" He finally came up with a word. "Can you imagine how many wedding plans are made in dark cars in the moonlight?"

Marisa smiled.

"Not quite the same as a business discussion at a kitchen table, huh?"

Once again, his perceptiveness stunned her. And brought mixed feelings. The past couple of days when she'd thought of his—proposal—and she'd thought of little else—she kept reminding herself to make the decision in her head, not her heart. This *was* a practical decision, not a romantic one. Fairy-tale dreams and wistful fantasies only got her into trouble. For her own sake, this discussion should be at her kitchen table in the glare of a hundred-watt bulb. But this felt right. And she appreciated him trying to put a little glitter on their coldhearted discussion of marriage, even if they were decorating with fool's gold.

"So what details did you want to discuss?" Josh brought her back to the practical—which was where she had to stay if this had a chance of working. He pushed a button and eased his seat farther away from the steering wheel.

The legal question was the first that popped into her head. "Do you want me to sign some kind of agreement? A marriage contract?" she asked, waving in the direction of her house. "I'm sure you have a lot more to lose if we...if this...if it doesn't work out."

"Absolutely not." He turned in his seat and tilted her face toward the moonlight. "We may be going into this for different reasons than the normal ones, but it's going to be the same kind of marriage everyone else has. The only marriage contract I'm making with you is in here." He tapped his temple.

She blinked once, blocking out his determined image.

"If I've learned anything practicing law," he said, his voice softening, "it's that a marriage works when nine-tenths of it is commitment. Signing a piece of paper doesn't cement a commitment."

"No, it doesn't."

"In a lot of cases, it's the easy out. The escape hatch. A vast majority of the divorces I handled were with people who went into it thinking they'd just get a divorce if it didn't work out. I don't want that."

"Me, neither," she managed to whisper.

"Good." The finger that had been under her chin idly traced her jawline, sending pleasant sensations down her arm. She caught his hand and drew it down to rest between them on the console.

"Distracting?" She sensed his grin even though she couldn't see it clearly.

"Yes. Yes," she said again when the first came out so raspy she wasn't certain he would recognize her answer.

"Good. Now what else? The wedding? What kind do you want?"

That was one thing she hadn't even thought about.

"The big, white traditional thing?" he continued.

"No." She'd quit looking at bridal magazines and dreaming of weddings when she was eighteen and pregnant.

"Good." His sigh was heartfelt. "I'm looking forward to *being* married a lot more than I'm looking forward to *getting* married," he said. "But if you want that kind—"

"No. Oh, gracious," she thought out loud. "My folks."

She looked up at him. "Janet. Your parents. Are they all going to expect…?"

"Probably," he answered. "Which brings us to the when. If they're all going to be here, we have to give them time."

"I don't want them here," she said, realizing it was true. "Do you?"

"Not particularly."

Acting like a couple had been easy tonight among strangers. Acting like a happily married couple in front of the people they loved, the people most difficult to fool, would be terrifying. Too daunting.

Would her parents approve of her cold-blooded approach to marriage? Maybe, she realized. Once they'd adjusted to her unplanned pregnancy, the most difficult thing for both of them—the thing they'd actually grieved over—had been that she'd given up her chance at a "normal" life. In one fell swoop, with one practical decision, she was redeeming the normal life they'd wanted for her. The life she'd wanted so much that she'd assumed it would be that way. You couldn't even call that a dream. It was an expectation. And now Josh was giving her one last chance.

"Unless we plan to tell them the truth…"

He didn't answer for a minute. His voice was low when he finally did. "What is the truth? Are you marrying me because you want to?"

She didn't answer directly. "You're marrying me because you want to get married," she said. "Not because you want to marry *me*. There's a difference."

"I do want to marry you," he insisted. "Is it my fault you didn't come along until after I decided I wanted to get married?"

She grinned as she assumed he'd intended.

"As far as I'm concerned," he went on, "I'm marrying

you for all the right reasons. But, no, I don't especially want to tell my family—especially Janet—all the details. It's none of their business.''

"They'll ask too many questions," she said. "I don't lie well."

"Me, neither. Although I've probably had more practice than most, given my profession." His words lightened the tone just that little bit that made so much difference. She didn't feel nearly as tense as she had a minute ago.

"So we agree we don't want a big wedding."

"Definitely," he said.

"I guess that leads us to what kind and when."

"As soon as possible," he said without hesitating.

When she didn't respond, he clarified, "Next week?"

Next week? The very thought took her breath away.

"I've been thinking about it since you said you'd like to go back to school."

"Yeah?"

"I did a little research with all the literature I'm accumulating about the area. I assume you're thinking about KU since it's only twenty miles away?"

She nodded.

"School starts in two and a half weeks."

He was taking charge of her life. The thought sent a tremor through her. However, he *was* helping her put into motion all the things she'd said she wanted to do but had never managed to.

"Wouldn't you like to start this semester?"

If she wanted to go at all, she could think of no reason to wait.

He put into words what she hadn't dared to think. "I guess it boils down to how sure you are you want to marry me." He let that notion settle. "If you truly know you want to, can you see any reason to delay?"

She couldn't think of one.

"In some ways, a small wedding at the courthouse and presenting—"

"Can we have a minister?" she interrupted.

"We can have anything you want."

"Okay. I want a minister, even if it's just us."

"And Ryan," he added.

"Yes. Ryan, too."

"And a minister," he reminded her. "A small wedding without a lot of fanfare, and we'll present it to our families and friends as a fait accompli. Seems to be the logical way to go, don't you think?"

It sounded immensely appealing.

"Where are we going to live?" she said, finally remembering one of the important things she'd planned to ask. "We haven't talked about that."

"I want to build a new house," he said. "That's one of the things I'd decided before I knew I was going to ask you," he admitted sheepishly. "You okay with that?"

The tilt of his head caught some of the glow from the streetlight two houses away. His face was half illuminated, half in shadow. The expression she could see reminded her of Ryan when he wanted a new Nintendo game. She felt a tender rush of some emotion. "Sure. I'm going to object to that idea." She dipped her head toward her front porch. "A house with all the modern conveniences and things that don't need repairing every other day? Oh, yeah, I think I'm going to protest."

He swooped in for a kiss, surprising her. "I can hardly wait to get started. I want a yard and a lawn mower you can ride."

She laughed and savored the pleasant warmth he'd left on her lips. "But obviously that's not going to be instantaneous," she said. "If we get married next week…"

He told her about his temporary arrangement with his landlord, one of the city councilmen. "I haven't even finished unpacking," he added. "So if you don't mind, I could move in here while we build."

"Seems logical to me. I do have the three bedro—" She broke off, realizing that technically they only needed two.

"Ryan's room, your office and *ours*," he said.

She nodded. "You can share my office, too," she invited, and he leaned forward and kissed her again, this time lingering. It was sweet, satisfying and oh-so-addictive. She sighed regretfully when he finally pulled away and leaned against his door.

"We can't do that anymore. Not if we're going to get anything else discussed," he added.

He was right. Thinking was easier if he didn't touch her, but in this case, thinking too much might not be a good thing either. Burying a slight panic attack beneath a deep breath, she leaned against the car door. "You mean the details?"

"The concrete plans." He nodded. "Date? Place? Time?"

Real, concrete plans would make it a solid, thoughtful, well thought out decision instead of some impulsive, emotional one, like it felt now. Writing something firm on the calendar—something she could see and touch—would surely make it feel as though she was doing the sane, sensible, logical thing. Wouldn't it?

"Date. Place. Time." Her voice sounded calm, even though her head was filled with the most ominous words from the wedding ceremony. Her heart was thumping. No matter how Josh made her feel when he kissed her, would marrying him be the right thing? It was truly time to speak now or forever hold her peace.

"So how about next week?" he asked with a warm, beguiling grin.

Chapter Six

"That's wonderful, Marisa." Evie Hanson hugged her and twirled her halfway around her kitchen table. Then the facts sunk in and she held Marisa at arm's length to study her. "But who?"

Marisa had time to open her mouth a smidgen.

"That guy? The brother of your friend from college?"

This time Marisa didn't try to get a word in edgewise. She just nodded.

"Oh, Marisa, that's wonderful," Evie said again. "But you've only seen him a couple of times," she added, suddenly very quiet—at least for Evie. "You knew in that length of time?" she asked eventually.

"You haven't seen him." Marisa smiled. "Oh, Evie, he's...he's..."

Her unfinished sentence worked exactly as Marisa had hoped it would. It had occurred to her last night when she couldn't sleep. If she could somehow convey that she didn't have words to describe Josh, it would divert some of the questions she didn't have answers to. And it summarized Josh exactly. He was indescribable.

"Oh, Marisa. I'm so happy for you." Evie hugged her again.

Marisa's sigh was totally unplanned, but the knowing look that came into her neighbor's eyes told Marisa it was an effective touch.

"So when?" Evie demanded. "And when do we get to meet him?"

"Well, that's what I came to ask. Would you mind keeping Ryan next Saturday evening?"

Evie looked at the calendar on the wall by her refrigerator. "Shouldn't be a problem, but let me check with Bob."

Marisa nodded. She explained their scare with the mayor and the newspaper last night. "So we told Ryan this morning—Josh took us out to breakfast."

"And how did Ryan take it?" The woman waved the question away as soon as she asked. "Never mind. He's been dropping Josh's name since the first night you went out. I'll bet he's in seventh heaven."

"He said, 'Cool,' then after Josh left, he asked a few questions. That was pretty much it." Marisa shook her head, still perplexed by Ryan's reaction. She'd expected questions, millions of them. "Right before I came over here, I heard him in his room, talking to himself. It sounded like he was practicing introducing Josh to his friends. Oh, I think it's going to be so good for him."

Evie's eyes narrowed. "That's not why you're marrying him, is it?"

Marisa felt a sudden urge to confide the whole mixed-up mess to Evie, but resisted. Exactly what would that accomplish? She didn't particularly want her friends and neighbors standing back, waiting and watching for her im-

petuous marriage to fall apart. "I'm marrying Josh for
me," she said truthfully. Her marriage *wouldn't* fall apart,
she thought determinedly, not as long as she remembered
the common-sense reasons and didn't get caught up in fantasies and false expectations. "But knowing Ryan is going
to benefit, too, made it much easier for me to decide."

"I know he was your first consideration when Josh
asked," Evie said. "But it's about time you took care of
you."

"And that's why I need you to keep Ryan next Saturday
night." Marisa finally brought the subject back to her original reason for coming over. "Since the paper managed to
cover Josh's reception without mentioning me as his fiancée, we decided to go ahead and get married *before* we tell
our parents. We're doing it next Saturday."

Evie's mouth dropped open. She bobbed her chin up and
down a few times, but no words came. "I thought you
meant next Saturday we'd get a chance to meet him," she
said finally. "Boy, when you decide to do something, you
don't waste time."

"It'll save lots of hassles. You know how my mom is."

Evie nodded.

"She'd be here with her fingers in the pie, planning an
event a lot bigger than anything we want or intend. Josh's
parents...well, his mother is the same. So we decided to
do it, then announce it. So that's why I need you to watch
Ry—"

"For one night? You said just one night? You aren't
taking a honeymoon?"

"I always take a week's vacation before Ryan starts
school, so I have next week off anyway. But since Josh
just started his new job, we thought we'd save the honeymoon till later." Till we get used to each other and into
some kind of routine, Josh had said and she'd agreed. A

honeymoon would put too much strain on all of them. "And since I'm going to quit my job so I can go back to school myself—"

"You're what?"

"I'm going back to school. And my classes start the week after Ryan's, so—"

"Why?"

"'Cause I've always wanted to teach. Josh said I might as well do what I want. I'm taking him up on the offer." She shrugged. "That doesn't give us a whole lot of time to plan a wedding. So we're just going to do it and get on with our lives."

"You *are* still going to live next door," Evie demanded.

"What? Afraid you're going to lose your baby-sitter?" Marisa teased.

"Hey, at the rate things are going, it may be a fair trade in a few years."

Marisa felt herself blush.

"You are going to have more kids?"

"Josh wants to."

"And you?"

"I want to, but…"

"But?"

"The thought scares me." She lifted a shoulder.

Evie frowned. "It's been a tough road, raising Ryan by yourself. I'd be a little scared, too."

Marisa silently thanked her friend for being able to put her fears into words.

"You're a terrific mother, Marisa," she added. "I always thought it was a shame you didn't have more kids."

"Well, we're not going to do anything to prevent it. I figure by the time we have one, I'll be ready."

"You will," Evie assured her with a smile. "So you *are* staying here?"

"For now. That was one of Ryan's biggest concerns. After he had a chance to think about it, he realized our marriage might mean moving and he didn't like that idea at all."

"I can imagine."

"I reminded him that Josh was moving in with us. And though Josh wants to build us a beautiful house someday, that would take time. Nothing would change right away. That eased Ryan's mind and now he seems excited."

"Well, staying where you are will definitely make the adjustment easier for you and Ryan. It's better if you don't change everything at once."

"And we don't need to worry about Josh's adjustment?"

"Men adjust more easily," Evie said as though she actually knew.

Marisa laughed and hoped Evie did know what she was talking about this time. If Marisa had any real concerns about Josh, it was that the shock of living with her and Ryan on a twenty-four-hour basis would be too much for him. He seemed so...orderly, together. No one would use those words to describe Marisa and Ryan's life.

For the next while, she and Evie discussed more of the details. And they *would* have a few guests at the ceremony, Marisa realized when Evie promised she and Bob would be there just as Marisa was leaving. Oh, well, they would need witnesses, she supposed as she wondered how to tell Josh the guestless wedding they'd planned wasn't going to work out exactly that way.

The minister at the neighborhood church Marisa had attended all her life was delighted to perform the ceremony and didn't seem to mind that they shied away from the premarital counseling he usually insisted on.

"You're both old enough to know what you're getting

into,'' he told Josh. ''But are you certain—'' he looked at Marisa ''—you don't want to wait until your parents can be here?''

Under his stare, Marisa felt as if she was Ryan's age again. But then, she'd felt ages older than her years since well before Ryan was born; it might be nice to feel young and outrageously daring once again. She assured him they wanted exactly what they'd said, a short, small, *quiet* wedding. Knowing her mother, the minister finally got it and smiled.

Ryan was Josh's best man and Marisa's son of honor. Bob and Evie, with family in tow, arrived on the hour to assume places in the front pew.

Marisa looked at Ryan, standing so tall and proud between them in his new dark suit. His hair was almost black from the water it had required to slick it into good behavior. He looked at both of them in awe.

Marisa smiled, knowing her portion of the stunned approval was for being wise enough to marry Josh in the first place. Josh's portion was hero worship, pure and unadulterated.

The ceremony was simple. Just the words. As Reverend Marks's quiet voice washed over them, Marisa studied the man she was marrying. Superman's X-ray vision couldn't be any more intense as Josh listened to the preacher. His broad shoulders, beneath the dark suit that Ryan had noted with pride was almost exactly like his, were firmly squared and looked as though they could carry the weight of the world. His chiseled profile—the strong, determined line of his jaw, his high, stubborn cheekbones—would rival any classical Greek statue's.

He was the most handsome man she'd ever laid eyes on. He could marry anyone he chose. Why was he marrying her?

It had to be more than deciding it was time he got married. Men didn't have ticking biological clocks, did they?

A desperate amusement bubbled up inside her. She didn't realize she'd giggled aloud until Josh's surprised gaze widened on her.

Under his look, she giggled again. She couldn't help it.

Reverend Marks joined Josh in frowning. His fuzzy salt-and-pepper brows came almost together over his eyes. He looked over his glasses at Josh as if to say, *Are you sure you know what you're getting into?*

Marisa managed to suppress the urge to giggle again—until the minister cautioned them about forsaking all others. *What others?*

The thought brought forth another giggle and more looks. She hadn't even had a date since right before she found out she was pregnant. This time, Ryan joined in looking at her, probably thinking of the "appropriate behavior" lecture she'd given him only minutes before the three of them had joined Reverend Marks at the front of the church.

By the time the ceremony was over, Marisa felt as if she would wilt like a limp noodle from the effort it took to keep her case of the giggles under control. Everything was funny. She even laughed when Josh kissed her.

"Sorry," she muttered against his warm and reassuring lips.

"Nerves?" he asked, supporting her with a lingering arm around her waist as they turned to face Evie and Bob.

"I think so."

"It's over?" Ryan asked, looking up at them.

"It's over," she managed with a sigh.

"You're married?"

"We're married," Josh confirmed.

"Cool." Ryan gaped for a moment as though trying to

think of something more to say, then gave up and ran to join his friend.

Bob, an amateur photographer who had insisted they would want pictures, snapped several informal ones. Then he began posing them. First with Ryan, then with Reverend Marks. Then just her and Josh. Josh diplomatically called it all to a halt ten minutes into the photo session.

"Let's go to dinner," he said. "Our reservations are for six."

Once they'd known Evie and Bob planned to come, Josh had suggested they adjust the time of the wedding to allow their dinner to include the children. "We aren't having any kind of reception," Josh had said when he invited them. "Please. At least help us celebrate with a nice wedding dinner. Ryan will enjoy it more if you're with us," he'd added, and they'd given in.

A reprieve of a few more hours. Marisa felt the tension ease from her shoulders. This was her wedding night. And no matter how she felt when Josh kissed her, no matter how much she savored and sighed over each and every one of those kisses, no matter how much she'd enjoyed having him around the past week, the thought of their wedding night scared her to death.

The rooftop restaurant where they celebrated—in the same hotel where Josh's reception had been the night she'd agreed to marry him—was beginning to fill with Saturday-night diners as they finished their early but elegant meal. The table was bedecked with flowers and candles. A small bottle of champagne, which even the children had had a sip of so they could join in Bob's toast, lay overturned in the silver ice bucket.

"You ready, Ryan?" Bob asked as the Hansons prepared to take their leave.

Evie came around the table to give Marisa a hug. "You're a beautiful bride," she whispered, then gazed at Josh, who was settling the check. "And your new husband is a dream."

The way Evie eyed him, Marisa knew she was complimenting more than his looks. "He's a very special man. I can't believe he wanted to share this with us *and* our kids." Her hand made a sweeping gesture of the restaurant in general. "It's been a wonderful experience for them."

"Thanks for coming." Marisa returned the hug.

"Oh, boy, do you have an interesting night ahead of you," Evie whispered in her ear.

Marisa extracted herself from the embrace and hoped Evie didn't feel the slight tremor that had started somewhere deep inside her and worked its way out. *The night ahead of them.* The very thought made her mouth feel as though she'd swallowed a bag of cotton balls.

Evie and Bob herded the children toward the door and left. Josh, meanwhile, added another five to his generous tip and looked at Marisa. "Shall we go?" He offered her his arm.

She nodded, unable to answer. They had the drive home and then...

She wouldn't think about it. If she could just concentrate on feeling—just think about the way his kisses made her feel. There was nothing in the world to be nervous about. So what if she had virtually no experience. So what if she disappointed him. He'd indicated he liked the idea of having a *convenient* lover. He hadn't said anything about wanting a *good* one.

The elevator that would take them to the lobby seemed forever in coming. As the rooftop was the final stop, when it finally arrived, they had it to themselves. Going down, it stopped on the twelfth floor. "Is there something wrong?" Marisa asked.

Josh held up a key. "We decided not to take an official honeymoon, but I wanted to at least do something memorable."

Marisa swallowed hard. She expected what came next to be memorable, anyway. She'd been praying for days she wouldn't make it memorable for the wrong reasons. Now the moment was at hand. "I...I didn't bring anything." She hung back although Josh had already stepped out.

He extended his hand as the heavy door started to close, then stepped in front of the sensor to keep it open.

"Shouldn't we at least go home first and—"

"Trust me," he said quietly.

If she didn't trust him, she'd just done something terribly foolish. She had no choice but to take his hand. But she couldn't meet his steady gaze.

The room he led her to was a corner room—a suite, she amended—overlooking the Plaza, a bustling upscale shopping area in the daytime, a touristy hangout by night.

Josh stood by the door, one hand in the pocket of his suit pants as she stepped hesitantly in. They had a small balcony, she realized, drawn immediately to the sliding glass doors. If things got too tense, if she made too big a fool of herself with her know-nothing clumsiness, she could always throw herself off it, she thought with a grim smile.

"It's about time you did that," Josh said from beside the still-open suite door.

"What?" she asked absently.

"Smile," he replied quietly. "I wondered if you were already having regrets."

"Not regrets," she assured him after a moment's careful consideration. *Not yet, anyway.* "Jitters," she said with what she hoped resembled more of a genuine smile. "I keep telling myself it's normal—even in a...a...normal marriage.''

"That's what we're going to make this," he promised huskily, finally closing the door. He walked slowly toward her as if afraid she'd bolt if he moved too quickly.

It was a thought, but she refused to give in to it. Not even backing away, she stood her ground and distracted herself by carefully examining the room.

At least this room didn't have a bed. She didn't dare look through the open French doors on the opposite side of the room.

A spectacular splash of red caught her eye. Roses. A massive bouquet of them graced a small table in the corner. She hurried to them and buried her face in the fragrance. "Oh, Josh, they're beautiful," she said.

"I hoped you'd like them," he said dryly. He was standing a few feet away. "Especially since you wouldn't let me buy you a real bridal bouquet."

"The silk ones were gorgeous," she said. "And they'll make a wonderful arrangement when we get a new house," she explained with a twinge of guilt. "A sentimental decoration with meaning. And what would I have done with a bridal bouquet? I didn't have anyone to throw it to."

She heard his sigh. "Are you feeling cheated?"

The twinge of guilt broadened to battering-ram size. Every romantic thing he'd suggested—flowers, candles, music, a limousine to bring her to the church for their wedding—she'd vetoed. She'd wanted to go into this with her eyes wide-open, with no silly, dreamy expectations. "Do *you* feel cheated?"

"You're more—much more," he murmured, almost as if he was holding his breath, "than I expected or anticipated. How could I feel cheated?"

His tone made her knees shake. She hid her face in the

roses again and hoped he'd still be able to say that after they... Later.

"I have an idea," he said. "It's early yet, not even dark. Let's go out and walk around. I'd like to check out the famous Plaza. Maybe we can find somewhere to dance."

The first natural smile she'd had all day burst forth. Dancing! That was exactly what they should do. Her body instantly remembered how his body had felt against hers at the mayor's reception. She hadn't wanted that dance to finish. She hadn't wanted the evening to end. Tonight it wouldn't have to. *Oh, please, let him make me feel that way again so I won't feel so cold and...terrified.*

"I'm going to change." He'd already headed for the bedroom. "It's too hot to wander around in a suit."

Marisa looked down at the clean lines of the cream-colored dress she'd chosen for her wedding. It would do, she supposed. It was simple and elegant, the most expensive piece of clothing she'd ever bought. But she wished she had something besides high heels.

"Evie packed you a few things," Josh said from the other room. "They checked us in when they got here and had the bellman bring our bags up."

Trust me, he'd said. She wondered how long it would be before she really could. She'd relied on herself far too long. But he was proving to be a very trustworthy man. He thought of everything, took care of every detail.

"So Evie and Bob were in on—" She stopped abruptly in the door. He'd taken off his shirt. His chest looked as good uncovered as it did in clothes. It was strong, sculpted without being overly muscular. It looked like a warm, sturdy place to rest her head. A swatch of dark, fine hair spread wide across his upper chest, then narrowed gradually to his waist and disappeared below the spot where the belt and fastener at his waist hung open.

Obviously he'd noted her gaping mouth and wide eyes. Before she made a fool of herself by backing out of the room, he smiled slightly. Picking up the slacks lying on the bed beside his suit jacket and shirt, he carried them toward the bathroom. "Yes, Bob and Evie were in on this," he said, answering the question she'd never managed to finish.

She hurriedly opened the familiar suitcase sitting on the bed. Evie knew her well. She'd put in her favorite slacks, added one of her nicer shirts. And her low-heel sandals were right on top.

Marisa peeled off her panty hose without removing the dress, then yanked her slacks on beneath it. With an eye on the bathroom door, she sucked in a deep breath. Drawing the dress over her head, she replaced it with the top in one smooth motion. She felt the tension ease from her shoulders as the door remained closed. With a sigh, she sank onto the bed and fastened the strap on her shoes.

She heard the bathroom door open behind her. "Ready already?"

"Almost," she said breathlessly. "I want to check my makeup, comb my hair." Nonchalantly she picked up her cosmetic bag from the suitcase.

"Take your time." He sounded amused. She didn't have the courage to look at him as she passed him at the end of the bed. "I need to hang up my suit. Shall I take care of your dress?" he called a moment later as she slapped cold water on her hot face.

"If you don't mind," she answered, pleasantly surprised by her husband's offer. *Her husband.* She was talking to her husband, she realized. And if he continued in the manner he was starting, he might just be very handy to have around.

Keep smiling, Maxwell, he told himself as he waited. But the grin he'd plastered on his face was far from genuine. Hell—heck, he amended—she acted almost like a virgin. What did he know about virgins?

Ryan—the very reason he had to start watching his language more carefully—was absolute proof she wasn't. Somehow that idea comforted him a little. He'd never in his life been with a virgin. Sex was sex. It had its own special category. But even his first time had been with an experienced older woman. She'd been nineteen and had known the ropes better than anyone he'd been with since.

Marisa was just nervous, he told himself. She'd never been married before. He'd swear in court that she'd been as hot as he was when he kissed her last night. He'd carried most of his still-packed boxes into her spare room and then lingered after Ryan had gone to bed. He'd left, pleased with himself for not pushing when she so obviously might have welcomed more.

One more night, he'd thought, and his days of taking cold showers were over. He'd savored the anticipation, certain that sex with Marisa would be sweeter than anything before—the closest thing to heaven. His toes curled, thinking about her. Making love to her was going to be well worth the short wait.

When she walked out of the bathroom a minute later, he gripped the back of the chair beside him and forced himself to look out the window. It probably wouldn't help her nervousness to see savage hunger on his face.

He didn't need to study the way the short silky blouse hugged her curves. His brief glimpse of the lightweight slacks gave the impression that her legs went on forever. She had a gift for imprinting her image in his mind.

Aw, hell—heck—who did he think he was kidding? He'd salivated over the way she'd looked in old blue jeans in the grocery store. And he didn't care nearly as much about how she looked with her clothes on as he cared about seeing her with them off.

"Should we call our folks now? Before we leave?" he asked, surprised that his voice didn't come out in an awkward teenage squawk.

Her stillness at the question drew his gaze. She'd frozen in the middle of the room. He cursed himself all over again. The tense lines around her mouth had reappeared. He'd brought them back. He prayed she wasn't regretting her decision to marry him.

"Let's wait until tomorrow," she said. "Don't you think it would be better to tell them after—" She broke off. Her voice acquired his squeak.

After what? he wanted to ask, but didn't dare. "Then, shall we go?" He rose and offered her his hand. *Let's go before I carry you to that bed and unwrap you like a wedding present.* He couldn't even think about it.

The leisurely stroll around the Plaza was too hot and too long.

They didn't find a place to dance. The clubs with DJs were loud and raucous. The few with live bands were even worse. And watching the patrons—most of whom looked too young to be there legally in the first place—made him feel old.

They found a jazz band where no one else was dancing, so they didn't, either. He spent the time enjoying Marisa's pleasure in listening.

"Shall I order a bottle of champagne?" he asked. The insinuation that it was an occasion worthy of celebrating brought back her tension. This time it didn't disperse, and shortly after the band's first break, Marisa stood up. Extending her hand to him, she looked at him determinedly. "Come on. Let's go back." *Let's get this over with,* he heard as distinctly as if she'd said it. It was there in her squared shoulders, in the line of her beautiful body.

Let's get this over with? he wondered as they walked quickly back toward the hotel. He had to keep increasing his stride to keep up with her. By the time they reached their room, he was firmly convinced she thought this was going to be worse than her notion of Chinese water torture.

Then why'd she marry me? He was starting to feel as uptight as she looked.

Her stone-faced resolve didn't end at the door of their suite. She crossed immediately to the bedroom and rummaged through the suitcase she'd left open on the bed. Following her to the doorway, he watched her scramble the contents Evie had packed so neatly. "She forgot..." He heard the frustration in her mumble. Then she found a box with the logo of an exclusive lingerie shop.

She lifted it. Surprise wiped the grim look from her face. "Open it," he suggested.

Marisa did away with the lid and stood staring at the ivory-colored fabric inside for a long minute. Finally she lifted a part of it, holding the shimmery, satiny material as if she expected it to explode in her hands. She blushed and glanced up at him. "I...she... I didn't think of this." She gnawed her lip. "I'm glad Evie did. I'm glad I have something...nice to wear for you." This last she whispered.

Before he could say a thing, she gathered up the rest of the lace-trimmed material and started for the bathroom, head held high as she swept past him.

As soon as the door closed behind her, Josh sank onto the edge of the bed. Whew!

I'm glad I have something nice to wear for you. That was a clue. Could she be worried that she'd disappoint him in some way? How could he be disappointed?

Unless... Something stilled and wilted inside him. He

would be disappointed if Marisa didn't desire him the way he desired her. If she only felt an obligation.

She *had* been shocked when she'd learned he was proposing a "normal" marriage. And she *had* asked—about a dozen times—what he expected of her.

He heard the bathroom door open and quickly busied himself moving her suitcase to the rack over by the closet. It would be best for both of them if he didn't look at her— no matter how much he longed to.

As soon as he heard her move away from the bathroom, he decided to make use of the room himself. On the off chance her reluctance came from shyness, he saw no need to intimidate her by stripping to nothing and presenting himself to her like a bull moose in heat.

As he passed her, she pulled the loose edges of the elaborate robe together. It was all he could do not to groan in disappointment as his brief glimpse of lace-covered breast disappeared. Was it modesty? Or reluctance to share?

It took him longer to decide what to do when he came out of the bathroom than it did to disrobe and brush his teeth. A little bit of cloth between them would be good, he decided, adjusting the shorts he'd decided to leave on and clearing his throat before opening the door.

"Lights out?" he asked cheerfully, pausing self-consciously just inside the bedroom and flipping off the switch. Could nerves be contagious? He didn't wait for a reply.

When he made his way to the bed and pulled back the covers on his side, he was surprised to discover she wasn't on the opposite side when he reached for her.

Damn! Hell! He no longer cared about his language. He held his breath as he heard the shiver of silk near him. In his mind's eye, he saw the lacy masses of sheer white fabric from the robe she'd had on land in a heap on the floor. His mouth watered.

Then the mattress moved, covers rustled and he felt her warmth as she slid into the bed. He wanted to speak, but he was speechless. He couldn't even breathe.

He heard her head nestle into the pillow beside his. He could feel her tension.

Silently he reached for her, planning to find her hand and lace his fingers through hers reassuringly. She was much closer than he anticipated and his palm came in contact with satin, low on her belly. He heard her gasp, felt a ripple of shock tighten her muscles. He warily eased his hand to his own chest.

Terror! She was terrified of him.

"Sorry," he muttered, then cursed himself. Dammit, he wasn't sorry. He wanted to touch her, wanted her to touch him. He wasn't sorry. She knew his intentions. "I...was looking for your hand."

She offered it, pale and wavering in the thin sliver of light sneaking between the drapes. He took it and then didn't know what to do with it. If he folded their entwined hands against his bare chest, she'd probably be as shocked as she'd been by his touching her. If he eased their hands back between them on the bed, he might brush against her body again. She was lying so close. Her soft fragrance engulfed him, drugging his senses. His breathing felt as shallow as his thoughts. He was paralyzed by the fear of frightening her again.

Not knowing what else to do with the hand she'd trusted him with, he brought it to his mouth, kissed her fingers, then drew it to his chest—over the covers.

They had to talk.

But lucidity escaped him. Feelings, exquisite longings so sharp they verged almost on pain, swamped him. A knowledge, something physical rather than mental, settled on him. This *had* to be right. It was important that this be right. He could make her want him, couldn't he?

He felt her bewildered gaze on him. In ways, she seemed more innocent than her son. Without thinking, he turned halfway to his side and reached over with his free hand to smooth her hair. Although he barely touched her, he felt her stiffen.

Dammit. It *was* an obligation. She didn't want him the way he wanted her. She was offering herself up like some sacrificial lamb.

Did he care?

Hell, no! She knew. He'd made his intentions clear from the very beginning.

He waited, heard her quietly inhale, then let some inner force guide him as he slowly outlined the shape of her face with the back of his finger. Her features were placid, calm. He could feel her tension ease slightly as she gave herself to the sensation. Her breasts rose and fell in a long, quavery sigh only inches from his arm. He marveled that his light touch could soothe her when it electrified him.

Tracing the side of her neck, he gently explored the hollow of her throat and lingered in awe over the graceful fragility of her collarbone. Following a course that seemed mapped out for him, his fingers stroked and tried to memorize the slope of her shoulder. A lacy scrap of fabric stopped him, making him feel quick and indignant frustration. The strap of her gown felt harsh and abrasive compared to the velvety texture of her skin.

She held her breath as his hand faltered over the obstacle. She expelled it carefully when he decided to ignore the narrow strap and go on with his engrossing investigation.

Then she flinched as one fingertip connected with the side of her satin-covered breast. He felt her whole body go rigid beside him again and something inside him came unglued.

He lurched to a sitting position on the side of the bed.

"Josh?" The rasp in her whisper was like acid poured on an open wound.

He couldn't answer. He could only sit, gasping for breath, wondering what had gone wrong.

"What is it?" Her voice was small. So very small.

"I promised you time," he finally managed. "All the time you needed." He bent, resting his elbows on his knees and dragged a hand through his hair. "This was a lousy idea. Bad idea," he repeated for himself as he rose and pulled the bedspread with him. Wrapping it around him, he started for the bathroom to find his clothes.

"Our marriage?" she asked so softly he wouldn't have heard if the question hadn't ended on a distraught little squeak.

"This honeymoon thing." Somehow he'd forgotten everything he'd told her in the beginning. He hadn't sugar-coated his proposal or his expectations. He'd been frank about what she could expect from him. But he'd also made promises he planned to keep. Surely he could give her the time she needed to desire him, too.

What fantasy had attacked him and made him believe a little romantic icing would get everything off to a good start?

He knew he should say more, but couldn't think of a thing. Sighing deeply, he reached around the corner into the bathroom and flipped on the light.

She was sitting up in bed now. Her face was pinched and almost as white as that crazy bridal thing he'd encouraged Evie to buy when she'd suggested it. Beneath the satin and lace, Marisa's perfect breasts heaved, taunting him.

He looked down at his hand, which was gripping the

bathroom doorknob. "We've got plenty of time," he assured her. "Plenty of time."

And then, as if the demons of hell were after him, he slipped into the bathroom, slammed the door behind him and locked it.

Chapter Seven

We have time. Plenty of time. Five days later Josh's words still echoed in Marisa's head. She wished they'd go away. She wished *he'd* go away.

She pulled her thoughts up short and took the idea back. She didn't wish that at all. Burying her face in her hands, she tried to sort things out. She liked Josh. She liked him a lot. Because of that she didn't understand what she'd done on their wedding night. She didn't understand why he'd slept on the small sofa in the sitting room once he'd finally come out of the bathroom. She didn't understand him or anything that was happening. So how could she explain her marriage to her parents with any degree of believability?

She'd expected a couple of minor changes: another person living in her house. Companionship after Ryan went to bed. But everything had changed.

No, not everything. She was still sleeping alone. The one thing she'd expected to be very different hadn't changed at all. She still felt the same aching needs she'd felt since the first night Josh had kissed her. She analyzed her feelings and their "honeymoon" for the thousandth time.

She knew Josh's actions on their wedding night had been her fault. She'd been uptight. But was a paralyzing longing to please him such a bad thing? She resented feeling guilty.

Before she'd agreed to marry him, he *had* promised her all the time she needed. Why didn't he understand that she didn't need more time, just a little…patience?

She looked down at the pad in front of her. So far, she'd written nothing but "Dear Mom and Dad." And doodles. And:

Mrs. Joshua Maxwell
Mrs. Josh Maxwell
Mrs. Marisa Maxwell
Marisa Maxwell

Crumpling the paper, she threw it at the wastebasket and blamed the miss on the ringing phone.

She was acting as if she was in junior high again. The only difference between those dreamy practice sessions using the name of her latest heartthrob was that she hadn't used any elaborate curlicues or dotted the *i*'s with hearts this time.

There was one other major difference, she admitted wryly. This was real. She *was* Mrs. Joshua Maxwell.

"Marisa?" Speak of the devil. Josh's low voice over the telephone wire sent strange sensations down her spine.

"Yes?"

"You busy?"

"Not really," she admitted. "I'm trying to write a letter to my folks. To explain…well, you know."

"I know." She heard his smile. "They seemed to take the news well, even if it shocked them."

She agreed. "Yeah. But if we don't want them on our doorstep soon trying to figure out what's going on, I thought I'd better write. So far, I'm not having much luck finding something to say."

There was a long pause. "I should probably do the same," he said. "But I figure Janet's keeping my parents calm since she *knew* this would happen." His tone was dry.

Marisa smiled. That was exactly what Janet had said when they'd called her with the news.

That call had been the most difficult to make because Janet knew both of them so well. It turned out to be the easiest. She'd done all the talking. She wasn't a bit surprised, she professed, since they were perfect for each other—though she was a bit surprised at how quickly it had happened.

"What's going on with you?" Marisa asked Josh, trying not to express her own surprise that he was calling her from work. It was something he hadn't done except the very first time, when he'd called to ask her to dinner.

"Could you meet me at my office in an hour?" he said. "I have something I want to show you."

"What?"

"Can it be a secret? Will you come, anyway?" His voice held wariness of her willingness to come if he didn't reveal his secret. *That* irritated her. When had she failed to do whatever he'd asked?

Whatever else was going on between them, she did trust him. He should know that. And he should trust *her* a little. "Sure I'll come," she said, then quickly added, "Oh, but that's the time Ryan will be home."

"You should probably be there since it's his first day of school." He sounded disappointed.

"Not necessarily," she said. "Except for kindergarten, I've never been here his first day of school. He's always gone to a sitter. It shouldn't be a problem," she continued, thinking out loud. "Let me talk to Evie. If she's going to be around, I'll come."

"Good." His enthusiasm returned.

In this at least, maybe she could please him. "If I'm going to be able to do this—" she glanced at the clock on the microwave "—I'd better get moving."

"I'll call you back after you've had a chance to talk to Evie?"

"Just plan to see me unless I call *you* back." She noted the neatly printed name on the auto-dial label. Josh's was the only one on the list that included both name and number. He'd assured Ryan he could call him anytime he needed to by pushing one button. She'd had the feeling that Josh had waited until she was in the room to have that conversation with Ryan. He was intent on taking care of them, and that was a very comforting feeling.

"See you in about an hour, then?"

"I'll be there unless Evie has a problem."

"Ask if she'll give Ryan dinner, too." The suggestion sounded impulsive. "If she doesn't mind, I'll take you out."

"I'll check." This time she suspected she sounded wary. Since they'd come home from their honeymoon, he'd avoided being alone with her. What did Josh have planned? She wasn't certain she was ready for any more surprises.

"Evie!" Marisa didn't have far to go, since her neighbor was lounging on the patio in the backyard, eyes closed as she soaked up sun.

The woman jumped, spilling a splash of the coffee from the mug she'd propped on the arm of her chair.

"Risa, you scared me." She flattened her hand against her chest.

"Sorry." Marisa sank to the edge of the other redwood chair.

"You enjoying your week off?" Evie asked lazily, closing one eye again.

Marisa shrugged. "Until today, things have been too busy to call it enjoyable."

"Getting Ryan ready for school." Evie nodded. "Thank heavens they're gone," she added with delight. "Hasn't it been a wonderful day?"

The day had been too long. Marisa was tempted to tell her friend the truth. She'd had too much time to think. She needed to talk to someone. But the friendship between Evie and her had never been *that* kind. They had little in common except a neighborly regard and their children.

In any other situation, Marisa would have called Janet. But since Janet was Josh's sister—and Marisa's sister-in-law—Marisa had lost some of her cry-on-your-best-friend's-shoulder privileges. It wouldn't be fair to Josh *or* to Janet.

"I know I've been taking advantage of you far too often and—" Marisa began.

"If you're asking me to watch Ryan this evening, don't go any further," Evie interrupted, holding up her hand. "I owe you so many times that he could move in for a month and we still wouldn't be even."

Marisa laughed. Evie always cheered her.

"Actually I need you now. *And* this evening. Are you going to be here when the kids get home from school?"

"Right here." Evie patted the arm of her chair. "I don't plan to move until someone makes me."

"Would you mind meeting the bus?" Marisa asked reluctantly. "Otherwise, Ryan will go straight home." She snapped her fingers. "Never mind. I'll leave him a note. I can tell him to come over here."

"I'll meet the bus," Evie said. "What's going on?"

She explained Josh's mysterious invitation.

"Well, don't worry about Ryan. Or his dinner. I'll expect you when we see you."

Marisa was halfway across her own yard when Evie called, "How 'bout lunch tomorrow? If you *really* feel guilty, that'd be a great way to ease your conscience."

"I'd love to." Marisa turned and walked backward several steps. "We'll fix the details later?"

"Later," Evie agreed.

Marisa had been to Josh's office only once—the week before when she'd come into the courthouse so they could apply for their marriage license. They'd gone directly from the office where they'd filled out paperwork to his. She'd been a little preoccupied at the time, so she had no idea where his office was.

At four minutes after four, she was standing in front of the directory, trying to decipher it. The city had posted vague department locations rather than specific offices or personnel names.

Two attractive men stepped off the elevator, and Marisa did a double take before she realized one was her husband. The sight of him still amazed and thrilled her.

"Marisa. There you are." He directed the man with him her way. "I thought you might be late. We decided to wait for you here."

Marisa bit her lip. Except on their wedding day, she hadn't been on time for Josh yet. She mentally resolved to try harder as he apologized for not giving her more notice.

He introduced his good-looking companion as Chris Johnson. About the same age and build as Josh, the two men were like handsome bookends. One blond. The other dark. One dressed casually in jeans and a plaid shirt with rolled sleeves. One in a dark suit.

Chris extended his hand. His blue eyes sparkled with appreciation as she took it.

"Chris is a developer," Josh continued. "We had business this afternoon, but when Chris found out you and I were going to be house hunting in the near future, he offered to show us some of the areas we might be interested in. Introduce us to a few builders."

Marisa gaped at Josh for a second, then managed to find her tongue. "That…that's very nice."

"Maybe I can use a little influence. Help you get a good deal." Chris winked. "Shall we take two vehicles, or would you like to pile in with me?"

"We may as well go with you," Josh said before Marisa could suggest they follow. She wanted to discuss this. "You can tell us more about the developments we're going to."

Chris chuckled. "They're all going to be mine, of course."

"I figured." Josh lightly took Marisa's arm and escorted her to the truck. She ended up crammed shoulder to shoulder between the two large men in the seat of Chris's bright shiny new pickup. Josh put his arm around her to give Chris room to drive, and Marisa found herself closer and closer, almost cradled with her back to Josh's chest, as they exited the parking lot.

They left city center, passing through some of the older residential districts. Chris pointed out various sections of town and mentioned when they'd been added to the city. He was knowledgeable about the city's history. The area her house was in had developed slowly in the late twenties and early thirties, he told them.

"That was when a builder built two, maybe three, houses a year. None of it was the cookie-cutter industry you see now."

"What do you mean?" Marisa asked.

"No two houses in your neighborhood are exactly alike, are they?" Josh asked.

Not that she could think of. "No," she said, noting that he'd said "yours," not "ours."

"That's what I'm trying to do," Chris said smugly. "You'll see. We're trying to make sure no two houses in my neighborhoods are exactly alike or even have the same floor plan. Similar maybe, but not close enough that you can stand outside and divide them into the 'ranch,' the 'split entry,' and so on. *And* we're trying to integrate several sizes of houses in each area so we can attract varied income levels to each neighborhood. Get away from the class system that has almost gotten to be a trend in typical suburban neighborhoods."

Josh nodded and Marisa listened to them talk about the legal technicalities in some of the city's zoning codes, and she began to understand why Chris had been to see Josh in the first place.

"Here we are," Chris said as they pulled up in front of a house in progress. "There are three houses going up on this block. I'm sure we'll find Mac, one of the builders," he explained, "at one of them."

Chris started up the concrete drive and Marisa put a hand on Josh's arm. "Are we house hunting, Josh?"

He looked perplexed as he took her hand from his arm. "Don't you think this is a great opportunity?" He laced his fingers through hers and started to follow Chris.

"I thought we were going to build."

"Before we can do that, we have to decide where we want to buy a lot. And if we find something perfect already built, that would be as good, wouldn't it? Did you have something specific in mind? Got your dream house planned?'' he asked with a tempting smile.

Since Ryan, she'd been busy surviving. She hadn't allowed herself dreams, let alone something as specific as a brand-new house. Her dreams were much more practical— a new roof, maybe a porch swing. But a dream house? She shook her head.

Until Josh transplanted himself and his dreams into her life, she hadn't thought beyond raising her son and getting him through school.

''If we build,'' Josh continued when she didn't answer, ''we'll need a builder. This is a chance to meet several and see what kind of work they do. Come on.'' He tipped his head toward the door Chris had gone through. ''Let's check some of these out. Get some ideas.''

She nodded hesitantly and followed.

It was the house of his dreams. It was the deck he'd seen himself and Marisa sitting on even before he'd officially met her—the day she'd run into his cart in the grocery store.

''Perfect,'' he murmured, then checked to see if anyone had heard him talking to himself again. He'd had to really watch himself at Marisa's.

That was one of their problems—besides being able to get out of the bathroom only if you knew Marisa's trick with the screwdriver. It felt like Marisa's house. He thought of it as Marisa's house. It *was* Marisa's house. Marisa and Ryan's. He felt like a guest, one not sure of his welcome. They needed a home of *theirs.* Neutral, mutual territory. And a yard big enough to require a tractor lawn mower.

What a great view, or at least it would be in another couple of weeks. Rough mounds of dirt would become a plush green lawn slanting down to the small grove of trees separating this property from the one behind. French doors led off the kitchen/dining-room area to his deck. He didn't have to close his eyes to see nice, solid deck chairs sitting there.

"Is this one sold?" he asked Chris, carefully keeping the eagerness from his voice.

"I don't think so." Chris's smug grin said he'd been certain he could show them something enticing. "Lemme check with Mac." Mac had been at the last house they'd toured. He watched as Chris walked out the back door, onto the deck and across the mounds of earth. Upstairs, he heard muffled bangs and thumps from the workers installing plasterboard.

"What do you think?" He turned to Marisa, who stood behind a pile of sawdust outside the door as if it was too high to step over and enter the room.

"Are you hoping to buy it?"

"Isn't it great!" He realized she was horrified. "What's wrong? You don't like it?"

"You said we'd build something. That this was just—" she searched for a word "—a trip to scope out neighborhoods, see what kind of house we might want."

"You don't like what we've seen so far? You don't like this house? You want to loo—"

"We can't move," she interrupted, a desperate note in her voice. "You said...I thought...when you said we'd build, I assumed it would take a while to find a lot, make plans, hire someone."

"I meant we'd get something brand-new. We could be here by Halloween." His heart thudded heavily in his chest. It would be *their* house. They'd all fit. They'd start feeling like a family. "No more screwdrivers to get out of the bathroom," he tempted. "No more slow-running ancient drains and creaking doors. Wouldn't buying this house be easier, more convenient, than actually building something?'' He lowered his voice. ''I love this house.'' His arm swept toward the outdoors. ''Don't you think Ryan would love having this yard?''

''It's nice. But Ryan's my worry,'' she said softly. ''The evening before we were married, he got very quiet after you left. I asked if he'd changed his mind about it. About us getting married.''

''And he said?''

''He was having second thoughts. He wanted you to live with us, but he didn't want to leave his friends.'' In the short time they'd been together, surely Josh had seen how important Brian was in Ryan's life.

''I told him you wanted to build a house. I promised we wouldn't move anytime soon. That we'd be where we'd always been, at least until school was out this year. He'll be changing schools then, anyway, going to middle school. Wouldn't that be a better time to move?'' She released an uneasy sigh. ''I like the house, Josh.'' She raised her hands in a helpless gesture. ''I know your intention is to make things better for Ryan and me, but give us time. We need more time,'' she said again on a whisper.

Time. Something they should have taken more of before. But marriage was like everything else, wasn't it? You grabbed the bull by the horns. You jumped into something with both feet, then conquered problems one by one as they came your way. Wasn't that how it worked?

He swallowed his disappointment.

''You'll be glad to know this house hasn't sold yet,'' Chris said cheerfully when he returned. ''You're the first to see it, in fact. It's being listed this weekend—unless you want to talk to Mac about not bothering to list it. He might give you a better price.''

"We're not quite ready yet. Thanks, Chris, for all your help. We do want this builder's name and number for later, though. Do you have his card?"

"Not with me, but I'll have my secretary send you one tomorrow."

Josh studied what would have been his backyard again. "It's a shame this'll be gone by the time we're ready. It's a nice house."

"Mac's houses go quickly," Chris warned.

"It's not a wasted trip. We do like it. You do like it, don't you?" Josh asked Marisa, who still stood by the door, looking totally miserable.

"I love it. It's beautiful."

Chris seemed pleased. "We'll get Mac to build something you like when you are ready. Maybe even one exactly like this as long as you're not interested in this area. I would hate to see you rush into something before you're ready."

Josh glanced at Marisa again. No. He had a feeling he was done rushing into things for a while.

"Thanks for having lunch with me, Marisa," Evie said the next day as they were led to a booth at Neighbors, the restaurant Josh had taken her to that first night, the night he'd asked her to marry him. "It's kind of a tradition to go out for lunch on the day the kids go back to school, but all my friends have gone back to work," she admitted. "I'm afraid I was feeling sorry for myself when you came over yesterday afternoon."

"Do you want to go back to work?" Marisa asked.

"No way. I like being a stay-at-home mom. I'm just irritated with all my friends. How dare they prefer money to hanging out with me?" She laughed, then turned the question back on Marisa. "It's not going to last long, but how are *you* liking it? How did Mr. Finegold take the news you were quitting?''

"I didn't quit," Marisa mumbled, looking at her menu. "Not completely, anyway. I ended up taking a couple of weeks off, but I told him I'd stay."

"You're going to work *and* go to school?"

"Mr. Finegold panicked. I didn't have the heart to run out on him after all he's been through with me. He offered to rework my schedule—part-time evenings—and shifted some of my responsibilities. Then he gave me a nice raise." She lifted her shoulders. "So I'm still employed." He hadn't had to talk too long or too hard, Marisa admitted to herself. The thought of giving up the job that had been her and Ryan's security for so long had been scary. And with the way things were going, it was probably best to keep it.

"Josh doesn't mind? He'll never see you."

"He didn't seem to," Marisa said. When she'd told him, she suspected he was relieved. He'd probably thought it would save the stress of having to sit and look at each other from across the room every evening.

"Did you get the classes you wanted?"

"Actually—" Finally Marisa had something to smile about "—it's better than I thought. I'll be finished in only a year. And I'm doing my student teaching this semester. After the first few weeks, I'll have the exact same schedule as Ryan."

"Oh, Marisa, that's wonderful."

"They haven't confirmed it yet, but I'll probably be student teaching at South, a block from Ryan's school. I'll be able to take the kids to and from school."

"They'll be thrilled. You know they think they're getting too old to ride the bus—with all the babies," Evie added in such an accurate mimic of her son, Marisa had to chuckle.

Here's a HOT offer for you!

Get set for a sizzling summer read...

with **2 FREE ROMANCE BOOKS**
and a **FREE MYSTERY GIFT!**
NO CATCH! NO OBLIGATION TO BUY!

Simply complete and return this card and you'll get **FREE BOOKS, A FREE GIFT** and much more!

- The first shipment is yours to keep, absolutely free!

- Enjoy the convenience of romance books, delivered right to your door, before they're available in the stores!

- Take advantage of special low pricing for Reader Service Members only!

- After receiving your free books we hope you'll want to remain a subscriber. But the choice is always yours—to continue or cancel anytime at all! So why not take us up on this fabulous invitation with no risk of any kind. You'll be glad you did!

335 SDL CPSS

**235 SDL CPSK
S-SE-05/99**

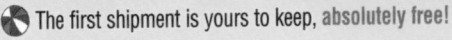

Name:		
	(Please Print)	
Address:		Apt.#:
City:		
State/Prov.:		Zip/ Postal Code:

► DETACH HERE AND MAIL CARD TODAY! ►

The Silhouette Reader Service™ — Here's How it Works:

Accepting your 2 free books and mystery gift places you under no obligation to buy anything. You may keep the books and gift and return the shipping statement marked "cancel." If you do not cancel, about a month later we'll send you 6 additional novels and bill you just $3.57 each in the U.S., or $3.96 each in Canada, plus 25¢ delivery per book and applicable taxes if any.* That's the complete price and — compared to the cover price of $4.25 in the U.S. and $4.75 in Canada — it's quite a bargain! You may cancel at any time, but if you choose to continue, every month we'll send you 6 more books, which you may either purchase at the discount price or return it to us and cancel your subscription.

*Terms and prices subject to change without notice. Sales tax applicable in N.Y. Canadian residents will be charged applicable provincial taxes and GST.

"I'll bet Evonne loves that."

Evie shook her head. "Vonnie'll survive. She gets a lot of benefits from having a big brother, so it doesn't hurt her to take a few of the slings and arrows." She took a deep breath. "I guess Ryan won't have a little sister any time soon. Not with your schedule."

"Not soon." Josh had said he wanted to get married so he could have a family while he was young enough to enjoy his children. They'd agreed that when and if it happened, it would be fine.

"Josh hasn't made love to me." The words sneaked out before she could stop them. She hardly realized she'd said anything until Evie gasped.

"What do you mean?"

"Exactly what I said."

"Not even..."

"Not even on our honeymoon," Marisa admitted.

"Guess he wasn't impressed with the negligee I chose."

"I'd be surprised if he even saw it," Marisa said. "He turned the light off."

"Oh?" Evie's eyebrows raised.

"Oh, Evie, things are so mixed-up."

"You don't think he's—"

"No." She knew exactly what Evie was thinking, and the thought was laughable. She had too much evidence to the contrary. At the mayor's reception, when they'd danced... His kisses were too warm, sweet—not that there'd been any since they'd gotten married. Except for last night, when they'd endured the enforced closeness in the cab of Chris's pickup, Josh avoided touching her. But Marisa could feel the heat of his gaze whenever they were near. "I think the problem is me."

"What do you mean?"

Marisa couldn't go into her theories without going into

more detail about their marriage than she wanted to. "I don't know what I mean." She was sorry she'd opened the discussion.

Evie put down her menu. "I have a theory," she said, leaning across the table. "Maybe this proves my theory right."

"What?"

"Well, you know men supposedly want sex but don't want to commit to marriage?"

Marisa nodded, though she couldn't accuse Josh of not wanting to commit to marriage.

"I've always thought that's a little cockeyed, that it's a lot more complicated than that. I've always suspected men want sex *and* they want marriage. Nothing will convince me they don't like the stability."

Marisa could testify to that. Wasn't it pretty much what Josh had said when he'd first proposed?

"They just don't necessarily want both sex and marriage from the same woman."

Marisa laughed. "So I should have slept with Josh, instead of marrying him?"

Evie grinned. "No. Not necessarily." She shrugged. "But I do think there is that Madonna thing."

"As in the singer?"

"No, silly. As in Madonna and child. Once you've married a man, he wants you to be virginal and pure and the type of woman he wants to raise his children. I goofed!" She interrupted herself to slap her forehead. "I shouldn't have bought that virginal white wedding negligee. I should have gone for the bright red vamp stuff. Slinky. Sexy. I debated it," she added, gnawing at the corner of her lip.

"It doesn't matter, since he didn't see it," Marisa reminded her. "Does this theory of yours come from personal experience? Are you saying Bob didn't sleep with you on *your* wedding night?''

Evie smiled slyly. ''Oh, he did. But that's where the theory comes from. That and after Brian was born. That's when we had trouble. He didn't touch me anymore. I could tell it wasn't because he didn't want to. It was because everything had changed. I was suddenly Madonna.''

''You're suggesting I seduce Josh? I don't think I'd make such a great vamp.'' She grimaced.

''If my theory is at all correct, you don't have to. It'll work out.'' Evie grinned slyly. ''Or he'll find a mistress.''

''Thanks. I needed that.'' Marisa didn't spare the sarcasm.

''You don't need to worry.'' Evie patted her hand. ''He's one of the good guys. I can tell.''

Marisa didn't disagree for an instant. Josh *was* one of the good guys. But he was also one mystifying husband. ''What *did* happen on your wedding night?'' Marisa summoned the nerve to ask.

''The usual,'' Evie said lightly. ''But my theory comes from the fact that I was pregnant when we got married. So nothing changed. I was the 'vamp' until I had the baby. *Then* things changed.''

Even if Evie was right, Marisa wasn't certain what her theory proved or even if it applied to her and Josh. But it was interesting food for thought. ''I'm sorry I dumped on you, Evie. I shouldn't have brought it up. Forget I said anything, okay?''

Evie nodded as the waitress appeared to take their orders.

''What'd you guys do last night?'' Evie asked after they'd ordered the soup-and-salad special. ''You weren't gone very long. You decided not to go out to dinner, after all?''

''I suggested we go home,'' Marisa told her. ''It seemed

pointless for the two of us to have dinner alone when I knew we'd sit at a table across from each other and either not talk at all or have another very civilized but meaningless conversation.''

''About what?''

''Josh's surprise was taking me to look at houses. I don't want to move until Ryan changes schools next year. The way things are going…'' She left the sentence unfinished.

''Marisa,'' Evie said in her Mother-knows-best voice, ''you cannot let yourself get into the frame of mind where you expect the worst. No marriage has a chance that way.''

Did Marisa's marriage—her one last shot, she believed—have a chance, anyway?

''You and Josh loved each other on sight. Enough to jump into this. Don't let yourself forget that.''

But we *didn't* love each other, Marisa thought. We were going to ''grow it.'' How could they grow it, she wondered? What could she do to nurture the feelings she thought Josh had had from the beginning? Or maybe she'd only imagined them. And maybe that was the problem. Was she letting fantasies creep in where practicality should reign? ''Sometimes…I guess I'm worried that we really didn't know each other well enough. I should have—''

She broke off as the waitress brought their soup.

When their server left, Evie reached across and patted her hand again. ''Marisa, there's no doing it over. You can't go back.''

She was right, Marisa acknowledged. Wishing she could change the past wouldn't get her anywhere. It would be a whole lot more productive to figure out how to improve things in the future.

''There was something about Josh that made you throw caution to the wind. Can't imagine what,'' Evie went on, jiggling her eyebrows suggestively. "But that isn't like you at all, is it?"

She'd married Josh for all the right and logical reasons. How had she made it look as though she'd "thrown caution to the wind" and jumped in with both feet?

"There are always adjustments."

Marisa nodded in agreement this time.

"So all you have to do is figure out where things went wrong. Go back. Start from there."

Start at being friends! That was where they'd been until the day they'd gotten married. She had to go back to thinking of Josh as a friend rather than a husband.

She could go back, she decided. She could be Josh's friend and companion. And maybe in the meantime, she'd buy something slinky, sexy and red.

At least she had an idea of something to try.

Chapter Eight

He'd made a mistake. There was no point in denying it any longer. Now how did he correct it? Josh wondered as he went directly to the appropriate section of the store for the bread Marisa had asked him to pick up on his way home.

He had every aisle memorized. And he'd thought grocery shopping would be a part of his past. Now he was stopping at the store on his way home every day.

He'd always been organized, making lists and going once a week. Marisa treated the store like her pantry, running to it whenever she needed something.

He didn't understand the way Marisa's mind worked at all.

He could admit to himself that it had been stupid to expect marriage to solve all his problems—or even one of them, he thought wryly.

Well, one had been solved. He wasn't talking to himself

anymore. He wasn't talking much to anyone. He couldn't risk saying the wrong thing and seeing that crushed look in Marisa's eyes.

He liked having Ryan around. The boy made dinner conversations interesting.

And he liked having Marisa around, too. He liked looking at her, hearing her motherly exchanges with Ryan. He loved being enveloped in her soft scent when she passed him. Never mind that her presence doubled one of his other problems—one he thought for sure marriage would take care of. Lord knew he wanted her, but she didn't seem ready to take the relationship to the next step yet. The way she froze when he touched her—something he hadn't tried since the 'honeymoon'—he wasn't sure anymore if she'd ever be ready.

So he wandered around in a constant, miserable state of arousal. How could he fix things? How did he get out of this mess he'd gotten himself into?

He wasn't a quitter. He couldn't just ask for a divorce. He'd made promises, for one thing. Whatever else he felt, he felt responsible. For her. For Ryan.

But he'd created a disaster. He had to find a way to rectify his mistakes.

The promises! He would keep the promises and *then* he could ask for a divorce. Some, like being a father figure to Ryan, were long-term, but he could get a nice start. Spend an hour with him a day. Get close. Get a pattern going. If they established a solid relationship now, they could continue it later—even after a divorce. He could get all the repairs at Marisa's house done, make sure she got her teaching degree…

By the time he arrived at Marisa's house—home, he corrected—he had quite a list of answers.

When he entered the kitchen, Ryan was sitting at the

table arguing with his mother. But it was comfortable, the kind of argument two people had who were easy enough with each other to say what they felt.

Marisa looked up at Josh. "Oh, hi," she said, as if surprised to see him. What? She didn't expect him?

Ryan brightened. "You tell her, Josh."

"Tell who what?"

"Mrs. Brack gave us homework," the boy said, gesturing at the workbook in front of him.

"On your second day?"

"That's what I thought," Ryan said. "But she said it was just practice. Doesn't that mean I don't have to do it?"

"How can you practice if you don't do it?"

Obviously that was the wrong thing to say. Ryan looked disgusted. "She isn't even going to grade it." He rolled his eyes.

"What exactly did Mrs. Brack say?" Josh asked. "About the homework, I mean."

"She said we'd have more homework this year than we've had before. She wants us to form a habit. She isn't even going to give us a grade on it," he said again.

"That doesn't mean you don't have to do it," Marisa said. "She expects you to turn it in whether she grades it or not."

"Your mom's right," Josh said. "It's practice for you, and she probably wants to see how everyone is doing in math. This will show her."

Ryan sat back in his chair and crossed his arms belligerently.

"You may as well get started," Marisa suggested. "'Cause you can't do anything else until it's done."

"I have all weekend," Ryan protested.

"You know the rules, Ryan. You do it as soon as you

get home. Just because you're going to have more this year doesn't mean the rules have changed.''

"It's a good rule," Josh agreed. "Wouldn't you rather have it out of the way?" he asked. "Hey, get it finished and I'll let you beat me at Nintendo."

You aren't supposed to side with her, Josh translated the look Ryan shot at him. Could he afford to alienate his one friend in the house? And Marisa had her back to him as she put something in the oven, so he couldn't judge her reaction to his jumping in.

She was smiling at him when she turned around. "We have about forty-five minutes before this is ready." She laid a hand on Ryan's shoulder. "You have time to finish that." Her nervous but hopeful smile at him tugged at Josh's heart—and other places, as well. "Would you like to sit on the porch with me, Josh?" she invited. "It's something I like to do this time of year."

"I…that would be nice," he managed. "Should I pour us something to drink?"

"I'll get it."

He took the glasses she'd taken from the cabinet out of her hands. "Let me. White wine?"

"A soda would be nice." She indicated the two-liter bottle sitting on the counter. "I'll wait outside."

She was sitting on the top step, her back against one of the porch posts, when he reached the door. She jumped up to hold it open for him so he could juggle their drinks.

As soon as she had hers and had sat back down, he took the post adjacent to hers. Leaning sideways against it, he propped one leg in front of him on the porch and let the other dangle over the side, not realizing he was imitating her position until he was settled. At last, some of those required classes in law school were coming in handy, he thought. Since he'd practiced mostly corporate and family law, he'd never had to mirror a witness's body language to put them at ease.

"Thanks for backing me up with Ryan," she said.

"Anytime."

"Did you have a good day?" she asked, sounding just like a dutiful wife.

"It was okay," he answered like a dutiful husband. It made him smile. They were searching for common ground. It was pleasant, a personal conversation that had nothing to do with the weather or the nightly news. Or Ryan.

"You'll be glad to know I bought a new doorknob for the bathroom this afternoon."

"I was thinking about the exact same thing on the way home."

She looked as though that pleased her. His gaze swept her long legs and he noticed that the toes of her shoes were practically touching him. He bent his knee a bit more, destroying the bookends image he'd had of the two of them. His new position increased the distance between them to half a foot, but there was no need to display what looking at her legs was doing to him. No one in his memory looked better in shorts. "Shall I fix it tonight?"

"If you want." She shrugged. "But I can call the guy down the street if you want me to," she said. "He's done handyman things for me before."

"I can fix it."

"Do you mind? I hate you to—" She bit her lip.

"What?"

"I hate to ask you to do anything when I know how you feel."

"How do you think I feel, Marisa?"

"You want a new house." She studied the melting ice cubes in her glass, poked at one of them with a fingertip.

"I know you think this place is a rat trap. I don't want you to spend your time or money on some—"

"I want you and Ryan to have the kind of house you deserve," he interrupted. "It's very difficult for me to feel at home here when you treat me like a guest."

"How have I treated you like a guest?"

"You wait on me." He pointed to his soda. "You realize this is the first drink I've gotten for myself since we were married?"

"I'm sorry." She looked stricken.

Despite the guilt he felt for that look, he felt better for getting it off his chest. "I don't expect you to wait on me."

She opened her mouth, closed it, then opened it again. "I was…I thought I was being a considerate wife. It didn't occur to me that you might feel as if I was treating you like a guest."

"I'm perfectly capable of doing the repairs. Let me be useful."

"I don't know if I have the necessary tools," she said.

"I have a few things," he said. "A screwdriver is probably all I'll need to change that knob. I have that and more. Some woodworking tools, as well."

"Oh, yeah. You *like* fixing things." She'd forgotten his boasting about his father's Mr. Fix-it skills. But that had been when he'd asked her to marry him and she'd been too dazed for anything to sink in.

"I hope to have a garage or some kind of shop eventually. I like working with my hands."

"Then we live in the right house, don't we?" Her smile said she was being facetious. But it dimmed immediately. "Still, I wouldn't want you to put energy into a house that's…that's…"

"A rat trap?"

"You also said any profits when we sell it should be put aside for Ryan's college education."

"You don't think that's a good idea?"

"Of course." She nodded. "But I hate for you to spend time—or money—on something you won't get some benefit from."

"I'm living here," he said. "That's not a benefit?"

She didn't look at him.

"I'm sharing home-cooked meals. Companionship. I didn't expect everything to be instantly perfect." Liar, he thought. That was exactly what he'd expected. Foolishly.

"You're not totally unhappy, then? You don't regret…" She finally looked him in the eye. Contrarily he wished she wouldn't.

He glanced at the door and wondered if he dared bring up the subject haunting them both. But Ryan might appear at any time. In another few minutes, she'd want to check whatever she'd put in the oven. Shoot, they were sitting on the front porch. Any neighbor could wander by and overhear. He couldn't bring up sex now. "Let's give it time, Marisa. Don't you think that's fair?"

"Can we go back to being friends?" she asked hopefully.

That was exactly what they'd lost when they'd said the magic words to make all this legal. If they could be friends, it would be easier to fix the damage he'd done when he rushed her into this. When he'd kept all his promises, *then* he could leave. "I think that's a brilliant idea," he agreed.

"How come you and Josh don't sleep in the same room?"

Josh knew that Ryan and Marisa hadn't heard him come in, knew that he should let Marisa know he was standing at the kitchen door. Mother and son were somewhere down the hall.

"Brian's mom and dad sleep together," Ryan went on. "Isn't that what married people do?"

Ryan was standing at the bathroom door. Marisa was probably putting on makeup, getting ready to go to work.

She cleared her throat. "Most of them do."

"So why don't you and Josh?" he persisted.

"He decided…we decided—" Marisa cleared her throat "—that we'd wait a while. Get to know each other a little better before we became roommates."

"Oh." Ryan seemed satisfied with her answer. "Brian said that's why people get married. You know. The sex stuff." Josh could sense the bright flush on Ryan's face from his tone.

"It's part of the reason," Marisa said. "But only part. People get married because they want to do things together. Other things," she added quickly. "Josh and I got married because we didn't want to be alone. It's sad to be alone."

"You have me," Ryan said.

Marisa laughed. Josh could imagine her touching him. She touched Ryan a lot when he said things like that. And Josh hungered for the same kind of touch. He caught himself leaning toward her voice and felt foolish. But it was foolishness with an ache attached.

"I won't have you forever," she said. "You'll grow up. Go to college. Decide you like your friends better than me." He heard Marisa's smile in the statement and pictured Ryan's frown as he wondered whether it was true already. "You may even get married someday."

Josh could imagine the horrified look on Ryan's face by her chuckle. Sometimes it felt as though he knew them awfully well.

"I guess if you don't *have* to sleep in the same room,"

Ryan finally decided, "it might be okay." He sounded skeptical.

"You're just spoiled," Marisa said. "A lot of kids have brothers or sisters and they have to share rooms. I'll bet you'd kind of like it if you had someone."

"Are we gonna have another kid?" The disbelief had returned to his voice.

Marisa cleared her throat again. "Would you mind?"

"You'd have to do…other stuff," Ryan said, every bit of the distaste he ascribed to the subject coming through loud and clear.

Obviously Marisa had taken sex education seriously. Ryan wouldn't be so free with his questions now if she hadn't already been open and honest with him.

But the last comment obviously left her fumbling. He heard Marisa stammer and stutter and her words become pinched, unclear. He moved farther into the hall.

"Then we *aren't* going to have another kid?" Ryan asked.

"Maybe someday," she said again. "But for now…" Her voice wasn't as assured as she probably meant it to be, but Josh didn't think Ryan would detect the slight waver. "A relationship—any kind of relationship—has to develop slowly," she said more firmly. "So it gets better all the time."

"Like Grandma and Grandpa," Ryan said knowingly.

"Like Grandma and Grandpa," Marisa agreed. "And you and Brian. Remember when you used to fight all the time? You weren't always best friends. That's why Josh and I are going slowly," she finished. "We want to be best friends."

"You won't have to kiss him all the time like Grandma does Grandpa?"

"Josh isn't… I don't think Josh likes me in that way."

How could she think that?

"You're pretty, Mom," Ryan protested indignantly.

"I'm glad you think so." Her voice was nearer suddenly as she came out of the bathroom. Josh held his breath. He heard her stop, say something else to Ryan.

Josh breathed out in relief when he heard her footsteps going the other way, toward her room.

Ryan's "Aw, Mom" followed her as Josh gingerly tiptoed back outside and made a noisy reentrance.

"How 'bout McDonald's tonight?" Josh suggested to Ryan a little later as Marisa made a hasty exit for work. She was going to be a few minutes late again.

Ryan scowled up at him and put in a bid for his favorite. "Taco Bell?"

Josh nodded his agreement.

"We going to play football again tonight?"

They'd been playing at least an hour most nights, especially the nights Marisa was at work. "I have a better idea," he said. "I want to surprise your mom. Will you help?"

Ryan looked as if he wasn't sure he wanted to help with any surprise Josh might have cooked up. "Not flowers or something, is it?"

"Better. Much better," Josh promised, and herded Ryan toward his car so they could go get dinner.

"Do you think my mom's pretty?" Ryan asked as they drove.

Josh turned down the radio Ryan had turned up. "Your mom is one of the most beautiful women I've ever seen."

Maybe he shouldn't have said it so reverently. Ryan looked at him suspiciously and Josh decided he'd better change the subject if he didn't want to get into a discussion similar to the one Marisa had just had with him.

"Did you have homework tonight?"

Ryan nodded.

"Done already?"

He nodded again.

"Good." After a moment he said, "I'll bet you make real good grades in school."

"Did *you* make good grades, Josh?"

"Had to. My little sister was a straight-A student, and she wouldn't have let me live it down if she'd made better grades than me."

"Janet?"

"Yeah." Josh grinned at his new stepson. "Janet. I keep forgetting you know her."

"Not really," Ryan disagreed. "I've never even seen her."

"But she talks to you on the phone."

"And sends me presents," Ryan added. "It's pretty neat that she's your sister."

"How hungry are you?" Josh asked, slowing and putting on his turn signal.

"Some," Ryan said.

"Let's stop here at the lumberyard first. Then we won't have to go out later or let our tacos get cold because we had to stop on the way home."

Ryan seemed game for anything. He was even helpful with suggestions about how to get the big box into the trunk of Josh's car. They ended up tying it closed with twine that the clerk supplied.

"Cool," Ryan said as they got back in the car.

"Think Marisa will like it?"

"Yeah," he said. "She's always wanted one."

"We're going to have it waiting for her when she gets home."

"Cool," Ryan said again.

One promise down. A whole list yet to go.

* * *

Marisa pulled into the drive at eleven. She'd only been working her new hours for a week and she was weary to the bone. Her school schedule left her plenty of time to get the day-to-day chores done, but that wouldn't last long. When she started student teaching, she might have to re-evaluate the deal she'd made with Mr. Finegold. He *had* been good to her. But he was already getting more comfortable with the way Mindy and Claire—the other two employees he'd divvied her responsibilities between—were handling things. He had Marisa coming in two nights a week basically to see if they were filing insurance claims correctly. She wasn't really doing anything but checking up on them and making him feel better.

But you never know when you might need the job, a contrary voice said inside her head. "Mr. Finegold would probably take you back in that case," she muttered and jumped as something tapped her window.

"Oh, Josh!" She placed a hand over her heart as he opened the car door for her. "You scared me."

"You going to sit in here forever?"

"Thinking about it." She was already feeling more energetic than she'd felt a moment before. Whatever else he did, Josh could jump-start her heart just by looking the way he did.

"Been a long day?"

She nodded and let him help her out. His hand wrapped hers lightly and sent a reassuring, solid warmth straight through her. "Ryan in bed?"

"Hours ago," he said.

"I sound like I don't trust you to do the most basic things, don't I? I'm sorry. I do. Worrying is a habit. He's been my sole responsibility for so long."

"You've done a terrific job." Josh laced their fingers

together intimately and she realized that in the past few weeks, they had made it back to friendship. "Did I tell you, Mrs. Maxwell, how much I like your kid?"

"No, I don't think you did." His eyes held a satisfied glimmer. His "Mrs. Maxwell" sounded pleasantly possessive as he steered her away from the back door of the house, where she usually entered. "What—"

"Let's go in the front way." He guided her in that direction. "Ryan is great company." He paused, then continued, "And great help putting together—" he gestured dramatically toward the corner of the porch "—porch swings."

"Oh, Josh." Marisa stopped in her tracks and stared.

"Come on. Try it out." He pushed her gently toward the steps. "Ryan declared it cool."

"I'll have to do something about his vocabulary. It's getting very limited," she murmured.

"It isn't the nicest swing," Josh said. "I couldn't figure out how to get one of the big fancy ones in my car. I had to go with the put-together kind that comes in a box."

"It's perfect," she said, sinking onto the swing without Josh's urging. "Oh, Josh, thank you." Bereft of words that would tell him how much his gesture touched her, she waved a hand at the seat beside her. "Aren't you going to join me?" she asked more coyly than she intended. At this rate, soon she'd be buying the red lingerie she hadn't had the courage to buy yet and batting her eyelashes at him.

"Just a minute." He held up one finger. "Here. Let me take that for you." He grabbed her purse and disappeared inside.

"Cool," she declared as she set herself swinging with a push of her foot.

"I wonder where Ryan got his vocabulary," Josh teased when he rejoined her. "Here." He handed her a wineglass.

He lifted his and tapped it lightly against hers. "To many happy hours in your swing."

To her horror, she burst into tears.

"Oh, Marisa." He plucked the glass from her hand before she spilled it, then set both glasses on the porch floor beside the swing. His arms went around her and drew her close to his wonderfully broad chest. "Shh. What's wrong, sweetheart?"

The gentle endearment shocked the sobs to a sudden halt. "Sweetheart" was probably what he called Janet. Reality! She grasped for it and came up with a handful of Josh's shirt. She didn't want to think about reality right now. His arms felt blissfully warm and secure around her. The cold ache that had been growing inside her for days and days became an agonizing burning pain.

"What's wrong, honey?" His hand stroked her back and brought her closer to him. She felt his heartbeat against her chest.

And she wasn't sure why she was crying.

Because this porch swing makes me feel cared for and...and spoiled, she answered herself. *And no matter how much I tell myself not to care, I want this marriage to work more than I've wanted anything in a very long time.*

"Marisa." Josh's voice rasped close to her ear. It was low, seductive.

She leaned away from him, tilting her head to catch his expression in the moonlight. "I'm sorry, Josh. I didn't mean to cry."

"I didn't mean to make you," he said quietly.

"I'm not used to saying I want something and having it appear," she tried to say lightheartedly. It came out fervently.

"Then you're long past due," he said just as fervently,

and his eyes rested on her lips. Then his mouth followed. His touch was gentle, tentative.

Marisa didn't have to close her eyes. She couldn't have kept them open if she'd tried. The sweetness of his kiss weakened her and made her whole body feel as limp as a paper doll.

He sipped at her mouth, holding back. She found herself pushing desperately nearer, struggling to get closer to him.

"Marisa," he said against her mouth, trying gently to tug her away from him.

She resisted.

His hands came to her sides, just far enough below her armpits that his palms brushed the sides of her breasts. And her breasts suddenly ached with the need for more of his touch.

He groaned and renewed his efforts to put her away from him. "Do you know where this is going?" he asked on a sharp intake of air. A cricket started humming as if in answer to his question. The night seemed to grow darker and closer around them, cocooning them in a breathless, heavy atmosphere. "I can't take it if you change your mind."

"Don't you want me?" she whispered. She felt feverish, possessed. She wanted to be possessed by him.

His only answer was another pain-filled groan. "I want you so badly I can hardly be in the same room with you," he said. "I'm always afraid of what I might do."

"Please, Josh," she whispered against his lips. "Make love to me."

He froze for a moment, then sighed deeply. "I'd be delighted to," he finally said, his voice so low and husky she almost didn't hear. "I'd be delighted to," he said again, then lowered his head to kiss her some more.

Chapter Nine

Josh carried her inside. After the heat of the early September night, the cool air-conditioning indoors was a shock to his system.

Marisa shivered and he felt a stab of fear that she might change her mind. He couldn't take it if she did.

Her bedroom door was open. He nudged it closed with his shoulder after they were safely ensconced inside. Her bed was old-fashioned, an antique four-poster, narrow. But that was good. He didn't intend to let her get out of touching range, and in this bed, it wasn't likely. He set her down carefully in the middle of it.

She gazed at him, her eyes wide and bright as he settled on his side next to her. "Marisa." He couldn't seem to stop saying her name. He couldn't stop even when he was kissing her.

He'd never tasted anything as addictive as her lips. His mouth watered as his hands slowly traced her shapely breasts. He leaned into her, letting his body mold to her gentle curves. She seemed content to concentrate on his kisses. Her hands cradled his shoulders, tightening from time to time as his exploration became more extensive.

She gasped as his hand slid beneath the silky fabric of the shirt he'd unbuttoned. He paused and held his breath, then pushed aside the material when she relaxed again. The sight he'd revealed took his breath away. He covered the gentle mounds above the white lacy bra with kisses. And he couldn't help smiling when he heard a gasp of pure pleasure as his tongue sneaked beneath the edge of the fabric.

Bliss. She was bliss. He unwrapped her as carefully as she'd unwrapped the few wedding presents they'd received.

She'd read the cards, admired the pictures, enjoyed each word. He read her expressions, admired the light in her passion-glazed eyes, enjoyed each tiny gasp of appreciation.

She'd savored the bows, touching and smoothing them. He savored her, touching and smoothing away her clothes.

She'd traced patterns and textures as she folded and preserved each bit of wrapping paper. He memorized the patterns and textures of her body.

She'd finally oohed and aahed over each gift. Everything in him was awed by everything about her.

No gift could ever be as perfect as the one he had in his arms, he thought as he sipped and tasted an inch of skin he was afraid he'd missed in the process of revealing it. Then he realized he still had every stitch of his own clothes on. Too uncomfortably impatient to be rid of them, he didn't wait for her to undress him.

His clothes were gone practically before she noticed he'd stood up to take them off. Her lovely hazel eyes widened briefly as he rejoined her on the bed and resumed lavishing her body with the attention it deserved. "Touch me," he pleaded as he pulled her close, memorizing the way her curves seemed to flow in perfect symmetry against him.

Light as butterfly wings, her hand fluttered gently to his chest. She let her fingers curl in the hair there. She moved against him shyly, moaning quietly as he circled and caressed one of her taut nipples with his tongue.

She was very inexperienced. It finally sank in.

Somehow the knowledge tempered his desire, sharpening it, making it stronger even while edging it with determination to be as careful of her as he'd be of a rare and precious gem.

With his lips he captured his name on hers when he finally took her.

When she whispered it again on a sweet, satisfied smile when the loving was over, he'd never felt as complete or satisfied.

The handsome man in her bed was her husband. And her lover.

The man in her bed had held her close all night, cupping her bare breast in one of his magical, mystical hands.

Marisa sat up slowly, drawing the quilted bedspread around her as she rose quietly, trying not to disturb him, trying to get to the alarm before it went off.

"Trying to sneak out on me," the man in her bed said, opening one eye and fixing her with a contented look.

"Yes," she said. Although the heat rushed through her face, she became aware that she was blushing when a delighted grin spread over his face. "Actually," she said, using her most dignified voice, "I was going to stop the alarm from going off so you could sleep a few extra minutes. I'll go make coffee." She clamped her hand around the clock and stopped it midring.

"Come here," he whispered.

She dodged his hand and slipped into the small walk-in closet, closing the door behind her. It opened again just as she let the quilt slip and reached for her robe.

The sight of him, standing as magnificently naked as the day he'd been born, shocked her more than her own nudity. Her whole body felt a fire reminiscent of last night as she grabbed her old tattered robe and hurriedly wrapped it around her.

"You are the most beautiful thing I've ever seen," he said on an indrawn breath.

"Thank you, kind sir." She curtsied, feeling tongue-tied and stupid. She couldn't stand here and carry on a conversation with a naked man—even if he was her husband and lover.

"You're blushing again," he taunted. "And smiling," he added, obviously pleased.

"Lots to smile about." She lowered her gaze, only to raise it quickly. Looking down wasn't safe.

"Good." He was suddenly serious. "You aren't sorry, then?"

"Definitely not sorry."

"Good." He stepped into the small walk-in closet, closing the door behind him. As daylight disappeared from the space, she saw him reach for her and stepped to meet him.

"Mmm," he sighed against her mouth. "Wish we had time…"

He didn't have to finish the thought. His body talked for him as he reached inside her robe and pulled her to him. Her body answered with a rush of longing that startled her and left her breathless. "How do you do that?" she gasped.

"What?" He nibbled her lips.

"Make me feel this way," she finally managed, letting

her head loll back as he left a trail of kisses down her throat. Her knees grew weak.

"Feels good, huh?" He dipped his head lower as his hands slowly ran the length of her back.

The closest she got to answering was a low moan.

"But we don't have time for this, do we?" he finally said on a husky groan. He backed away a step but seemed incapable of letting her go. "Guess I'll go take a cold shower." He reluctantly reached behind him and let the daylight back in.

She couldn't help her wide smile. It'd probably stay fixed in place today. "I'll go make coffee," she said again. "But hurry. I don't need to get Ryan up for a while. We can have our first cup out on the porch swing."

"Now that's incentive to hurry." He pulled on his jeans without bothering with the underwear that lay crumpled by the bed. His parting shot caught her halfway down the hall. "That porch swing may be dangerous," he warned.

"I know," she said without turning, and smiled.

The way Josh made her feel, everything—including mundane things like washing dishes or taking out trash—might be dangerous with him around. She definitely needed to watch her heart.

The early morning hinted at the kind of day it was going to become: hot and muggy. But right now the sky was rosy, the breeze fresh and intoxicating. By the time Josh joined Marisa on the porch, she'd lulled herself into a contented stupor with steady, gentle swinging.

"I love my porch swing," she told him, scooting over for him, then leaning into him as he sat down and put his arm around her shoulders.

"I suspect I'm gonna love it, too." He sipped at his steaming coffee. "May I ask you something?"

Marisa nodded, a little nervous about what might be coming, given the hesitant tone of his voice.

His hand tightened on her shoulder. "If I didn't know better—I mean, unless Ryan was some kind of miracle or something…"

She knew exactly what was coming.

"…I'd swear you were a virgin." He let his expression ask the question. "Before last night, of course," he tacked on in case she hadn't noticed that her virginal status had changed.

"Not exactly." A disturbing thought popped into her mind. She felt her cheeks flame, but she had to ask, "Did I do something wrong?"

Josh's reaction was immediate. He tipped her face up to his. "Not a thing." He stared into her eyes. It would be so easy to get lost there. "Not a damn thing." He planted a quick kiss on the corner of her mouth. "But practice makes perfect," he promised slyly, and Marisa smiled.

It felt right, starting the day with him. Everything seemed more real than it had yesterday, more sharply defined. Even the orange of her neighbor's poppies across the street seemed brighter.

The slight breeze lifted a strand of her hair, and Josh smoothed it back into place. "Could you define 'not exactly'?"

She had to think for a moment to remember the question. She grimaced. "Ryan's a walking, talking testament it only takes once," she said. "The night I got pregnant was my first and only time."

His frown turned dangerously dark. "You weren't raped?"

"Raped? No. It's called stupidity," she said. "I felt so invincible then. It was the night of my senior prom. My boyfriend—"

"Ryan's father?" Josh interrupted.

She nodded. "My boyfriend smuggled in booze. He had his mom and dad's big luxury car. I felt so mature. So grown-up. So in control of my life. I knew where I was going to college. I knew what I wanted to be. I thought Jimmy and I would eventually marry." She lifted her shoulders, bringing herself out of the past she'd visited.

"You loved him?"

"I thought I did." She laughed mirthlessly. "You want to know what's really funny?" She didn't wait for him to answer. "I barely remember it."

"The sex?"

She nodded and felt her color rise again. "What little I do remember was *nothing* like last night," she said. The corner of her mouth tilted wryly. "I'd hate myself for the whole sordid event if it wasn't for Ryan. He was the only good outcome."

Josh took her hand. It seemed to be attached directly to her heart. She felt a tug in that vicinity, and a mishmash of emotions made tears spring to her eyes.

"And last night?"

"Was special," she admitted even though she couldn't continue to look at him. "Very special."

"My pleasure," he said, smiling at her. He lifted his mug and downed the rest of his coffee. "And as much as I hate to do this, I'd better get moving."

She started to follow, but he shook his head and held out his hand. "Give me your cup. I'll get you a refill. You have another fifteen minutes or so before you have to get Ryan up, don't you?"

She nodded.

"You may as well enjoy it—in your porch swing," he added. "I'll enjoy thinking of you here while I'm driving to work."

"I'll enjoy being here," she said as he bent to kiss her. The scent of his cologne lingered with her long after he'd gone.

"I have tickets to KU's home opener tomorrow." Josh waved them around proudly when he got home the next evening. Ryan stopped whooping and hollering long enough to stare when Josh wrapped his arm around Marisa's waist and kissed her enthusiastically.

Marisa prayed Ryan wouldn't comment. She had no intention of continuing in front of Josh the discussion she'd had with him the other day.

She sighed with relief and let herself enjoy being danced around the room by Josh as Ryan turned disgustedly back to his homework.

"Any chance we could knock Ryan out early tonight?" he whispered. The words—and the promise they evoked—sent shivers down her spine.

"Not likely," she whispered back.

He looked disappointed but not surprised. And she found herself pulling away and going back to what she'd been doing. The overnight change in Josh was miraculous.

Shoot, she'd been shocking herself all day. She'd found herself humming under her breath, even in class. She'd wanted to twirl dramatically and burst into song. She hadn't done anything so silly since high school.

But the excitement of being a newlywed would wear off. She couldn't let herself get tangled up in emotions. She'd married Josh for purely practical reasons. She knew how easily she could get carried away with fantasies and feelings that had nothing to do with logic.

"Here." Josh took the package of hamburger she'd been about to open out of her hands and put it in the fridge. "Let's go out to dinner."

''Where?'' Ryan was suddenly interested in the conversation again.

''I was thinking of someplace nice.''

Marisa went to get ready while Josh offered to help Ryan with his homework.

Football tomorrow? She wrinkled her nose at her reflection in the mirror. She didn't find the thought appealing. She'd planned to get ahead in the housework department.

But she couldn't disappoint Josh. He'd seemed so pleased with himself.

Didn't she have to avoid any wonderful, fairy-tale, we-do-everything-together fantasies about this marriage if she was going to remain rational? ''That's exactly what you have to do,'' she ordered her reflection in the mirror.

Her image nodded in agreement.

Josh drove to three restaurants before finding the one he wanted. Ryan had been to the first place with a friend. Josh was tired of being the odd man out, the only one unfamiliar with everything.

The second was too relaxed. He wanted the evening to be a little extraordinary, even if Ryan's presence kept it from being exactly a date.

After the waiter took their order, Ryan asked to be excused to go wash his hands.

''He's very conscientious,'' Josh said.

Marisa laughed. ''He's casing the joint. He has to check everything out when we go somewhere new,'' she said. ''It has nothing to do with wanting clean hands.''

''Poor Ryan. You're too good at this parenting thing. How's he ever going to get anything past you?''

''I hope he doesn't have too many secrets.''

Josh squirmed inside and studied the other patrons

around them. Things were going really well. He didn't want to talk about secrets.

"You're doing fine, too," she said, then modified the compliment. "Better than fine. I'm amazed at how well you've taken to this parenting thing."

"Two-thirds of the time, I sound just like my father." He laughed. "Surely, with a little practice, I'll be able to come up with some original lines."

"You want some extra practice?" With her fingernail, she absently started to draw designs in the condensation on her glass. "Would you mind if I didn't go to the football game tomorrow?"

He had no particular fondness for the team. He recognized right away that his rush of disappointment stemmed from his expectations of this marriage—like the house. He'd visualized certain things. "You don't like football? I thought—"

"I'd really like to go—some other time. It's just…well, I had a lot of things I planned to do tomorrow. I didn't realize I would have to go into the classroom full-time almost immediately. Things are going to get really hectic when I start student teaching next week. I'd hoped to use this weekend to get ahead." She looked in the direction where Ryan had disappeared. "But a day out—just you guys? He'd be thrilled."

It wasn't what he wanted or remotely what he'd planned. When he'd decided to get the tickets today, he'd liked the idea of his little family sitting in the stands, hugging one another excitedly on the good plays. Kissing to celebrate touchdowns. He still needed excuses to touch her. But he could see himself exchanging high fives with Ryan. Maybe it wasn't such a rotten idea.

"I'd planned to clean out my closet tomorrow. Make space for your things in my…*our* room," she said shyly.

"Excellent idea." Best idea he'd heard in years. "Maybe we should start when we get home tonight."

"I was…kinda hoping to do other things tonight." Her tiny smile rocked him to his bones. He watched her long eyelashes hide her eyes and waited for the inevitable blush. It came and he could hardly wait for dinner to be over. Damn, she had good ideas sometimes.

Ryan was slowly winding his way back to them through a section of tables. Josh forced his mind to practical matters. "Would it be a good idea to ask one of Ryan's friends to join us, use the extra ticket? Or would it be better if it was just Ryan and me?"

"You've spent a lot of time with just him. I'm sure he'd love to ask one of his friends," she assured him. "Especially since his friends have included Ryan so many times. He'll love being the one handing out the invitation. He'll love the chance to show you off," she finished as Ryan joined them.

Marisa slid over to let her son into the booth beside her.

Josh filled Ryan in on the change of plans. The come-hither smiles Marisa kept aiming at him more than made up for the disappointment regarding the football game.

One night of amazing lovemaking didn't automatically fix everything about this marriage, he reminded himself as he'd done a hundred times that day.

But two? Maybe.

"I'm going to Brian's, Mom," Ryan yelled as they got out of the car at home. "I have to ask him about tomorrow."

"Don't hurry," Josh muttered, and Marisa laughed.

"*That's* not a very fatherly attitude," she teased.

"Bet it is." As soon as they were in the door, he took her in his arms. "I'll bet any man who looked at you for hours and didn't want his kids to either go to bed or leave would need his head examined.''

She loved the way she fit against him. She snuggled closer as he deepened his kiss. There was something extremely heady about him.

''Josh, you know Ryan will be back any time. We can't—''

''I know.'' He took her words away with another kiss. ''But there's nothing that says we can't practice for later. After he's in bed.''

''I thought *that* was the practice.'' She giggled.

''This is practice for the practice.''

His nonsense did nothing to distract her from the sensations he was creating in her body. His hand cupped her breast and his thumb lazily circled its peak. She felt the nipple grow rigid even under all the layers of clothes.

She suspected her knees weren't going to hold her, and Josh must have read her mind. He swept her up in his arms and carried her to the couch.

''Josh, we'd better—''

''Practice makes perfect.'' He sat down, cradling her in his lap. His hand stroked her leg, then edged beneath the skirt she'd put on before they'd gone to dinner. ''These have to go,'' he said, and deftly started removing her panty hose.

''You know what?'' She struggled hard to keep her sanity as he struggled to make her lose it.

''What?''

''I suspect you don't need any practice. You're very good at this.''

The kisses didn't stop. They just became less consuming. ''Does that bother you?''

''Not really,'' she said, then immediately revised it.

"Well, a little, but I know it isn't very logical or practical. Does it bother you that I don't have much experience?"

"I'm looking forward to teaching you anything and everything you might need to know." The teasing note left his voice as he sat up and began straightening their clothes. He tucked her panty hose between the cushions. "In case Ryan comes," he explained.

"Without thinking about it, you automatically hide the evidence." His amused laugh rumbled the hand still splayed against his chest. "What's so funny?"

"I thought I was done with this sneaking-around stuff when I asked you to marry me. It didn't occur to me that having a kid in the house would be the same as parents or a roommate."

"You sure know the tricks," she said wryly. "What have you been doing? Having illicit affairs with married women?"

"Never." His voice held an edge. He smoothed her hair away from her face. The gesture seemed to soothe him. "I haven't done any of this in years and years. Not since I was a teenager."

"Ah. Teenage years. Ask me if I'm looking forward to having Ryan there in another few years." Her face brightened. "You're going to come in handy, though, knowing all this."

He didn't chuckle like she anticipated. Instead, he frowned. "I'm not as good at noticing sneaky things as I am at doing them."

"It surely won't be that bad." She slid off his lap to take a seat beside him.

"No." He absently studied their clasped hands. "You want to know the real reason I took the job out here?" he said, totally changing the subject. "Sold my share of the partnership?"

She wasn't at all sure she wanted to hear whatever he was leading up to. "You said you were tired of corporate law."

"I was. But the main reason was a woman—one of the other partners. We'd been seeing each other for three years. I assumed we'd eventually get married."

The stab of jealousy that twisted in her chest shocked her. Marisa held her breath, even more uncertain she wanted to hear.

"One night after working late, I stopped by her apartment and found she was seeing one of the other partners, too."

"Oh, Josh. That must have hurt."

"Not really," he said. "That's when I started worrying. I decided I was doing something backward."

"What do you mean?"

"I hadn't asked her to marry me because I was waiting to fall in love with her."

"You didn't love her?"

"I cared about her. But I was busy working toward that partnership. I thought I'd fall in love with her eventually. When I had time," he added wryly.

Marisa shivered and wrapped her arms around her waist. This sounded chillingly similar to what he'd said about growing love. "So why didn't it happen?"

"I've thought about it a lot. I think our relationship died from sheer neglect. I fell into my dad's workaholic habits. I thought she understood I was putting in so much effort for us. For her. For the future. I expected her to be there when everything fell into place. I thought I'd fall in love with her."

"Aren't you glad you didn't fall in love with her and then find out she wasn't faithful?" Marisa asked.

"Oh, she would have been."

Marisa laughed. She was beginning to love his blind optimism. He must do a daily everything-will-be-fine mantra.

"It's true," he protested. "I know it's true. She just got tired of waiting for me to fall in love with her."

"But you never got around to it."

"I never did."

"So that's when you decided you'd do it the other way—get married and *then* fall in love?" She wanted to ask him if he was doing it right this time, if he was falling in love with her. The dreamier side of her—the unrealistic side, she assured herself—probably wouldn't like his answer.

"That's when I started thinking about it," he admitted.

"And so you sold your partnership."

"Not right away. Things weren't really awkward until they announced their engagement."

"How long did they…see each other before that?"

"Two years."

Marisa didn't try to hide her surprise. Two years wasn't exactly impulsive. He'd been thinking about shopping around for someone to marry for two long years? It didn't become "impulsive" until he'd selected a candidate? She wasn't certain how that made her feel. "What happened after they announced their engagement?"

"Both of them started acting uncomfortable around me. That made things less than comfortable for me, too."

Shimmers ran up her leg from the idle patterns he was drawing there with his finger. "So you sold out and came here."

He nodded. "I sold out and came here. And now you know—" he lowered his voice dramatically "—the rest of the story." He sighed and glanced at the back door. "I guess it's not very practical to start this again." Gingerly tugging her skirt back over her knees, he stood and jammed his hands into his pockets.

Marisa moved to the edge of the couch. "You want to help me in my closet?"

His eyebrows raised. "Ooh. I didn't think about the closet. That should be a fairly safe place to do…whatever we were going to do."

She grinned but didn't rise to the bait. "*I* was going to clear some space so I could transfer your clothes tomorrow."

He held out his hand to help her up. "That's the second-best idea you've had all day." He didn't have to say what he thought her best idea was.

But Marisa had a feeling she might just learn to like cleaning out closets.

Chapter Ten

Marisa smiled to herself as she realized she was singing again and turned the corner down the hall. The noise of the vacuum cleaner buried the fact that her voice wasn't what it used to be. And songs from *Camelot* seemed to fit her mood perfectly. Discovering the "simple joys of maidenhood" was more thrilling than she'd ever imagined.

Marisa glanced around her little kingdom and shut off the vacuum. It was time to finish moving Josh's things.

Stacks of boxes lined the walls of the guest room. He'd suggested they put some things in storage—until they moved to a bigger house. He'd looked away when he mentioned the house. She felt a guilty sting, remembering.

It wasn't right that he'd had to resort to living out of boxes. That they didn't have enough room. But it wouldn't be right to break her promise to Ryan, either. There had to be some sort of compromise.

She lifted a stack of Josh's knit shirts from one of the

boxes. Holding them to her nose, she was disappointed to smell only the clean, fresh scent of detergent as she carried them to her room. *Their* room, she amended. She had to start thinking of everything as theirs, instead of hers. That would help.

And she'd be more careful about making Josh feel he belonged here, too. And then next year...

A rush of warmth filled her heart as a vision of the spacious, modern ''castle'' Josh wanted to provide for them filled her mind. A dream house to go along with her dream husband. She sighed and realized how wonderful it was to finally allow herself to dream again.

She snapped her fingers as a brilliant idea struck. The compromise! It wasn't really a compromise. It was what she'd thought they'd do all along, but it was time to get started. Tonight when Josh and Ryan came home, she'd suggest they go looking for a lot. They needed to get house plans. They needed to start dreaming together. Surely actually starting would ease his impatience.

With a song about happily ever after in their own Camelot in her heart, she went back into the guest room.

She'd also go through his boxes of household goods, put some of his pots and pans and dishes in the cabinets. She'd take some of hers out—put them into storage. Wouldn't that help him feel at home here?

She opened the box marked ''kitchen'' and smiled. His stuff was better than hers, anyway. She hit a high note as she realized she might as well just throw some of her things away. His pots and pans actually matched, while hers were mostly excess from her mom's kitchen or scavenged at garage sales.

She found herself singing ''I Feel Pretty,'' from *West Side Story.* She did feel pretty, and even sounded good on the tra-la-las. Josh would be pleased, she thought, closing the cabinet beside the stove an hour later. But just in case, she'd carry out her box of throwaways *after* she'd had a chance to gauge his reaction.

Back in the den she decided she should do more. She'd never gotten around to cutting articles of interest out of the old magazines she always saved. Josh's legal books and magazines could occupy some of the space if she tossed out a few of her stacks. He might actually prefer working here, instead of staying late at the office—as he'd done several evenings—*if* she put some of his books on the bookshelves. She felt confident that working late wouldn't become a habit after everything he'd said last night.

And *if* she cleaned off the desk. She sidestepped boxes to do exactly that. The house had good-size rooms and closets, but the desk had almost been overwhelmed by his boxes and her clutter. It was hidden from view.

Josh had obviously used it, though. The heavy leather date book he carried everywhere was on top of one of her stacks of papers. She set the date book aside. A yellow legal pad covered with Josh's neat script was beneath that. She started to move it aside, but the bold underlined word at the top, "Marriage," caught her eye. It took one second to realize she shouldn't read it—it was Josh's—and another to know she didn't really want to know what it said.

The paper that fluttered to the floor from beneath the pad as she pushed it away changed her mind. It was a purchasing contract. His signature mocked her from the bottom line. It was for the house. She felt something wither inside and picked up the yellow pad.

At first she tried to convince herself it had been written before they were married. Even if it wasn't for the date at the top of the page—five days after their marriage—the third item down on the "cons" side of Josh's list would have convinced her otherwise.

The "pros" side had two items: Ryan, and not talking to himself. The "cons" side had sixteen. But the list beneath that was even worse. He'd titled it: Promises to Keep. Number one on that list was "porch swing."

Marisa sank slowly to the floor and stared at the pad she'd let fall to her lap. Beneath the list of nine promises was one word in large letters and underlined twice. He obviously had to do the nine things to reach his goal at the bottom: Divorce.

"Marisa, we're home," Josh called as he entered the house. "Well, *I'm* home," he corrected himself as Marisa came down the hall. "Ryan went home with Brian so they could tell Bob about the game." Josh wiggled his eyebrows suggestively and started toward her. "I encouraged him to take his time."

The ball game had been okay, but he'd never been so happy to see a fourth quarter start. It had taken forever to tick to an end. He'd been anxious to get back here, to help clean closets, whatever, to be with Marisa. Josh stopped under the glare of light from the window.

She looked as though she'd been crying. Some insane premonition told him it had something to do with him and that it wasn't good. Then he saw the legal pad in her hand.

"You want a divorce?" she asked, holding the pad toward him.

Josh's mouth had never been so dry. He wasn't sure he could open it to answer her. "No."

"Isn't that the ultimate goal? You go through this list of promises to keep?" She waved the yellow pad. "Then you feel you can ask me for a divorce?"

He had to clench his hands into fists to keep from grabbing it from her. He wanted to tear every page on it to bits.

But she'd read it. She wasn't going to forget what he'd written just because he destroyed the evidence.

"Maybe we should forget all the garbage in between and skip to the end."

"I wrote that ages ago, Marisa. Before—"

"We haven't been married for ages." She glanced down at the list. "And you have a habit of dating everything."

"But that was before—"

"Before you made love to me?" Marisa finished for him when he'd been silent too long. "Sex is the only thing that makes this marriage worth keeping?"

No. He didn't believe that at all, he realized with gut-wrenching fear. Sex had definitely made things better, but he wanted them to make it for other reasons—wanted it more than anything he'd ever wanted in his life.

Not a day had gone by since their marriage that he'd felt lonely. Or lost. Or as though he was killing time, waiting for the next day.

She excited him. Made each hour and minute and second rush by too quickly. Since their marriage, time had sped past even when he'd had doubts. Even when he'd lived on pins and needles, afraid to touch her, afraid she might flinch, he'd always looked forward to the next day.

"Marisa, I was confused. I thought we'd—" He bit his tongue. He was going to make it worse, dammit. He should be able to make a case for himself. He'd done it often enough for others.

"Made a mistake?" she asked when he didn't finish. "You'll be glad to know on that point we agree."

"I couldn't figure out where we'd gone wrong. I couldn't think what to do."

"Well, you've made a start." She looked down at the list in her hand. Then, glancing around, she picked up a pen from the counter and began marking through items.

"The porch swing. You've done that one. If you'd like," she said with saccharine sweetness, "I'll give you a list of my own of things that need to be done so you can 'fix up the house.' That should help us get that one out of the way more quickly."

"Okay. I was doing the right things for the wrong reason," he said flatly. "But things have gotten better, haven't they?" He stepped closer, took the list from her hand and set it on the counter. He reached for her. "Marisa…"

She dodged him.

"You asked if I wanted a divorce. I said no." Josh stepped closer. "Give it…give us," he amended, "a chance."

He wanted to take her in his arms. The set of her shoulders said his attempt to do so would be shrugged away. But there weren't any words. Nothing he could say would make up for the hurt he saw in her eyes, on her face. Her whole body seemed bent by it. And knowing his list had caused it…

"Is that why you're buying the house? So you'll have somewhere to go when you complete your promises?"

Oh, Lord. She'd found the purchasing contract, too. He rammed his hand through his hair. "I was going to tell you. It…there hasn't been a good opportunity. I wanted it to be a surprise. You did say you loved it."

She looked at him skeptically.

He hoped he didn't look as sheepish as he felt. "Okay. That's *one* of the reasons I bought it. I do want it for you. For us. But the day after we looked, Chris brought by the builder's card like he promised. We talked and I realized the way things are growing around here, a house would be as good an investment as some of the others I've made with money from the buyout." He shrugged. "I figured if you still liked the house next spring…"

Her expression softened a little. Not much, but a little.

"Okay. I want it," he admitted.

She finally smiled, slightly. But tears shimmered in her eyes.

"I have no desire to move there until Ryan is ready," he added firmly.

"You could have talked to me about it."

"That's been our problem, hasn't it? You have your ideas and I have mine, and we blithely imagine they'll meet and match somewhere along the line."

She sighed. Some of the tension was gone. If he could only explain the list as easily. It was how he thought things through.

He shook his head. From the way his list looked, she had every reason to believe he *had* thought things through and wanted their marriage to be over.

He took her in his arms. Their lovemaking had to mean something. If he couldn't convince her mind, he was certain he could her body. He knew more about her responses to him than she did.

"Marisa—" He lifted a hand to her hair. "We're finally on the right track. We've both made mistakes, haven't we?"

She slowly shook her head.

"Can you forgive me mine? Can you forgive me for writing all this down? I make lists sometimes to come up with answers. Ideas. They help me think things through."

She smiled sadly, almost to herself. "I guess I did the same. Only I tried to come up with ideas to improve things," she added with more than a hint of accusation. She met his gaze. "When I asked if we could be friends? That was my idea for improving things." She smiled slightly. "I liked the porch swing better. That was a *good* idea."

"I liked it." He felt as if they were sharing a private joke. It felt intimate and nice.

She withdrew from him. She was calmer now, but it was a steely calm. It was almost more unsettling than the emotional storm that seemed to have passed.

"I want to go on. Like we've been. I want to stay married to you. I want us to keep doing the right things, for all the *right* reasons."

She lifted her chin and looked him straight in the eye. "I won't sleep with you again."

That left him momentarily speechless. "How can we have a normal marriage if…if we don't act like a normal couple?" He stepped closer. One kiss and she'd be pliant, wanting his kisses, wanting him. "You can't tell me you haven't enjoyed—"

"I'm not taking the chance of getting pregnant and *then* having you decide again you've made a mistake. Been there. Done that." She swung around, showing him her stiffened spine. "If that's all you want from this marriage, we probably *should* get a divorce."

"That's not all I want. I don't want a divorce. I've never done this before. I didn't know what to expect. How could I have known that you didn't have much experience? I would have done a lot of things differently if I'd known—"

"That I didn't have heaps of experience?" She cleared her throat. "Is that what you were looking for?"

The pain in her voice was contagious. "It's what I expected," he said. "I just assumed… It wasn't something I thought about."

"Sorry to disappoint you."

"Expecting one thing and getting another doesn't necessarily mean you're disappointed." Disappointment was as remote from how he actually felt as anything could be.

"You have to agree that Ryan makes it logical to assume—"

"It only takes once. Believe me. I know."

"But since then—"

"Raising Ryan hasn't left me with a lot of time or energy to find someone to teach me what everyone assumes I know. But it doesn't matter. What happens now is up to you. But I won't be foolish again."

"You think making love with me—with your *husband*—is foolish?" It was heaven. How could she call it foolish? The palm of his hand tingled with the memory of touching her. "Don't compare something that happened a decade ago with now." Her one previous experience in the back of some arrogant ass's car couldn't possibly be similar. Could it? "Ryan's father." The words left a bitter taste in Josh's mouth. "He hurt you?"

"I was well anesthetized." She laughed without humor. "I have such memorable experiences to mark the special occasions of my life. Prom night, I lost my virginity. I woke up sick to my stomach the morning of graduation. Mom credited it to nerves and I prayed she was right. My wedding night, my husband didn't want me."

"You thought I didn't want you?" The answer was in her eyes. "You were terrified. Trembling. I assumed you were offering yourself up like some kind of sacrifice. *That's* when I thought we'd made a mistake." His voice lowered. "I want kids. Why would I decide we'd made a mistake if you found out you were pregnant? Is that what happened with him? Did he just desert you?"

She nodded. "I guess you could call it that. School was out by the time I knew for certain. He and his parents got together with us to discuss what we should do, and he spent the time trying to convince all of them I was the school slut—whore is the word he used, I recall. According to him,

Ryan could have been anyone's. His parents believed him, of course.'' She shrugged as if to say that was that.

''And after Ryan was born? He still didn't believe it?''

''He never saw Ryan,'' she said. ''I wouldn't subject my son to *that*.''

''He should have been responsible for some of Ryan's support.'' He sounded more like a lawyer than a husband. He hated that. ''Where is he now?''

''He went to college in California somewhere. His parents moved a year or two later. I haven't seen or heard from any of them since.'' Her look said, I don't know or care.

''You could have made him take some of the responsibility. At least financial support.''

''My parents and I agreed that if we forced him to accept that, he could expect certain rights. It wasn't worth it.''

''So you went on,'' he said softly.

Her nod was abbreviated. ''And now we're here.'' The last word sounded as if it got caught in the back of her throat. She turned away from him and he watched her gather herself. Her shoulders sagged for a moment. Then she straightened.

''You can't think I would be like that,'' he said.

''Not really,'' she admitted, examining her hands. ''But this has got me thinking.'' When she turned back toward him, her fingers were pressed solidly against her lips. He saw them tremble as she lowered her hand to her side. ''As shaky as this marriage is, do we want to bring a baby into it? Is it worth the risk? Is it? For any of us?'' The last was said on a whisper as she quickly cloaked the pain in her eyes with a dull glaze. ''We were on the right track *before* we actually got married. Going through the legalities, living in the house, seemed to change things, to make us expect different things.''

"Maybe we didn't make a mistake. Maybe we just went a bit too fast," he suggested.

She looked relieved. "That's what I think," she said. "I want to slow things down. I need time. *You* need time. Do you want to feel trapped into...into staying if you really want to leave?"

His mind raced for some reassurance. He couldn't think of a thing. He couldn't even argue with her logic. "I don't want to leave."

"Since I know I will never try marriage again, it doesn't matter," she said bluntly. "It's up to you."

"Will you at least promise you'll let me..." He hesitated.

"What?"

"Try. Can't we keep trying, Marisa?"

Her mouth twisted. "As long as you understand and don't try to...to seduce me. I won't wind up pregnant and alone again." She turned to leave the kitchen.

"You could go on the pill," he suggested. It was obviously the wrong thing to say.

She laughed. It wasn't a pleasant sound.

"Or I could do something," he quickly added. Maybe her reaction was some indignant feminist side coming through.

"You don't get it," she said calmly.

He frowned.

"This marriage was the most impulsive thing I've ever done. But because this marriage—" she waved a hand "—made some sort of...insane sense to me, I convinced myself it wasn't impetuous. I thought neither of us expected too much. I thought it would be all right."

"It still makes sense," he protested.

She went on as if he hadn't interrupted. "I thought that since I was making decisions with my head—not my heart—we'd both get what we wanted without any emotional distress.''

He couldn't think of a thing to say. Somewhere, deep in his gut, he knew none of what either of them had said during this whole discussion had been based on logic.

''I like making…'' She shook her head and frowned. ''I like having sex with you. But it feels dangerous. It does something to my emotions. I don't want it clouding my common sense.''

''Love's an emotion. How can we grow it without…feeling things?''

She closed her eyes, sighed, then pointedly glanced over at the list before she met his eyes again. ''I think I'd rather grow trust before I grow some great, all-consuming emotional attachment to you.''

She looked small and vulnerable and he wanted to take her in his arms and hold her. But then he'd want her in other ways, and physical needs would come into play and mix things up. ''I see your point,'' he said diplomatically. He didn't like it, but he saw it. ''You don't trust me now.''

''I don't know if I do or not. I don't know if I really did even before. That's the problem. I want to,'' she added hopefully. ''So if you want to keep trying—'' she paused ''—that's okay with me. But if you want…'' She became engrossed in massaging one fingernail with her thumb. ''I know you wanted—expected—a normal marriage, sex and everything.'' She cleared her throat. ''I'll understand if you don't want to stay. But if you want to keep trying, I need time. That's all I'm saying.''

Quitting wasn't an option. He didn't like the other choice much better—it felt like going backward—but he didn't need to think about it. ''What will *you* be doing while I'm trying?''

"I won't put up any roadblocks, if that's what you mean. I'll be friendly."

"Like roomies?" he said half-sarcastically.

"Friendly, optimistic roommates." She tried to soften her decision with a tentative, hopeful smile. "Can we go from there?"

He nodded, and she turned and started back down the hall. "What if you're already pregnant?"

When she turned back to face him, her face was white. "No one could be that 'lucky' twice in a lifetime." The horror in her voice was so thick he could almost see it.

It twisted something inside that she didn't want *his* child. "You said Ryan was the best thing that ever happened to you."

"That doesn't mean I want to go through it all again by myself."

"You wouldn't be by yourself if you were carrying my child," he promised.

"I don't want to find out the hard way." She started for the bedroom—her bedroom once again, he assumed—as Ryan yelled something across the yard to Brian from the back porch. She stopped, her face drawn and weary. "Guess I'd better see to dinner."

"Let me," he offered. "I'll do the honors."

"Would you mind?" She looked at him gratefully.

"Not at all." With a thanks, she started down the hall. "Damage control," he murmured as she closed her bedroom door. "It's the least I can do."

"What's wrong with Mom?" Marisa heard Ryan ask a couple of weeks later as she came home from her evening job at the drugstore. It was also her second full day in the classroom where she'd be student teaching.

"She's exhausted," she answered before Josh had to say

anything to incriminate himself. She tried hard to sound normal. Too weary to catch the screen door, she let it slam behind her as she stepped inside the kitchen.

Ryan and Josh were sitting on the floor playing Nintendo just the other side of the wide arch that separated the living room from the kitchen. "She's exhausted," Josh repeated to Ryan, and gave her a seductive, charming grin. She refused to let it tug at her heart, but her heart responded, anyway.

"Why don't you quit that job?" Josh suggested as she dropped her books and gear on the kitchen table.

"Yeah, Mom. You're never home anymore."

"I'm thinking about it." She joined them in the living room and sank onto the couch.

Josh glanced up at her, obviously surprised and very hopeful.

"Mr. Finegold has quit worrying quite so much that no one else can do my job," she explained. "He's depending more and more on Rebecca Croft."

"It's a good time then," Josh offered. "Turn in your resignation again, see how he reacts."

Josh helped Ryan put the game back in the cabinet beneath the TV and resettled on the floor in the middle of the room, one long leg stretched before him and his hands linked loosely around the other knee. "We miss having you here in the evenings," he said quietly. "Don't we, Ryan?"

"Yeah, Mom," Ryan agreed.

"If I quit that job," Marisa said, "I probably still won't be home three nights a week." She tried not to let Josh's frown affect her. She turned her attention to Ryan. He was the one she had to be worried about. So far, he didn't seem to mind at all that he and Josh were left to fend for themselves. She suspected he liked it, since Josh gave her son his undivided attention. It was good for him.

Ryan's self-confidence had gone up and up since Josh had been around. He wasn't as quick to question his abilities, because Josh was always saying, "You can do it." He'd picked up Josh's cocky walk, though it still needed some fine-tuning if he was ever going to do it as smoothly as Josh. "Develop a fatherly relationship with Ryan" had been number four on his promise list.

"Why wouldn't you be home if you quit your job?" Josh asked.

"The thing that got me seriously thinking about it again is another job offer," she said. "I think I want to take it."

"I thought you wanted to quit because you're tired," Ryan said.

"This is different." The very thought of this job invigorated her. The idea of sitting in the same house with Josh every evening terrified her, because the way he looked at her—as he was now—made her skin tingle and memories of his lovemaking flood her mind. With Ryan as a built-in audience, there wasn't much danger of doing anything too impulsive and getting carried away by the moment. But Ryan's presence brought another kind of pressure. Playing the role they'd assumed was an emotional drain.

"What kind of job?" Josh asked.

"Actually it doesn't really pay much, so I shouldn't call it a job. More like gaining valuable experience. They've thrown in some compensation, so whoever takes it can pretend they aren't just an unpaid volunteer."

Josh firmed his lips. His generosity kept money from being an issue, she realized.

"It's something I've always wanted to do, but I didn't think I'd get a chance until I actually got a teaching job," she added. "I want" was becoming a magic phrase in this household. Marisa had become nervous of using it too often because things magically appeared or happened. "I've been asked to direct the fall musical at the high school."

"Cool."

"Isn't that normally the drama teacher's job?" Josh asked suspiciously. "They're going to let a student teacher do it?"

She nodded. "Mr. Pelt wants to help coach his son's city-league soccer team," she explained. "It's the last year he's eligible to play, and Mr. Pelt's had to miss most of the games in the past because there's always a fall production. So he ran the idea of offering the position to me past the administrator."

"And *he* didn't have a problem with giving the position to a student teacher?"

"*She,*" Marisa corrected him with a smile. "My advanced age seems to be a positive in this case," she said, tongue in cheek. "My father gave the administrator her first teaching job," she added for clarification. "That little coincidence didn't hurt."

"So you're in if you want it?"

"I'm pretty sure. The experience will be an asset when I'm applying for a permanent teaching position next fall, don't you think?"

"It's a big job," Josh warned. "You'll still be tired."

"I know I can do it. The director I had in high school was excellent, and over my four years, I did everything— I was even student director. And this school has a big budget for productions, so I'll have lots of paid technical help for costumes and lighting and things like that."

"You do what you need to." Josh's tone was encouraging even though he didn't sound overjoyed at the idea. "We'll get along, won't we, Ryan." Josh reached over and made a mess of her son's bright hair. Ryan didn't shrug away as he did with her. Jealousy surged through her, but she wasn't sure who she was jealous of. Ryan, for having Josh's easy, affectionate attention, or Josh, for being able to do things like that without a negative reaction from her son.

"Sure, Josh."

"Then you don't mind?" she asked Ryan.

"Nah."

"We'll still have time right after school on the nights I'm going to be out," she promised him.

"So you can make me do homework," he muttered.

She didn't take the bait. She wasn't going to get into it with him again.

"If she didn't make you, I'd have to," Josh defended her, and Marisa's automatic smile of appreciation was heartfelt.

"It isn't fair," Ryan said. "You guys gang up on me."

"No," Marisa said with a laugh that felt almost real. "You guys gang up on me. Two guys, one girl. No fun. That's why I have to have an evening job—to get away from you." It was too close to the truth. She shouldn't have said it. She glanced at Josh.

He was smiling. "You guys gang up on me," he protested. "The old-timers and the Johnny-come-lately. I'm always the odd man out."

She and Ryan looked at him, then at each other. Then they both smiled and moved at the same time.

"See? See what I mean?" Josh yelled as Marisa helped Ryan knock Josh over, then stood back to watch. For a minute Josh let Ryan have the upper hand, then Josh turned the tables and pinned the boy to the floor. They rolled around, roughhousing, until she started to walk away.

"We gonna let her start this brouhaha, then just leave?" Josh asked. Ryan didn't need a second invitation. He launched himself at her.

Marisa turned and held out her hand. "No." Her voice said it all. Ryan stopped in midleap, surprised.

"No," she repeated more calmly. "It's...been a long day," she said to soften her refusal to join in.

Ryan took it in stride. He knew her moods and was probably chalking it up to a mom thing. She could see him rolling his eyes, even though he'd already turned away.

Josh's face went stony, but his eyes said he got the message. She didn't want him touching her. And his translation was exactly right.

"I'm going to change clothes." Unable to meet his gaze, she resumed her flight to the bedroom.

As soon as she closed the door behind her, she leaned against it, then stumbled to the bed. Leaning back against the headboard, she cradled a pillow to her chest.

Josh was right. She couldn't bear to have him touch her, but not for the reason he thought. How could she stand it when playtime was over and there was nothing more? Would she be able to walk away after Ryan went to bed?

Her brief glimpse of heaven with Josh made her want more. She was having a lot more trouble accepting this friendly, standoffish incarnation of their marriage than he was.

She pressed her hand to her stomach. And she certainly didn't feel like roughhousing. She felt fragile. Already, the strange, gentle, protective feelings were there.

Two days late. You're only two days late, she reminded herself.

But what if she was pregnant?

Again.

Chapter Eleven

"You're certain you want to do this?" Mr. Finegold had asked as she'd cleaned out her desk.

No, she hadn't been sure she wanted to quit. She'd done it and she *still* wasn't sure. She sniffed, misting up again as she looked at the cardboard box she'd brought home and set on the bed. It held eleven years of memories.

What was she going to do with useless mementos, things she'd received from friends and fellow employees over the years, things she couldn't throw away? Normally it would go in the den, but that was Josh's space now.

When, she wondered, would he leave, go to his nice new house, give up on them? Soon, she hoped, then immediately took the thought back. She didn't *hope* Josh would leave; she expected it. Everything in her believed Josh had been sincere when he'd said he didn't want a divorce after she found his list. But she also knew he'd been just as sincere when he'd made the darn list in the first place. Wasn't it realistic to expect him to decide he wanted a divorce again? She was trying to prepare for it.

When she'd told Mr. Finegold her decision, he'd shaken his white head. "I knew this was going to happen," he'd said.

Then she'd placed a box on the counter beside the cash register and said, "My last purchase with my employee discount."

Mr. Finegold's eyes had lit up and he'd refused to let her pay even the discounted rate. "No charge." He'd lifted a finger and added, "*If* you promise to get your vitamins here. Now I know why you're quitting," he'd added happily. Although she'd explained again about the extra job at the school and that it would be invaluable experience, he'd been a lot happier about her leaving for other reasons.

She smiled through a layer of sentimental tears and picked up the small box he'd carefully tucked on top of all the office junk.

At least she knew what to do with *this* particular item, she thought, staring at the blue and pink markings on the box. Her emotions swung wildly between hope and despair.

If she *was* pregnant, she'd have an excuse to swallow her pride. Josh had been wonderful the past few weeks. Keeping a safe, friendly distance was becoming impossible.

But she'd been through this before. Alone. It was the last thing on earth she wanted to do again. She was beginning to believe she *wouldn't* do it alone again if she was pregnant with Josh's child.

And Josh could make love to her again. That thought left her mouth dry and made her knees weak. She sat on the side of the bed, causing the box to tip toward her. She shakily grabbed the items that spilled out and threw them back in the box she'd righted.

If straightening up the pieces of her life could only be as easy.

If she *was* pregnant, she'd have every reason in the book to try *everything* to make things work out. The only risks would be in not taking an opportunity available to bring them closer. Deep in her heart, she wanted that excuse to throw herself at him, but did she want to hold him with a baby?

She rose slowly. Wondering and wishing wouldn't get her any answers. Finding out, one way or the other, would. Then she'd know what to do about it.

Josh crumpled the paper and threw it at the wastebasket in the corner of his bedroom. He didn't exactly need another sheet of paper to add to his new list entitled "Marisa." In almost a month he'd thought of only one item: Be patient.

How could he be patient when he felt as *impatient* as he'd ever been in his life? In his six-week-old marriage, he'd had less than a week of bliss. But those days had been worth every second of frustration in the weeks since.

He could add: Be nice. But that was what he'd been trying to do. He was getting nowhere. Except occasionally, he'd catch some indefinable look on Marisa's face, a tentative smile, the way her eyes lit up, and he knew something was happening. Surely if he kept planting the seeds and then waited...

Since their setback—which is how he thought of it—Marisa had treated him almost like she treated Ryan. Ryan was treated with respect and consideration. But also affection. That was the missing ingredient in *his* relationship with her.

He squelched a pang of envy. He *couldn't* let that feeling

grow. He couldn't let it root out the father-son relationship, which was like a tender plant that needed nurturing.

He should find it amusing that the list he'd made of ways to get out of this marriage was getting him deeper in—if he felt like laughing.

Ryan was at a friend's birthday party, staying overnight. Josh knew opportunity when he saw it. He wanted to use it, but couldn't come up with a single solitary game plan. If he could just get her to talk to him. Really talk. But he could think of nothing to do but…be patient.

He started at the light tap on the door.

"Can we talk?" Marisa asked quietly.

"Sure." He opened the door and stood helpless to do anything but gaze at her. How could she get more beautiful with each passing day? The pink of the sweater she'd paired with slacks matched the soft flush on her face. Whatever she wanted to talk about clearly made her nervous. "Come in," he suggested.

She glanced at the narrow bed. "Can we talk in the living room?"

"Sure." He followed her down the hall, managing not to drool as he watched the sway of her hips.

The sky was dark and cold for late September, and Marisa moved automatically to close the miniblinds over the windows. "I was afraid you'd work late again," she said conversationally.

He flipped on the floor lamp behind the sofa and felt a ray of hope. It had to be progress that they were together in this room when Ryan wasn't here.

He smelled her subtle perfume as she passed him to take a position at the other end of the couch. He caught himself leaning toward the scent and savoring it.

"Anything in particular you wanted to talk about?"

She wrung her hands and looked at him. Her mouth moved, but no words came.

"Maybe I should get us a glass of wine," he suggested. If the expression on her face was anything to go by, he might need one.

"No." She caught his hand and he settled back beside her. "I can't drink." She looked at him expectantly.

"Oh?" was the only response he could think of.

"I'm pregnant," she said so quietly he wasn't sure he heard.

"What?" He definitely wasn't sure he'd heard right.

"I'm pregnant," she said, louder this time, and cringed as he reached for her. Her reaction startled him.

"Marisa—" his hand hovered near her hair, but he hesitated to touch her "—you did say what I thought you did, didn't you?"

She nodded and entwined her fingers in her lap. In the circle of light the lamp cast over her, she looked golden. Her hair looked like a halo.

"You're pregnant?" he asked, not because he hadn't heard. It was the sort of news that seemed to need repeating before it could truly be believed. A bubbling joy struggled for ownership of his soul, but he couldn't let it take claim before he was absolutely certain. "My baby?"

Her sidelong glance held irritation. "I won't use it to try and keep you. This isn't a trap." Her voice held the quiver of wariness.

"Oh, Marisa." This time he couldn't help it. He reached for her—too late because she moved at the same time, jumping up and pacing away from him. He followed.

He caught her and wrapped his arms around her, pulling her close. He silently thanked his lucky stars and anyone who would listen. "We're going to have a baby," he stated, but his expression asked for confirmation again as he put her at arm's length and looked at her.

She nodded.

"Marisa. Oh, Marisa," he said again, pulling her to him. He couldn't decide whether to laugh or cry or whoop and holler. "Why…how…? Do you know what I was doing when you tapped on my door?" He felt her shake her head. He was holding her too close to actually see her. "I was trying to make a list of ways to get back in your good graces. Soon." He stepped away. "Tell me this changes things, makes a difference."

"I thought you'd leave weeks ago."

"Where would I go?" he asked, then held up a hand. "No. Don't answer that. I know what you're going to say. It was crazy of me to buy the house without telling you. And I only want to live there if you and Ryan are with me. But that's not the point. There are lots of places I could live. But where am I going to go with my life?"

"You don't want to leave?"

"I'd be lying if I said I hadn't toyed with the idea. The last few weeks have been hell." He hoped his smile wasn't twisted with the truth of that statement. "But I can't. What I have here with you and Ryan—this is what I want. I want a family. You. Ryan. And a baby?"

She nodded again, smiling slightly at his question. "If you ask if it's yours again, I'll hit you."

"I didn't ask. It was amazement." He laughed and fought the urge to dance her around the room. Instead, he pulled her close once more and tightened his hold on her. "I'm trying to get used to the idea."

"A baby isn't going to solve our problems."

"No, but look at us already. We're talking about something besides the weather again. For the first time in a month you're not closing me out. We've only given things a superficial try up to now. Can you imagine where we could be if we really put our...our souls into it?''

With a nudge from his knuckle, he tilted her face up to his. She met his eyes briefly, one bright searching look before she veiled them again, her lush golden lashes shadowing her cheeks. Her lips parted slightly. She inhaled a shaky breath and her breasts brushed his chest.

He'd make her want him, he thought determinedly, lowering his head.

The kiss she returned was tentative, then sweet, then hungry. He opened his eyes to make sure he wasn't dreaming. Then closed them again and enjoyed. In the state he'd been banished to for the past month, he knew he couldn't keep doing this without some ultimate reward in sight. He was the one who drew away.

She sighed, but she still hadn't opened her eyes.

''What are we doing here?'' He smoothed her hair, tracing her cheekbone with his thumb. ''Tell me what you want.''

She looked at him with hopeful skepticism. ''You still believe a marriage between us can work?''

''Absolutely. I believe it with all my heart.'' He felt the words to his bones. ''We can be a family,'' he promised.

''That's what you want?''

''It's what I've always wanted. But not like we're doing now.'' He felt her withdrawal as surely as if she'd physically pulled away from his arms. But she was still in his arms. There was still hope.

''It's time I moved to your room,'' he said. ''*Our* room,'' he corrected himself. ''We can't make a marriage with nothing more than a piece of paper.''

''A marriage license? Or a list?''

''I love your sense of humor,'' he said sincerely.

She stilled.

"I've missed it. But do you have to rub things in? I think we should make a rule that you can't use my mistakes against me."

"Oh? We're making rules now? Maybe you should write them down," she teased.

"I didn't mean to hurt you."

"You didn't mean me to find it," she said.

It took him a heart-stopping second to realize she was still gently teasing. "That too," he admitted.

She sobered instantly. "I didn't mean to get pregnant. I hope you…"

He rocked her in his arms. "Marisa. I'm thrilled. I *want* another kid."

"You've been great with Ryan. You'll be a good father to your own child."

He would. Dammit, he would be a *great* father. But some bittersweet emotion tainted the moment. Was a father for her children all Marisa wanted? Some impractical part of him wanted Marisa to want him for herself. "I *want* a family." He tipped her face up to his and gently covered her lips. "I want you."

"Still?"

He couldn't even answer. He groaned and kissed her, instead, putting all the longing into it he'd been holding inside for what seemed like forever. "I can't imagine a day without wanting you," he whispered against her mouth.

She suddenly giggled. It had a hysterical edge and her hand trembled against his chest. "It's not like I have to worry about getting pregnant."

He groaned again, hesitant to take her words as an invitation, wanting to reassure her in some way. "I'm glad you're pregnant," he said softly. "But not because I want the baby—"

Her sharp intake of air was almost painful.

"—as much as I want another chance with you," he hurried on. "I want the baby. But mostly I want another chance to do this marriage thing right."

Her breath escaped in a quavery sigh.

"I want to make love to you." He decided to make his intentions perfectly clear. "That's one of the problems. When I first decided to get married this way..."

"Before you thought of me specifically?"

He nodded. "I assumed the physical relationship between us could develop slowly, the same way the other aspects of a marriage would. I thought it would be like...like..."

"Hiring a new secretary?"

"Not quite," he said with a wry smile. "I've never been desperate to make love to my secretaries. With you, I haven't been able to think of anything else."

"And this was all supposed to be rational, something that evolved," she offered, understanding perfectly what the problem was.

"It didn't occur to me that I would want you so much, that the physical attraction would be instantaneous. It's made things more complicated than—"

She shushed him with a fingertip against his mouth. "Ryan won't be home tonight."

"Instead of hiding in my room, we can hide in yours," he suggested. At her slight nod, he lifted her in his arms.

"Ours," she said.

"Ours," he agreed, and carried her to her room. He finally let her feet touch the floor when they were by the bed.

"The thought of never making love to you again has been making me crazy," he whispered, his tongue tracing a path down skin he revealed as he removed her sweater.

She gasped.

"I couldn't leave even if I wanted to, because I couldn't live with that possibility."

His shirt joined her sweater on the floor. Piece by piece, he removed their clothes, intent on driving her just as insane with desire as he had been with his caresses. Before he was done with her, he was determined she would want him as desperately as he wanted her. Iron will tempered his burning need.

He savored the silken texture of her breasts, teasing one hard peak with his tongue and teeth while his fingers circled and taunted the rosy nipple of the other. He couldn't suppress a satisfied smile as she writhed impatiently, trying to close the distance between them. He couldn't help pressing himself against her, either, but quickly decided he couldn't afford to feel her luxurious, inviting warmth if he was to maintain his control.

He gently placed her on the bed and moved to lie beside her. Moving his hand slowly down her body, he explored her gentle contours. He let his palm linger over her slightly concave belly and gave way to the awe of knowing his baby was there, unseen and unimaginable, right beneath his hand. Soon the growing child would reshape her. He could hardly wait to see the fascinating physical changes that would tell the world of his claim on her.

And he could hardly wait to make love to her again. But that wasn't the thought to entertain if he was going to drive her mad with desire for him.

He bent to place a quick and reverent kiss on her stomach and was reminded of her inexperience as her body tensed.

Returning his attention to her face, he showered each exquisite feature with kisses and let his hands return to a slow, roaming worship of her body. With a slight move, he was on his back and she was on top of him. He savored each sensation as she molded herself against him.

She was beautiful. Even with his eyes closed, he could feel her beauty. One hand spanned the width of her waist as he explored the length of her back, memorizing where the hard, silken planes ended and the soft rounded slopes began. His searching fingers found secret places, and she opened herself to him. Her whole body seemed to quiver in anticipation. His own throbbed with impatience as he fit perfectly against her moist warmth. And he felt his control slip. One impatient thrust and she'd be his again.

He had to have distance. Gently moving her to his side, he renewed his determination that she would want him as he'd been wanting her for so long. She moaned as his hand skirted her slender hips and found her velvety mound. He ignored her tension and let his hand linger a moment between her thighs. He covered her gasp with his mouth as his finger slipped inside her. Savoring her rhythmic, automatic movement against him, his tongue duplicated his hand's tender efforts against her sweet mouth.

Her own hands had finally begun a tentative exploration of their own. Her fingers closed around him convulsively as he quickened his gentle strokes. It was his turn to gasp as she weakly tried to draw him closer. "No," he whispered with the part of him that was still conscious enough to want her desperate with desire for him.

He felt her groan more than he heard it. It echoed his growing distraction.

"What…are you…trying…to do? Are you…trying…to…torture me?" The last word was spoken on a breathless moan.

"Yes." He nibbled at one breast as he tried to take his mind off the desire coursing through him. "I want you to want me as much as I want you," he finally managed.

"I want you," she said impatiently. "I want you," she

begged in a whisper that was almost more pain than pleasure. "Please, Josh, make love to me."

Triumph was quickly replaced by pure impatient desperation. "Gladly." He repositioned himself. *Gladly.* The word echoed in his head as he thrust inside her and felt her silken warmth tighten around him. He could do nothing more than savor the sensation for a moment out of time.

Then they began to move in perfect unison in an ageold rhythm that quickly demolished any conscious thought. Somewhere, in some reality, he heard her whispering his name. The sound became a quiet sob as she reached her peak. He quickly followed her to a perfect ecstasy.

"You're crying," Josh said softly as he held her in his arms later, her head against his chest. He'd rearranged them, pulling the covers over them somehow without getting an inch away from her or letting her go.

"I know." She felt foolish, but that didn't seem to stop the silent tears. All she had to do was close her eyes and they sneaked from the corners and down the side of her face.

"You're getting me wet." He brushed the moisture from his chest and held up his finger as if he had to have proof before she'd believe him.

"Sorry." She managed to smile as she swiped at another tear that was threatening to fall on him.

"You wanna tell me why?"

"I'd forgotten how wonderful..." Her voice creaked to a stop, her throat too thick with emotion to finish.

"I haven't forgotten a thing," he said huskily.

"I'm so relieved..."

"Poor, sweet Marisa." The kisses he left on each of her eyelids made the tears start again.

"You really believe we can make this work?" she asked, still needing something more from him.

"Not can. *Will*," he said determinedly. "How long have you known?" he asked after a moment.

"A few days," she admitted. "I waited until Ryan wouldn't be around so I could tell you with-out...without..."

"Your son has made things a little more complicated, hasn't he?"

"Thanks for being so wonderful to him." The unending mist of tears clouded her eyes again as she looked at him.

"It hasn't been tough. He's a great kid." Josh's smile filled his whole face, his eyes. "We're going to be terrific parents. I'm excited for our baby."

"I'm glad he's going to have you for a father."

"He? Do you know something I don't?"

She giggled.

"You didn't say when this was supposed to happen. Never mind." He held up a hand. "I can probably figure it out, given the facts." He'd propped his head on his hand and started making patterns on her body with one finger.

She knew she was blushing as she pulled the sheet up under her arms to lessen the distraction. "There's at least one advantage of not having much experience," she said. "I can always figure out when my babies are due."

He swooped over her to leave a kiss on her lips. "What did the doctor say?"

"I haven't been to the doctor," she admitted. "A preg-nancy test, courtesy of Mr. Finegold, confirmed my suspi-cions. My last employee benefit."

"So we aren't sure?"

"I am." She took a deep breath and willed herself not to react defensively.

"Those tests have proved fairly accurate, haven't they?"

Now he was using his finger to explore the bare skin just above the sheet. With every pass, the sheet seemed to inch lower.

She nodded, wriggling slightly away from him to maintain her concentration.

"But you will go to the doctor soon." He left a small peck on the curve of breast he'd just revealed. Somehow the small action moved him closer than he'd been a second before.

"I have an appointment in two weeks."

"Good." He stole another kiss. "Good," he said again. "You have to start taking all those vitamins and things," he added.

"And how did you become such an authority on all this?" she asked as sweetly as she could, given the way her body was tingling and jolting at his touch.

"Janet filled me in regularly on every aspect of her pregnancy while I was home," he said. "Made me jealous as hell of my dear sibling," he added, then looked pleased. "I can hardly wait to tell her."

"Let's not get too excited," Marisa protested. "Can't we enjoy the idea ourselves for a little bit? Oh, no," she said with a moan. "My mom and dad are going to be camped on our doorstep as soon as they hear."

"It's time for me to meet them, anyway," Josh said absently. He was becoming more and more intent with each little bit of her he exposed to the air. "When are we going to tell Ryan?" His hand sneaked under the sheet to continue his explorations.

She held her breath for a second. "Can we wait to tell him?"

"Why?" The look on his face said this conversation wouldn't last much longer.

"Let him get used to the idea we're sharing this room,"

she managed to say coherently. "We won't have to answer nearly as many questions."

"But you answer them so well," he said with a smile as he leaned closer.

She frowned and he kissed it away.

Gently, carefully, Josh focused his attention on seducing each and every one of her senses again. She felt like the most delicate, precious thing in his world.

Not precious, she amended, willing herself not to name whatever he might be feeling. If she thought about it, she would cry. She *wanted* him to think she was precious, valuable, but that would mean he loved her. He didn't. He didn't even pretend to. And that, she realized with astonishing clarity, was what she'd hoped when she'd asked if he still thought this could work. She'd wanted to know he no longer wanted just anyone. That no one but her would do. She'd wanted him to say his initial plan to "grow love" had worked, that he'd fallen in love with her.

He hadn't. She had.

She was in love with him.

Despite all the good intentions to let her head rule, he'd stolen her heart. And now she was going to have his child.

He nipped tenderly at her ear, begging her undivided attention. The hand sneaking slowly up her thigh got it.

She was delighted to put her troubling thoughts aside and give herself up to his magic.

Chapter Twelve

"I have to go out of town next week for a couple of days," Josh said as they shared their first cup of coffee on the porch swing the following Tuesday morning. "I meant to tell you last night." He took her hand in his and grinned. "I got distracted."

"We're going to have to get rid of that Nintendo game," she said.

"That isn't exactly what had my undivided attention." The devilish gleam in his eye made her feel as steamy as the coffee. "But it does keep Ryan busy. The game definitely comes in handy sometimes."

Marisa felt the heat rise to her face. It was difficult enough to go into the same room with Josh each night when she knew darn well Ryan was taking note of the new sleeping arrangements.

His hand, still holding hers, settled on her tummy. "What are you going to do with yourself while I'm gone?"

he asked, his voice filled with the longing she was fast becoming familiar with.

"You asking me or the kid?" She could almost believe Josh was in love with her. Almost. But Josh was in love with being a happily married man. He was in love with the *idea* of being all the things he wanted to be: Husband. Father. Family man. Lover.

"You." He patted her gently. "This little guy's going to be busy just growing for the next few months."

"Maybe I'll buy some wallpaper. For the baby's room," she said when he gave her a questioning look.

He was shaking his head before she'd finished. "I'll wait for you to put it up," she promised. "You think I'm going to do *all* the work myself?"

They'd worked on the other house over the weekend. They'd measured rooms. They'd bought wallpaper for the kitchen. They'd looked at furniture. Josh had mowed the lawn with his new garden tractor. They'd be bringing the baby home to a new room. Marisa had a feeling that once they actually bought bedroom furniture, they'd be staying there on weekends. By the time Ryan was out of school, he'd have lots of friends there.

"You'd better not." Josh tightened his grip on her hand.

"Where you going?" she asked, returning to their original conversation.

"Denver. I have to attend a regional meeting of some association the city belongs to. It's geared for city administrators. Alana wants me to participate. You want to come?"

"Sure." She grimaced. "I'm certain they'll let me take several days off from student teaching if I just mention it."

"Timing isn't exactly right, is it?"

"Not exactly." She would have smiled again if her jaw hadn't dropped. At the corner a lumbering vehicle turned onto their street. The slightly tinted windows of the motor home coming toward them kept her from seeing who was inside, but the oversize home on wheels certainly looked like the cream-colored one her parents owned, right down to the light turquoise stripe gracing the length of its side.

"What's the matter?" Josh asked.

She pointed vaguely. "My parents, Josh. I think my parents are here."

Marisa looked like her mother. The older woman's face had a network of soft lines Marisa's hadn't acquired yet, and her body was a bit plumper. Her hair was darker and less...vibrant. Hair dye, Josh realized. She was probably covering gray. He looked at Marisa and tried to imagine gray lacing hers.

He couldn't help liking his new mother-in-law, especially when her first comment was a charmed "You make a wonderful couple." He liked anyone who thought they were a wonderful couple. She followed it up with a contented sigh as she took Marisa in her arms.

The hug Muriel gave him when Marisa introduced them felt stiff and awkward. But when she pulled away, there were tears of happiness in her hazel eyes.

His new father-in-law was less enthusiastic. He stood to one side, waiting for Marisa to formally introduce him.

"It's a pleasure to meet you, sir." Josh extended his hand.

"Call me Al." He gripped Josh's outstretched hand firmly. "It's about time we met," he added gruffly.

"Where's that grandson of mine?" Muriel saved Josh from having to say anything.

"Still in bed," Marisa answered as Josh glanced at his watch.

"But it's time to get him up for school. I'll wake him," Josh offered. "You stay and welcome your parents."

Marisa was telling them how happy she was to see them while explaining they had arrived at a less-than-perfect time. "Ryan and I only have forty-five minutes before we have to leave. And with the wedding and school, and Josh and I both starting new jobs..." Josh could picture her delicate shrug as she paused apologetically. He heard the new storm door he'd installed click closed as they all followed him into the house. "We aren't going to be able to take off much time to spend with you."

His new mother-in-law protested that neither of them expected their daughter's undivided attention as he slipped into Ryan's room and flipped on the light.

Marisa looked frazzled when he met her coming down the hall a few minutes later.

"I'm sorry," she whispered. "I should have warned you we could expect th—"

He silenced her with a far too brief kiss. "Your father's right. We should have invited them to visit as soon as we got married." He wrapped her in his arms. "I'd be checking out anyone who wanted to marry *our* daughter."

"I thought it was a son."

"I'm talking about the *next* one."

"You're definitely getting into this." Her smile was a bonus he didn't expect. "Thanks for understanding."

"I'm glad they're here." He tasted her mouth between words.

She sighed. "Mmm." Her eyes stayed closed as she licked her lips, savoring the kisses. "I'm supposed to be putting on my makeup and getting ready for work," she finally whispered.

Ryan thundered out of his room, stopping in his tracks to gaze at them with the disgust he displayed whenever he caught them kissing. He slipped around them sideways, careful not to touch them, then resumed his dead run. "Grandpa?" he hollered.

"I have to be on my way." Josh pulled away reluctantly.

"See you later?"

"This evening." He whistled under his breath as she pulled out of his arms and went into the bathroom.

Muriel was already fixing batter for pancakes for Ryan when Josh reached the kitchen. Al stood by, ready to offer a critique of her flipping technique, from the looks of things.

"I hate to run the minute you get here," Josh apologized.

"At least you have a steady job," Al said.

Muriel eyed Josh sympathetically and placed two perfectly browned pancakes on a plate.

After grasping for something to say, Josh decided no answer to Al's comment was necessary. "Gotta be on my way, Ryan." Josh touched the boy's shoulder as Muriel set his breakfast before him.

"See you tonight, Josh," Ryan said absently, already reaching for the butter.

With a salute to the room in general and another good-bye, Josh made his way to the outer door. It wasn't quite closed behind him when he heard his father-in-law ask, "Is he treating you well, Ry?"

Josh unabashedly listened for Ryan's glowing tribute and was disappointed when the boy only mumbled an answer.

"So, do you like him?" Marisa asked her mother late in the week. It was a rare night; they all were going to be home for a meal. Marisa had spent several evenings at play practice since her parents had arrived. Josh and Ryan had been left to entertain them most of the time. Tonight Josh and her father had accompanied Ryan to football practice while Muriel and Marisa stayed home to cook a sit-down meal they could all eat together.

Muriel looked over the top of the magnifying glasses she used when doing her needlework projects. "I like him."

"Could you be a little more specific?" Marisa asked dryly.

Her mother smiled. "He's an admirable man, a little intense," she said. "I get the feeling he'd like to mold all of us into something a little more—" she searched for a word "—efficient?"

Marisa laughed. "You caught that, huh?"

"You are driving him crazy, Marisa, with your haphazard planning," Muriel informed her unnecessarily.

"Ryan and I have always lived minute to minute. I know it isn't especially good, but I'm trying to do better."

"Josh was impressed with your meal plan for the rest of the week," Muriel said.

"You offered to get groceries for me," Marisa pointed out. "That makes planning ahead a little easier."

"I'm glad I'm taking some of the load off you, even if it's only for a few days." An intricate stitch held her concentration for a moment. "Your father and I could move in and I could take care of all of you."

Marisa froze with dismay until her mother glanced up and sent her a "just kidding" grin. The twist at the end said, "Gotcha!" Marisa hoped the tense sigh she eased from her lungs wasn't too obvious. Her parents moving in with them was all she and Josh needed. Things had changed since they'd arrived. On the surface everything seemed all right. Underneath it felt as if she and Josh had reverted to the polite strangers who'd shared this house right after their marriage.

"He'll get used to your ways eventually," Muriel assured her as if she could read Marisa's mind.

Marisa could only hope so.

"What about you, Marisa?" Muriel pinned her daughter with a steady gaze. "Do *you* like him? That's a more important question."

One that left her speechless. "I love him," she finally managed. *If only I didn't.*

"Good. That's why we came. I had to know. We weren't sure..." She hesitated.

"You weren't sure of what, Mom?"

Muriel let her embroidery hoop sag to her lap. "It happened so fast. I was afraid you'd married him for...the wrong reasons."

"What do you mean?"

"Lots of things. Not every man wants to take on a wife *and* someone else's kid. It seems odd."

"You thought I'd done something impetuous again?" At her mother's nod, Marisa continued, "There wasn't one thing about our marriage that didn't make sense. That's why neither of us could see any point in dragging it out once we'd realized..." She searched for the right word and saw the satisfied gleam enter her mother's eye. She didn't need a word. Her mother could fill in the blank.

"You have a good heart, Marisa. Sometimes you just don't let it lead you. I worried that you wouldn't let it be involved if you ever did get married."

Marisa rearranged herself in her chair, folding her legs under her and layering her arms over her stomach. "I'm not sure what you mean."

"You've made a good life for yourself and Ryan," her mother said. "But you're too self-sufficient and proud. You don't even let your father and I help you unless you're in dire need."

"You've helped me a lot," Marisa protested. "Like the

time Ryan was in the hospital. You helped with the bills. You stayed with him while I went to Janet's wedding.''

"We wanted to help. We would gladly do more. But when you called to tell us you'd married Josh, your father had to pick me up off the floor. That I know of, you haven't let any man close enough to get to know you, let alone marry you. It made me terribly sad. You're a beautiful, wonderful woman. It seemed such a waste.''

"You're not prejudiced in the least," Marisa teased.

"Only slightly." Muriel picked up her embroidery and resumed stitching. "I hoped you'd find something like Al and I have. I'm just glad it finally happened for the right reasons.''

"What would be the wrong reasons?" Marisa couldn't help but ask, although she wasn't sure she wanted to hear the answer.

"A father figure for Ryan. Security."

"You think I'd marry someone for money?" Marisa squeaked indignantly, uncomfortable at how close her mother was to the truth.

"I didn't say that. But I do think you react more from the head than the heart these days. It isn't necessarily good.''

Marisa wandered to the window to adjust the blinds. "And what would some mythical, sainted man who let me marry him for those reasons have to gain?"

"Companionship. Regular sex," Muriel replied.

"Mother!"

"You asked." Muriel concentrated on another intricate stitch.

Marisa busied her own restless hands straightening the folds of the Priscilla curtains her mother had taken down and washed the day before. They smelled of sunshine in a room that had become stifling and airless. "You thought that's why Josh married me?"

"We didn't know what to think. It was so unlike you."

Marisa laughed out loud. "You've always said I'm *too* impulsive, that I make *too* many decisions based on my emotions."

"I haven't thought that for a long, long time. But it's what I hoped for this time. I'm delighted to be way off base for once."

Marisa squirmed. She opened the old-fashioned sash window to let some of the crisp fall air in. She propped it open with the strip of wood she kept between the panes.

"I'd think you would applaud my good sense if I'd...if we'd married for those reasons," she finally said, trying to make a joke of it.

"All I can say is thank heavens you didn't." Muriel held her hoop to her mouth and nipped at the thread with her teeth. "Close your mouth, Marisa. Nothing I said is *that* shocking."

"I'm stunned."

"Why? Because I wanted you to marry for love or because I'd almost given up on the idea of you marrying at all?"

"I'm stunned at how many times you warned me not to do things without thinking. How many times have I made mistakes because I *didn't* take that advice?"

"I've made mistakes, too, you know," her mother said. "When you got pregnant with Ryan, we got carried away with the idea that you shouldn't let it change your life. How can a baby not change your life? How could we have thought waiting a couple of years to finish college would ruin everything?" She shook her head.

It *would* have ruined everything. Marisa wouldn't have met Janet. Without Janet, she would never have met Josh.

"Look at Ryan," her mother continued with a smile. "Your impulsive behavior gave us the best thing in our lives. I can't even imagine a world without Ryan."

Marisa couldn't comprehend such a world, either. The idea made her eyes mist over. It scared her to death that she'd begun to feel the same way about Josh. "So what do *you* think of Josh, besides liking him?"

"He's been a pleasant surprise," Muriel admitted. "We were a little concerned that he wasn't very stable."

Josh unstable? "Why?"

"Besides rushing into marriage with you, he quit a partnership in a well-established law firm. That didn't make much sense."

"He wasn't especially happy there. He wanted a change."

"One of his partners is marrying his former girlfriend. Things were a bit strained," Muriel said primly.

Marisa couldn't hide her surprise. Josh had obviously discussed the subject with them. "He told you that?" It wasn't something he'd hurried to share with her.

Her mother looked smug. "I asked why he gave up a partnership in an established practice to take this job."

"And he told you all that?"

"Was it a secret?" Muriel asked.

"No, but..."

Muriel nipped another thread. "Josh is very open."

Marisa almost wished her mother had been around for the first couple of weeks of her marriage. "What'd he say about my...our marriage?" Marisa asked, not sure why she couldn't leave well enough alone. Did she really want to hear what he'd told them?

The dreamy look in her mother's eyes told Marisa that whatever he'd said, her mother thought it was romantic. "He said you bowled him over in the grocery store and that was that. He was lost.'' She sighed contentedly, then reached for another skein of embroidery thread from the fishing-tackle box she took everywhere. "Sounds like a fairy tale, doesn't it?"

It is a fairy tale! Marisa wanted to say. Trust Josh to make the truth sound better than good. He must be a brilliant lawyer. The man was brilliant at saying the things people wanted to hear. Except that he loved her.

Would he say that, too, she wondered, if she gave an indication it was what she wanted? She could almost imagine him arguing with himself that it was for the common good. Then she could blindly believe and be happy in her ignorance. Ignorance *was* bliss.

"I'm just happy that our fears were unfounded. I'm so glad you didn't just *settle*," Muriel added pointedly. "I know now that you and Josh can be very happy."

She *had* been willing to "settle." Then she'd fallen in love with Josh, and knowing he didn't feel the same was slowly eating at her soul. How long would settling do when she was emotionally starved for more?

Forever! she told herself determinedly, drawing away from the window and the cool breeze. She ran her hands down her arms, then crossed them over her flat stomach. Now she had Ryan *and* a baby to think about. Settling had to be enough. It didn't matter that anyone would do. She could live with the fact that any halfway presentable woman could take her place as Josh's wife. It was all she had. "I'd better check the chicken."

"I'm just happy to see that you and Josh love each other," Muriel called as if she had to have the last word.

"I'm glad you're glad," Marisa mumbled as she peeked into the oven and wished she had play practice tonight.

* * *

"We have news," Muriel said toward the end of their meal.

"So do we," Josh said, taking advantage of the opening. With all the activity the past few days, the normal hustle and bustle plus guests, they hadn't had a good chance to tell her parents. He'd wanted it to be a family occasion. A celebration.

Marisa gripped his arm, her fingers biting in like a vise.

"We're heading back to Arizona tomorrow," Al said.

Why had Marisa panicked when he only wanted to share their news? Her parents had just announced they were leaving tomorrow. When would they have a better chance?

A fool's paradise! That was what he'd created, Josh thought as he listened to Al and Muriel's plans and looked around him at his happy little family. It was fake.

Since Marisa's parents had come to stay with them, he'd smiled too much. He'd answered far too many questions. He'd been the perfect father, gaining strange looks from Ryan from time to time as the friendly relationship they'd established up to now subtly changed.

Marisa had changed, too. The capable, independent woman he'd come to admire had given up her quiet confidence overnight. Since her parents had arrived, she seemed to need someone's approval before she could decide even what to fix for dinner. And it wasn't him she turned to for it.

His suggestion for steaks cooked on the grill tonight had been put aside the minute her mother suggested oven-roasted chicken. "Al should be watching his cholesterol," she'd said. Not that Al needed to for any medical reason; he just should—as they all should.

Josh was still the outsider, and it bugged the hell out of him. The sales job he'd done when he pitched the idea of marriage to Marisa had been *too* good. He was a father figure—not a father. He was a Mr. Fix-it—but not in his own home. He'd given her the chance to pursue her dreams—and she had little time left for being "family." His physical presence completed her picture—it meant the kids she was directing in the school musical could call her Mrs. Maxwell and their parents could look at her with respectful approval.

And what did he have to show for it? Hers. Hers. And hers. Her house. Her kid. Her parents.

His own baby wasn't even a blip on the radar. Her mind-numbing sexy body didn't hint a thing. And she panicked the minute he hinted that he wanted to lay claim to the one thing that was truly his.

Marisa's grip loosened only when Josh gave her a look to reassure her. He'd gotten the message. He wouldn't say a thing.

He placed his fork on the edge of his plate. The chicken tasted like chalk, anyway.

When everyone finished and there was a lull in Marisa's conversation with her father about this teacher and that school policy, Josh suggested, "It's about time for dessert, don't you think? Anyone for ice cream?"

Ryan was out of his chair immediately. Marisa rose more slowly. "Let me clear the table first." She started stacking plates.

Josh's hand on her arm stopped her. "Let's go for ice cream," he said quietly.

Marisa glanced at his dear mother-in-law, who was picking up a serving bowl from the middle of the table. "This will only take a few minutes," the older woman said, unconsciously taking sides with Marisa. "It will give dinner time to settle a bit."

"The short walk will do the same." Josh kept his voice

soft, even though he wanted to shout. "The fresh air will help."

Marisa's gaze swept to his face and her mouth fell open. "Let's go for ice cream." Her tone matched his as she spoke. She set the plate she held back on the table. "This can wait."

Josh gave her his approval whether she wanted it or not.

The "What's wrong?" was still in her eyes by the time everyone had shoes, purses and assorted paraphernalia for the expedition. Ryan raced ahead as usual, dragging his grandparents in his wake, showing them things.

Marisa held back, glancing sideways up at Josh from beneath her bent head. "You're upset because I didn't want you to tell them about the baby?"

He felt his jaw clench and then, by sheer will, he relaxed it. "Why didn't you want me to?"

She casually laced a hand through his arm and he jammed his hands into the pockets of the khaki slacks he wore. She withdrew her hand and seemed at a loss for what to do with it. She settled for clasping her arms beneath her breasts, drawing his attention to that portion of her anatomy. Studying Marisa's various parts didn't lead to intelligent conversation. He focused his gaze on the trio in front of them. Marisa's parents and Ryan were almost half a block ahead of them now.

"Well, we don't want..." She started over. "I haven't been to the doctor yet. We haven't told Ryan. It..." She stammered, something she'd never done before. "It's too early."

"Are you sure you're pregnant?" he asked.

"I am. I'm sure. It's just..." Her face reflected her misery.

"Don't worry. I'm not getting any wild idea that you

made it up," he said. "I can't imagine that you'd let me touch you if you weren't certain."

"I wouldn't." So much for thinking they'd made progress.

The trio was waiting at the corner. Josh and Marisa slowed their pace even more. "You must have another reason for not wanting to tell your mom and dad."

"I know it sounds silly, but Mom's in some romantic fog about all this, and I don't want my parents to think we got married because we had to." She looked at him uncertainly.

"I see." He stopped in his tracks. "What everyone else thinks is what counts?"

"Yes. No..." She sighed. "You don't know what it's like, having everyone disappointed in you."

He suppressed a tug of sympathy. He certainly knew what it was like to *be* disappointed. But not in her. How could he ever be disappointed in Marisa?

"I'm sorry," she whispered. "If you want to tell them..."

He shook his head. "It won't hurt to wait."

"Thank you," she said quietly.

"You're welcome," he returned. "Come on, you guys," he raised his voice for the others. "We may not get ice cream until breakfast time at this rate."

Muriel herded her segment of the family across the street, and Josh decided he was lucky Ryan didn't decide to point out that it was Josh who was dawdling.

"You never did say what your news was, Josh," Muriel said as he held the door at the ice-cream shop.

"I guess it mustn't have been important," he said. "I don't remember." They separated to join the two lines of customers.

"Two scoops?" Ryan asked Josh when it was almost his turn to order.

"You getting green-bean parfait?" Josh asked.

Ryan made a dubious face.

"What's our deal?"

"I clean my plate if I want two scoops of ice cream."

"You didn't eat your vegetables tonight."

Ryan looked surprised that he'd noticed. "The green beans tasted funny." He wrinkled his nose.

"So much for serving something right out of someone's garden." Muriel shook her head. "I thought fresh would be a treat."

"I *loved* the fresh green beans," Marisa said, grating on Josh's nerves.

"What can I get you?" The girl behind the counter asked Ryan.

"Chocolate," Ryan chirped. "One scoop?" He slanted a look at Josh, one meant to charm him into changing his mind.

Josh didn't have to shake his head. The frown was enough.

"You didn't clean your plate, either," Ryan mumbled to Josh as the girl handed him his one-scoop cone.

"I'll have green-bean parfait," Josh told the clerk. "Two scoops."

Ryan hooted.

"Be careful what you ask for—you may get it," Al warned as the girl behind the counter looked at him as if he was crazy. "If this was one of those three-million-flavor places, I'd worry."

"I'll have what he's having." Josh pointed at Ryan. "One scoop," he confirmed when she started to ask.

Be careful what you ask for. Al's words echoed in his mind as the girl handed him his cone. That was *exactly* what he'd gotten from Marisa. He'd asked for an imitation marriage. He'd made it clear the only thing that mattered was that they pretend it was real. He and Marisa knew the truth. Why *wouldn't* she care more about what everyone else thought than she cared about his perceptions? How could he be disappointed when what he asked for was what he got?

Even rich chocolate ice cream didn't erase the bitter taste in his mouth.

Chapter Thirteen

With her parents' departure, the tension between her and Josh eased slightly. But Marisa was almost relieved that Josh left on his business trip the next day. Things would be back to normal—at least normal for them—when he got back, she promised herself.

But in the meantime nothing was right. She felt sluggish when she got to school. By afternoon, her stomach was cramping. She expected to wake the next morning to the short bursts of violent morning sickness she'd experienced during her pregnancy with Ryan.

She *wished* that was what was happening when she discovered she was spotting. Terrified, she made an emergency appointment with the doctor and called in sick at the school. After getting Ryan off to catch the school bus, she curled up on the couch and prayed.

This baby meant everything to her—and to her marriage. She and Josh finally had a common goal. They'd decided

to make the best of the situation. If there wasn't a baby—
his baby—there wasn't a situation to make the best of.

The spotting turned to a flow by the time she went to
her appointment that afternoon.

"We've met, you know," the young doctor who'd replaced Dr. Winston said as he entered the examining room.

"Oh?"

"At the mayor's reception to welcome your husband,"
he reminded her.

She didn't remember and wished he was Dr. Winston.
The older man had cared for her through her growing-up
years, up to and including Ryan's birth. She knew she'd
feel a lot less scared with his reassuring, familiar presence.

"You *were* pregnant," Dr. Norman said after he'd done
his examination. "You've lost the baby, probably some
time in the past twelve hours or so. I know it probably
doesn't seem that way now, but it's for the best," he added
gently. "It's just nature taking its course—God's way of
taking care of imperfect embryos."

From an imperfect marriage, she thought with bitter despair.

"Your system is cleansing itself now," he explained.
"We may have to do a D&C later, but let's wait and see."

He gave her a speech about how millions of women lost
babies at this stage and never knew they were pregnant in
the first place. She was certain he intended his words to be
comforting. She fought the urge to scream at him. After
giving her detailed instructions, he told her to go home and
take it easy.

"And extend my regrets to your husband," Dr. Norman
said before he closed the door to the examining room. "I
am sorry."

The cold but formerly sunny autumn day had turned gray
to match her mood as she drove home. All the brightly

colored fall leaves seemed to have fallen off the trees in the time she'd been in the doctor's office. It felt like winter inside and out.

By evening Marisa's heavy flow accompanied cramps that made her want to cry. Everything made her want to cry.

When Ryan finally went to bed, she went to her own, cradled Josh's pillow and cried herself to sleep.

Josh came in whistling from the airport right after school got out the next afternoon. Ryan met him at the door with the football. "Give me a chance to change clothes, Ryan, my boy," Josh pleaded, throwing an arm around his shoulders.

Marisa, who had been lying on the couch most of the day, sat up.

"And greet my wife," he added.

He bent to kiss her.

"Mom's sick," Ryan said, sitting on the edge of the coffee table in front of them.

Josh looked concerned. "Morning—"

He broke off abruptly at the look she shot him. She was more relieved than ever they hadn't yet told Ryan and her parents. Relieved and sick with sorrow that they couldn't join her in her grief.

"Miss me?" He gave her a look filled with heat and hunger. The disturbing gloom he'd left with was gone. He rested his hand possessively on her empty stomach. "I missed all of you," he said, including Ryan with a sideways grin.

It took everything she had not to burst into tears. Ryan rolled his eyes as he got up and grabbed his coat. "I'll wait outside."

"Rest up," Josh ordered Marisa. "We'll be in charge of

dinner tonight, won't we, Ryan,'' he added loudly just before the screen door banged. ''I was going to suggest we go out, but...''

She shook her head, confirming that she wasn't interested in leaving the house.

With another quick kiss to the side of her mouth, he changed clothes and joined Ryan. Marisa went to hide in the bedroom.

How would she tell him? She hadn't dealt with it herself yet.

There had been little joy during her first pregnancy, but Ryan had been special from the moment he was born, simply because he was Ryan. This baby had been special from the moment she'd begun to suspect its presence because it was Josh's. She huddled beneath the quilt her mother's grandmother had made, dry-eyed at last.

Maybe she should just get pregnant again. That would give them time. Time for him to grow to love her as she'd grown to love him. Time to move into his house and make it a home. Time to nurture dreams they could dream together.

She couldn't do anything about it for a few days, but getting pregnant had never been exactly difficult for her. He wanted a baby. A family. He was the one who had wanted to get married.

What was selfish about giving him the things he wanted? He was the one who said they could grow love. It had been true for her. Couldn't it be true for him?

When Josh came in again, he flipped the light switch in the bedroom, chasing the deep shadows to the corners of the room.

''Marisa?'' he said quietly.

She pretended to be asleep. His weight rolled her toward him as he sat down on the side of the bed.

"Marisa," he said again, stroking the hair back from her face.

She opened her eyes and blinked nervously, sure he'd be able to see her guilty thoughts.

"Still feeling lousy, huh?" he asked. "Morning sickness? Is it lasting all day?"

She didn't say anything. She couldn't. The lump in her throat choked off speech.

"Anything in particular you'd like for dinner?"

She shook her head. She wanted to confess that if this was morning sickness like she'd had with Ryan, the word "dinner" would have had her running for the bathroom. His tenderness brought tears again. She wanted him to hold her, kiss her, but then she'd have to tell him...

"Aw, sweetheart, I'm sorry." He reached to take her in his arms and she turned away.

"Sorry." Confusion filled his voice. He stood and backed away. "Ryan and I are going to run to the store," he said.

As soon as she heard them leave, her crying turned into noisy sobs.

Leave one day and everything falls apart, Josh thought as he and Ryan pulled into the grocery-store parking lot. He'd driven to the modern one closer to the suburbs, the one with the fancy deli where they could find something to stick in the microwave and put on the table.

Yeah, he and Ryan were going to fix dinner. That didn't mean he wanted to spend hours at the task.

"Let's have pizza," Ryan suggested, heading for the frozen section down the aisle from the deli.

"Let's not," Josh called after him.

Ryan kept going.

Your mother has morning sickness, he wanted to add. *Pizza probably wouldn't sit well.*

He scowled at the deli case in front of him and wondered if the same thing wasn't true of everything he saw.

"Mr. Maxwell?"

Josh turned toward a deep voice behind him. A man about his age extended his hand. "Tim Norman," the man introduced himself. "We met at the mayor's reception?"

Josh wasn't sure he remembered meeting him, but that wasn't surprising. He'd been high on his coup with Marisa that night and he'd met a steady parade of people that week, not just that evening.

"Nice seeing you again." Josh took Norman's hand, noting that they were soft despite the strength of his grip.

"I've been appointed to the Community Emergency Preparedness Committee," Norman went on. "I hear you'll be visiting one of our future meetings to discuss liability." He chuckled. "I guess even emergencies attract lawsuits."

"Unfortunately emergencies seem to bring out the lawsuit mentality in people who wouldn't consider it otherwise." Josh looked over Norman's shoulder for Ryan. He was at the far end of the aisle in front of the ice-cream case. Ice cream might agree with Marisa.

"I don't know if your wife mentioned me," the man continued somewhat hesitantly, "but I'm also her new doctor. I took over Dr. Winston's practice when he retired."

Dr. Norman. The name clicked. Josh remembered being introduced to him, and Marisa's commenting later that she hated the thought of getting used to a new doctor.

"She didn't mention you by name," Josh said, and felt his chest expanding. Should he tell Norman that Marisa would be in to see him soon? She had an appointment to confirm their good news.

"How's she doing? My nurse did call today to check on

her.'' The doctor looked down at his feet. ''Marisa said she was okay, but you know how that goes. They always say that.''

''She isn't feeling well,'' Josh admitted.

''I am sorry about the baby. I know you both must be very disappointed.'' He touched Josh's arm. ''It isn't much comfort, but as I told her, it is for the best.''

Josh couldn't catch his breath.

''I know it doesn't make losing this one easier,'' Dr. Norman added, ''but Marisa's very healthy. In another six weeks, you'll be able to try again.''

He lifted his hand in a salute and started to leave. Josh caught his arm. ''Marisa *is* okay, isn't she?''

''She will be,'' the doctor acknowledged. ''I'm supposed to see her the day after tomorrow, but don't hesitate to call me if there are problems before then.'' With a vague wave over his shoulder, he pushed his cart away.

She lost our baby? Josh felt a shiver chase up his spine. The pain in his gut made him want to double over.

''What, Josh?'' Ryan tugged his arm. ''What'd you say?'' he asked when Josh focused on him.

''Nothing,'' Josh whispered. ''Nothing,'' he said again, more clearly this time. ''I was thinking out loud.''

''Mom does that, too,'' Ryan said in a matter-of-fact tone. ''Can we get ice cream, Josh? They have peanut-butter fudge. It's on sale.''

''Sure,'' Josh said, and slowly followed him to the ice-cream case. ''Peanut-butter fudge sounds fine.''

She was asleep when they got home. Josh stood at the door of the bedroom watching her, then went to prepare the soup and grilled cheese sandwiches he and Ryan had finally settled on.

Josh sat at the table with Ryan, his hunger gone. "No one ever guaranteed life would be fair."

"What, Josh?" Ryan gave him a "never mind" look and shook his head. "I know. You were just talking to yourself."

"Yeah, I was, wasn't I?"

"Aren't you gonna eat?" Ryan asked.

"I thought I'd wait for your mother."

He watched his son slurp the last of his broth from the side of the bowl without comment. He knew he should tell him that just wasn't done, but he didn't have the heart. By the time Ryan was old enough to need manners to keep from being a social outcast, he wouldn't do it, anyway. At this stage of the game, his friends probably ate exactly the same way.

Something in Josh's heart ripped. A heavy ache expanded in his chest. He could feel tears there.

His baby was gone, his and Marisa's. Everything had instantly changed when she'd found out she was pregnant. The baby had been the tiny, tenuous thread holding them together, giving them a chance, finally getting them off to a promising start. How could he even address losing the baby with her? What else would they lose?

He couldn't lose Ryan, either, the child Marisa had shared with him. That would be a triple blow. He loved the kid.

Josh suddenly sat up straight. He'd thought of him as his son a minute ago.

"Ryan." Josh's voice cracked slightly.

Ryan put the last crust of his sandwich down.

"Ryan," Josh started again, "would you like to call me Dad?"

Ryan thought about it a minute, then shrugged. "I don't know. It might be hard to remember."

It wasn't the answer Josh had hoped for.

"Would you get mad if I didn't remember?"

"Of course not," Josh said. "Everything new takes some getting used to."

Ryan's face twisted in concentration. "If I call you that, do you get to yell at me?"

Josh smiled. It hurt, but it was a nice kind of pain. Pleasantly bittersweet. "What makes you think I won't yell at you, anyway?"

That brought another shrug. "Ya haven't yet."

"That doesn't mean I won't."

This required thought. "Well," Ryan finally announced, "I guess I could try calling you Dad if you want me to."

"I'd like that," Josh said.

"Okay." Ryan rose from the table. "I'm gonna see if we can get a game of touch football going." Every kid in the neighborhood had been spending every possible evening outdoors the past few weeks. It was as if they knew they only had another week before they lost daylight saving time and the longer hours of light. A few more weeks after that, cold weather would set in. Ryan headed for the back door, then stopped there. "You'll remind me if I forget?"

"How 'bout we leave it that you'll call me Dad if you remember and Josh if you don't." Josh smiled. "That be okay?"

"Cool," Ryan said, and was out the back door.

Josh hollered the boy's name as he took a flying leap off the step and would have been gone.

He charged back.

"Get the door," Josh enunciated carefully when Ryan stuck his head back inside.

Ryan looked stunned for a second. The eyes that were so much like Marisa's lit up, and his face split in a wide grin. "Okay... Dad," he tacked on. Then he was off again.

"What have you done?"

Josh swiveled in his chair. Marisa stood at the kitchen door, her face pale, her hair in a bunch at the side of her head.

"Marisa!" He hurried toward her. "Ryan and I had soup and grilled cheese. Can I get you some?"

She backed away. He finally saw the fury in her eyes. "What in heaven's name have you done?" she asked again.

"What do you mean?"

"Why did you tell Ryan to call you Dad?"

He grinned. It was the wrong thing to do.

"How dare you!" She pushed past him and crossed the room to look out the window.

"It's no big—"

"How can you say that?" she interrupted, turning on him. "How can you mess with my son's life like that?"

"Like what?" His hands landed in fists on his hips. "Exactly what have I done, Marisa, besides...besides treat him like a son? I thought that's how you wanted me to treat him. Wasn't that what you wanted? Part of why you married me?"

"What happens to him if you decide to leave?"

"I went to all that trouble to get a marriage license and a preacher because I planned to leave at the drop of a hat?" He tried to squelch the fury building inside him. What the hell was *she* getting angry about? Wasn't he meeting the obligations he'd committed to in their verbal marriage contract? "If that's what you think," he added, "we haven't made a lot of progress, have we?"

Her face turned a grayer shade as she swung toward him. "You got everything you bargained for," she said. "Everything you said you wanted."

"Oh, yeah. A wife. A wonderful, modern, convenient house." He waved his hand at the ancient faded wallpaper.

"A kid I'm supposed to treat like my own son but who isn't allowed to call me Dad. You're *determined* we won't make it," he said. "Every little thing becomes a reason for you to pull back. What is it exactly you expect of me, Marisa?"

She opened and closed her mouth twice.

"I have a loving wife who doesn't have to work but takes on every extra job that comes along so she can leave the house the minute I come near it. A loving wife who can't decide if she wants me or not." He grimaced. "Oh, yeah, I've gotten everything I wanted."

"And the deal I got was so good?" she finally managed to sputter.

"What did I promise that you haven't got?" His hands came up defensively, erasing the air. "Correction—what do you *not* have if you'd *let* me give it to you?"

"You're still mad about the house."

"I was never mad about the house," he protested. "But don't blame me if you haven't got everything I promised."

"Oh. We're back to the list! No wonder I feel so secure in this wonderful marriage," she said derisively.

"You work hard at being insecure, at pushing me away." He wanted to shake some sense into her. "You work hard at not trusting me."

"And things like your list couldn't have a bearing on that, I'm sure?"

He wanted to spit nails. He wanted to take her in his arms and kiss her senseless so she couldn't remember. He crossed his arms over his chest. "I can't take it back, Marisa. I can't go back and wipe out that whole incident." He forced himself to lower his voice. "What is it that you want?"

He saw her lip tremble. It was all he could do to maintain his distance. But he couldn't let her get to him the way she'd gotten to him every time they discussed the basics. Nothing would ever get fixed. They'd go from one muddle to the next, making things worse. "What do you want?" he repeated.

"I want the right not to..." The big hazel eyes—those wonderful eyes that had trapped him that first night in the grocery store—filled with tears, trapping him again. "You barged in here with all your promises and we gave you everything you said you expected—except one thing. You forgot to tell us you expected us to be clay figures you could pose and fit into some perfect image you have in your mind of a family. We don't fit. We'll never fit."

"The only thing about that image that doesn't fit, Marisa, is me. I wanted to be in that picture. You've done your darnedest to keep me out."

"How?"

"Don't let me and Ryan establish a *real* relationship. Don't let me repair the house. Don't let—"

"You don't even like this house. You don't want to be here. You said that when we sell it, whatever profit it brings will go for Ryan's college. You've taken over the payments when it isn't even your house. How fair would—"

"And that summarizes it, doesn't it? It isn't my house. I rest my case. This isn't my life. It's yours. I'm supposed to stay on the fringes."

"You got everything you said you wanted," she protested.

"And you didn't?" She said nothing for a minute. "I'm here for Ryan, aren't I? When you'll *let* me be," he added quietly. "You're pursuing your dreams, aren't you? At the cost of mine, I might add." Even knowing sarcasm wouldn't help, he couldn't keep it out of his voice.

"You got companionship. A fam—" She broke off.

"A family?" he asked, suddenly remembering what this

was all about. She still hadn't told him. "And great communication with my wife? I've got that, too, haven't I, Marisa?"

She met the open challenge with silence.

"My wife loses my baby and I have to find out by running into her doctor at the grocery store. But I'm not allowed to ask her son to call me Dad without talking it over with her first."

Marisa's face turned ashen. "You know?" The question came with a total lack of sound.

"You didn't plan to tell me?"

"I…if you… When did I have the chance?"

"When I called last night. When I came home. Ten minutes ago. Couldn't you have told me when I got home? You didn't think it was important enough to mention?"

Marisa burst into tears. He took one step toward her, then planted his feet on the kitchen floor. She should have told him. He wasn't going to let crocodile tears—however real they looked, filling her eyes, streaming down her face—trick him into feeling he was in the wrong.

His indignant stance faltered when her hands came up to cover her eyes and her shoulders sagged.

He took a step toward her, arms extended. "We should be—"

She jerked away, hiccuping in her attempt to stem the flow of tears.

…*comforting each other.* He'd bite off his tongue before he made that effort again. "It was my baby, too. I really cared…" Emotion prevented him from saying more.

She nodded and finally seemed to get her broken sobs under control.

"Don't I have the right to know what happened?"

"It was an…imperfect—" she snagged a deep breath

and swiped at her moist face ''—embryo. The doctor said it was for the best.''

''He told me the same thing.''

''I'd lost it by the time I saw him,'' she said, her voice calmer now. ''He said it was nature taking its course.''

Her eyes were red and puffy. Why hadn't he seen it before? The telltale signs that she'd been crying had been there when he'd first come in from the airport. But he'd missed her and Ryan so much while he was gone and he'd been so intent on making up for his foolish jealousy of her parents, he'd come in reading some inane script and barely noticed that she wasn't playing her assigned part.

She wasn't supposed to be distressed. She was supposed to be thrilled to see him. When she didn't feel well, he simply altered the script slightly. She needed his tender, solicitous care.

''Here.'' He gestured toward the table. ''Let me get you some soup. Ryan made the cheese sandwiches, but I haven't grilled ours yet. It will only take a minute.''

''I'm not hungry.''

''You have to eat.''

''I don't have to do anything,'' she said quietly. ''You don't have to do anything.'' She added, ''Neither of us has to do this anymore, Josh.''

''What do you mean?''

''I mean...doesn't it seem like a good time to admit it was a good try, but maybe a lousy idea?''

His brain should be functioning, keeping up with her, making a comeback of some sort. It was dead. ''Marisa?''

''We should cut our losses. Move on.''

''Aren't you happy with the way things have been going?''

She couldn't answer that question. It wasn't allowed. She couldn't say that to go on now, she needed his love. She couldn't bear being a stand-in for his idea of the perfect wife. She wanted him to love her. Not her as a place holder for a wife, but her, Marisa. She tossed his question back at him. "Are you?"

"Happy enough," he managed. "I can live with it."

"So we should just keep pretending?"

He nodded. "We can be as happy as two-thirds of the rest of the world."

"And that's enough for you."

"I can live with it," he said again.

She stared at him for a long time. "I can't," she finally said, so softly he had to step closer to hear.

"I see."

"I thought I could," she said. "I thought we could just live meeting the practical needs. I thought it would work."

He felt hope take hold.

"But it isn't just us anymore," she said quietly. "Now Ryan's involved in the playacting, too. What happens when he starts to believe it all? What happens if he starts to call you Dad and suddenly you aren't there? What happens when everything falls apart?"

"Marisa, I gave you my promise. I won't back out on that. I won't just leave. If nothing else, in the past few weeks we've proved things can be good, haven't we? Once we knew we had something important at stake, we proved we could make things work."

"What would happen if one of us—you or me—fell in love with someone?" she almost whispered. "Would a pretend marriage still be enough?"

He frowned and looked confused. "Why would that happen now?"

She released a long, quavery sigh. He couldn't have said it more clearly. He would never fall in love with her. "Why wouldn't it?"

"We aren't looking," he said as if that made a difference. "You don't think we can grow to love each other?"

She was quiet for a long moment. "What happens in the meantime?" She didn't wait for him to answer. "Ryan starts to depend more and more on you? I get pregnant again? We have another child to complicate things?" She paused. "I get to follow the dreams I would have survived without. You get an imitation family." Her voice softened. "I've seen the disappointment in your eyes, too, Josh. What happens when you realize you've settled for something when you could have so much more?"

"I don't want more. I'm not giving up," he said determinedly, stepping toward her, intent on taking her in his arms. Just what she didn't need.

She closed her eyes and drew in a deep breath. "I am. I'm kicking you out. *I* can't live the way you described. I thought I could be happy in a practical, realistic, loveless marriage. I was wrong."

He watched her for what seemed like forever, waiting for her words to sink in, hoping for some sign that she didn't mean them. Then he carefully moved past her, not daring to touch her again. "I'll pack."

Chapter Fourteen

What else could he do? Josh wondered. What was he fighting this for? The chance to get everything he said thrown back in his face? He pulled out his suitcase and opened it.

What a devil's bargain he'd made. He'd bargained for a sane, practical marriage where feelings would grow like tidy hothouse plants in a well-tended garden. No weeds.

Whatever crop they had sown, it certainly hadn't produced what he'd expected. They'd actually been yelling at each other. Was that the kind of marriage he wanted? So much for rational and practical.

But in a way it was an improvement, he was surprised to realize. For the first time they hadn't had a polite exchange between strangers. It was a heated discussion. The kind he and Janet had often had. The kind he'd heard between his parents. One that any two people whose emotions were involved might have.

He wanted to stay. He wanted to be there to listen when Marisa needed to cry and hold her when her emotions were spent. He wanted the right to share her deepest passions. He wanted to share her sorrow and grief. It had been *their* baby. Why, when he needed to hold her to ease his own pain, was she sending him away?

He loved her.

The thought stopped him in his tracks.

He loved her. He wasn't sure when or how it had happened. He only knew it was true. And it had been from almost the beginning. The idea of leaving her now made his heart feel as though it was being torn from his chest. He sat on the side of the bed, propped his elbows on his knees and buried his head in his hands.

Technically, loving Marisa made all his promises null and void. He could no longer guarantee her the calm, cool unemotional marriage he'd offered. He wanted the roller coaster of excitement and anticipation and expectations he knew his marriage to Marisa could be. And lots and lots of emotion. He wanted the rapture she'd shown him in this bed to color every aspect of their lives. He raked his fingers through his hair and rose.

He'd take just enough for a couple of nights, he decided. Yanking a couple of suits out of the closet—Marisa's closet, where he wished he'd made love to her the morning after they'd become lovers—he put them in a garment bag. Clothes would give him an excuse to come back early next week. Marisa needed time. She'd rethink her decision. She had to.

In his wildest dreams he couldn't imagine not sharing another meal with them, not laughing with Ryan. Not being Marisa's lover again. The thought was like a body blow. Only the frantic need to hurry kept him from sagging to the side of the bed again to recover his breath.

Get out fast. Take only what he needed for a day or two. Come back after she'd had a couple of days to miss him. Come back the day after that and the day after that, getting a few things at a time.

He went to collect his toothbrush and shaving gear from the bathroom. The kitchen door banged open just as he remembered he still had all those items packed from the Denver trip.

Suddenly he heard Brian yell, "Marisa, Ryan's hurt! Come quick!"

Josh stopped what he was doing and raced into the kitchen and out the back door. Marisa and Brian were by the back steps.

"Where? What happened?" Marisa was asking Brian.

The boy was breathless, white-faced. "Old Mrs. Leitner's tree," he gasped, and grabbed his side.

Josh sprinted around the two of them, then realized he had no idea where Mrs. Leitner lived.

"The corner." Marisa pointed. "The giant marigolds."

Marisa had admired them every time they'd passed them. Josh was on his knees at Ryan's side before Marisa and Brian made it to the sidewalk.

Tears coursed down Ryan's cheeks, but he was alert and well enough to be moaning loudly. "It hurts, Josh. It hurts."

"What hurts?" Josh asked.

"My leg." Ryan's leg lay at an odd angle.

"Just the leg?" Dusk and the shade from the big tree made it hard to see. Josh ran his hands over the boy's small body. "Do you hurt anywhere besides there?"

"I don't think so," Ryan answered as Marisa arrived and dropped to the ground beside him.

"Are you having any trouble breathing?"

Ryan seemed to consider it. He shook his head. "Just for a minute."

"Knocked the wind out of you, huh? Any pain here?" He gently probed Ryan's bony chest.

"Just my leg."

"Your back or neck?"

Another thoughtful pause. "No." He started to prop himself up on his elbow.

"Lie still." Josh braced Ryan's slender shoulder against the ground. "Get the car, Marisa. My car," he added, reaching into the pocket of his jeans for the keys. "It's bigger. We can get him in and out of the back seat more easily."

Marisa touched Ryan's cheek, then looked up at Josh, her eyes wide. Her face was as white as the boys'.

"You going to be okay?" He reached across Ryan to touch her cheek, imitating the comforting motion she'd just done on Ryan.

The question seemed to be all she needed. She nodded. "Fine. I'm fine," she said, and got to her feet. "I'll be back in a minute," she promised Ryan.

"I'm going to lift you slowly," Josh said. "At the slightest bit of pain—anything that even feels funny—you cry out," he ordered. "Okay?"

After a few fits and starts with Josh checking and re-checking Ryan each step of the way, he had him off the ground. Perfect timing, he thought, turning to see Marisa pulling up at the curb.

"You taking him to the hospital?" Brian asked.

"Yeah."

"Can I go?"

"Your folks won't know where you are," Marisa said as she opened the back door of the car. "Go tell them what happened. I'll call your mom and let you all know what's going on as soon as we know anything," she promised.

Within minutes they were on their way. Josh drove as Marisa alternated between giving directions and soothing Ryan.

Ryan had calmed considerably by the time they reached the emergency room. Marisa had even managed to cobble together a loose idea of what had happened.

They'd been testing the rubber-band rockets they'd made as part of a science project. Ryan's had lodged in one of the branches of Mrs. Leitner's tree. He'd climbed up to get it.

"From our yard to there?" Josh asked.

"Yeah."

"Good launch," Josh said.

"Yeah." Ryan's brief burst of pride turned into a moan as Josh finagled to lift him from the car.

"You're lucky you didn't hit a window," Josh said, trying to distract Ryan from the pain.

"I didn't think it would go that far, Dad."

A bittersweet burst of pleasure turned to pain when he saw Marisa wince at what Ryan had called him.

"A window would have been easier to fix," she said shakily, stepping aside to let them go first into the emergency room.

It seemed like hours since they'd hauled Ryan away for X rays. Surely it wouldn't be much longer before the doctor came back with a report. Marisa didn't look as if she could take much more.

"You think it's broken?" Marisa asked Josh.

"I'll be surprised if it's not."

She nodded her head as if it was the closest she could come to finding words.

Guilt stabbed him at the tiny tremor of relief he felt. Thank heaven Marisa couldn't read his mind. He was sitting here actually anticipating how he might benefit if his son's leg was broken!

"You look exhausted." He raised his hand to touch her, then let it fall back to his lap.

Her slight smile looked genuine. "I was just thinking the same thing about you," she told him. "But the way you said it was kinder than what I thought."

"That bad, huh?"

"I was thinking you look like hell."

He heaved a deep sigh and raked his fingers through his hair. "What a week it's turning out to be."

"How'd your meetings go?"

He wavered between blaming a series of grueling meetings for the way he looked and being honest. He'd spent two days in Denver wishing he was home. Wondering why her eagerness to please her parents had bugged him so much and willing himself to be content with what he had, since that was what he'd told Marisa he wanted. He settled for something in the middle.

"I wish I'd been here with you. I'm sorry you had to go through the miscarriage alone."

"I should have told you about the baby the minute you came home." Her voice quaked at the mention of their loss.

He took her cold hand. "You won't have to go through this alone," he promised. "I'll stay, of course. You won't be able to carry a boy Ryan's size around with a cast on his leg."

"Let's just hope it's not broken."

The doctor came in from one end of the room, and Marisa stood. He motioned them to the examining room where Ryan lay totally out of it. Obviously he'd been given something for pain.

"This is Dr. Spencer, an orthopedic surgeon." The first doctor introduced the man standing beside X rays of Ryan's frail-looking bones. The break was very obvious.

Dr. Spencer pointed out several things, then said, "We're going to have to do surgery to set it properly," as he finished with the gory details. "We've scheduled it for seven in the morning."

Marisa looked up at Josh, uncertainty in her gaze. "Why morning?" Josh asked.

The doctor indicated the inflatable cast they'd put on Ryan's leg. "This will stabilize the leg, keep everything in line. We'll elevate it, get some of the swelling down. That will make the surgery much easier. I suggest you both go home, get a good night's rest and be back here by five tomorrow morning."

"I couldn't. Ryan may—"

"Your son is very sedated and I plan to keep him that way all night so he'll be rested for the surgery tomorrow." The doctor's voice lowered. "You don't look so good yourself, Mrs...."

"Maxwell," Josh supplied.

"Maxwell," the doctor continued. "Would you like me to get you something to help you rest?"

"I'm fine. Dr. Norman said I'm fine," she murmured.

Dr. Spencer directed a concerned frown at Josh.

"Miscarriage," Josh said quietly, and Marisa visibly wilted. Josh pulled her closer. She felt so good against him. "She'll get some rest," Josh promised both doctors as two more men entered the cubicle, intent on moving Ryan to a room.

The doctor reassured Marisa he would see them in the morning, prior to Ryan's surgery, then left and came back with a pill. "It's very mild. It will help you relax so you *can* rest."

She started to protest again.

"Let's get Ryan into a room, then I'll take you home," Josh said. "*I'll* come back and stay with him. Okay?" He didn't plan to let her argue.

She seemed dazed as together they followed the men taking Ryan out on their cart.

Josh blessed the night nurse for helping him convince Marisa she needed to go home. "You look weary to the bone, sweetie," the woman said as she checked Ryan's vital signs for the third time after they'd settled him in his room. "I guarantee you he isn't going to wake up anytime soon." She indicated the syringe she'd brought in with her and jabbed it into the tube of the IV they'd put in Ryan's arm. "He's going to need you bright-eyed and bushy-tailed tomorrow. So don't wear yourself out before the really tough part starts. I promise, we'll take good care of him."

"She's right." Josh had held out a hand to Marisa. "Let me take you home." She'd given up her protests only when he'd again promised to return and stay with Ryan himself. As thankful as he was for that small display of trust in him, he suspected she needed him more than Ryan did.

Wishful thinking, he admonished himself as they climbed into the car a few minutes later. Even in the dim light, he could see the pallor of her face. He started the car. She didn't *need* him or she wouldn't be sending him away.

The wind had turned as frosty as his thoughts. As they left the parking lot, brown leaves drifted up from the gutters and fluttered in the headlights. Marisa's teeth chattered.

"You're cold." Their seatbelts prevented him from pulling her close so she could share his warmth. Would she have let him anyway? His hands tightened on the steering wheel as he guided the car around a corner.

"I guess I'm not ready for this."

"I'm not either, Marisa." He knew she meant the colder weather, but he took the opening she offered. "I'm not ready for any of the things that have been happening with us." He spoke reluctantly, not sure if this was the right time to bring things up again but certain he couldn't wait any longer. "I'm not ready for Ryan to be hurt. I'm not ready for you to be in pain." He chanced a glance in her direction, hating that her face was a shade paler than it had been. "I'm not ready to leave. I'm not ready to give up on us."

She was so still as she stared straight ahead. She finally blinked two times.

"We said things earlier in the emotion of the moment." He cleared his throat and softened his tone. "Even if things were perfect between us, don't you think losing a baby would be devastating? We'd be under a lot of stress and strain. If we hadn't lost the baby, I *know* we would have been fine."

"But we did lose the baby," she said, retreating farther to cuddle up to her door. "I'm just weary of pretending."

Her statement startled him. "Pretending?"

"That everything is wonderful. Perfect. For the baby, I could have kept on, but I'm not sure I can now."

"I want to try," he said stubbornly. "Nothing's changed. I still want…and need," he added, "a family. Someone to talk to at the end of the day."

"And regular sex?"

"That was good, too." His quick smile died as he caught her meaning and realized she was pointing out that he wasn't saying anything he hadn't said before.

She couldn't help her wistful smile. "It isn't enough." She belatedly wished the sadness from her voice.

"No, it isn't," he suddenly agreed, surprising her. "I realized while your folks were here that I want more. A real marriage," he said as if it hurt to mention it. "I do want love."

Too shocked to speak, Marisa sat stunned, holding her breath. He hadn't said he wanted love from *her*. He hadn't said he wanted a real marriage with *her*. Why was her heart leaping and struggling to attach a meaning to his words that wasn't there?

Her teeth chattered again. He flipped on the heater and reached out to hold his hand to the vent to see if it was warm. Turning the cool gust off again, he released an impatient sigh. Something in his chest tightened to the point where he almost couldn't breathe. "I have enough for both of us," he managed to say.

"You have enough *what* for both of us?" she finally squeaked.

Thank heaven they were almost home. Her voice... Damn, he wished he could see her. Josh wanted to take her in his arms and kiss her senseless to show her exactly what he meant. He stepped a little harder on the gas and the car leaped forward. The hand Marisa had rested on his arm clutched at his shirt.

Josh turned into the drive and screeched to a halt, almost forgetting to take the car out of gear before he reached for her. "I have enough for both of us, Marisa," he said, trying to see her face clearly in the dim light from the dashboard.

"Love? Are you talking about love? Do you want love from me?" she asked in a small, thin voice.

"Oh, Marisa, my sweet." He drew her as close to his heart as he could, given the space between their seats. "I've never wanted anything more in my life than your love. But if you can't give it now, I can—"

"Are you saying you love *me?*" she interrupted. Her tone was stronger, gaining hope.

"With all my heart," he answered, then bent his head

to touch his lips reverently to hers. He prayed that all the love he felt was in the tender kiss. He wasn't sure he had the strength to say it outright. What would he do if she didn't accept it?

"Oh, Josh," she whispered. The passion and peace in her voice made him want to whoop and holler…and carry her into the house and make never-ending love to her.

"Come on," he said huskily, taking her hand. "Let's go in."

She tightened her grip on his shirt. "You and Janet are alike in a lot of ways. She was almost famous for her never-say-die attitude. You aren't just too stubborn to give up? You aren't just saying this now because you think it's what I want to hear?"

"Why would I think it's what you want to hear?" he asked against her mouth. "I'm still terrified you'll send me away."

"If you love me, why would I send you away?"

"I keep adding things I want from you," he said. "Every time you turn around, I ask for more from you than I told you I'd expect. From the start, nothing went the way I'd planned, but I *liked* being with you and Ryan, anyway. I couldn't understand all the wild emotion, the desperate need for you. I thought I'd lost total control." He laughed softly. "I wanted to live in the suburbs. You didn't want to move." He held up a hand when she might have spoken. "I understand. We need to make the transition when it's appropriate for Ryan. One or both of us ends up going to the grocery store every night." He went back to his list. "I never make it anywhere on time if I'm going there with you. I *had* lost total control. My well-ordered life was suddenly chaotic," he admitted sheepishly. "And you know what?" He didn't allow her a word. "I still loved living here with you. I still love being here with you. You brighten my days and make them more exciting and intense than anything I've known in my life.''

He paused for breath and saw the sparkle of a tear in her eye. ''Oh, Marisa, please don't cry. When Ryan's better, I'll go if you want me to. But please don't cry.''

She stunned him by laughing. ''You think I want you to go?'' Her hand gently shaped itself to his face. ''I love you so much. These are happy tears,'' she added as he brushed one from her lashes. ''Why do you think I asked you to leave tonight?''

He was so startled by her announcement he could only shake his head.

''I was afraid for both of us if you stayed. Almost from the start, in my heart, I've trusted everything you do and say. Too much. I scared myself every time I realized it. Then something would happen—like your list.'' She covered his mouth with her hand when he would have apologized again for hurting her. ''I used it to tell myself I couldn't let down my guard. I couldn't let my emotions guide me. I had to rely on good judgment.'' She took a deep breath. ''I know you would never leave me with a baby to raise on my own. Why do you think I didn't want to tell you about…our loss? I didn't want to risk your leaving,'' she answered her own question.

''Oh, Marisa.'' The kiss he gave her landed on her cheek as she lowered her head. Her fingers softly covered his mouth again.

''I have to finish. You have to know the truth.'' She licked her lips and he wanted only to taste them again. He had to force himself to concentrate as she went on, ''I'm only human. I knew if you stayed, I'd get pregnant again and I *would* use it to keep you here. I couldn't bear the thought of doing that to either of us.''

"You love me?" he asked, still stuck on the wonder of her revelation.

"I think I knew the night you gave me the porch swing. I just wouldn't admit it," she said reluctantly. "I was so certain I was being sensible. Then, when I couldn't deny it any longer, I wanted to stamp it out before it was hopelessly irreversible," she said. "Even then," she chuckled "I think it was too late. I was *so* relieved when I found out I was going to have your baby."

"But you were still fighting it," he said.

"And you weren't?" she asked between the kisses he was showering on her face.

"Maybe just a bit," he said. "I think it was more a case of not believing that it was possible I'd fall in love with anyone. It just didn't occur to me." He shifted restlessly, trying to gain access to more of her and not having much luck. "Do you know how hard it is to show you how much I love you from so far away?"

A tap on the driver's-side window startled them both. Josh tried to peer through the steamed glass, then rolled it down.

"Good grief," Evie said, hugging herself and rubbing her arms. "I keep forgetting you two are still newlyweds. You're out here fogging up the car windows when it would be a lot simpler—not to mention more comfortable—if you went into the house where you have a bed."

Josh laughed.

"How is Ryan? I saw you pull in the drive and when you didn't answer the phone, I decided I'd better come find out what was going on."

"Oh, damn," Josh whispered.

"What?"

"Ryan. I have to go back."

Marisa kissed the corner of his mouth. "They promised to call if he needs us."

"You'll miss it because you're out here in the car making out," Evie said dryly. She refused their invitation to go into the house with them, so they gave her a quick update. "Call me as soon as you have news tomorrow." She waved and started back across the yard.

After Josh and Marisa hurried inside and checked the answering machine, he pulled her back in his arms. "Where were we?"

"You were showing me how much you love me," she murmured against his lips since he didn't wait for an answer. When he finally lifted his head, she sighed.

"I love you, Marisa Maxwell." He generously spread kisses down her throat.

"I love you, too," she replied as soon as he let her.

He put her gently away from him. "I have to go back to the hospital," he said. "I promised you. Would I have gotten you home otherwise?"

"Probably not," she admitted. "But Ryan needs parents who love each other. In the long run, this is going to do him a lot more good than one of us sitting by his bed, watching him sleep." She traced a finger down the open collar of his shirt.

"I'm certain you're right." He pulled Marisa back into his arms. "But will you get any rest if I stay here?"

She grimaced. "Probably not."

"And that was the point, wasn't it?" Kissing her, he walked her backward toward the front closet. They were in perfect step. "If you're not going to get some rest anyway, tomorrow we'll both feel guilty that we weren't at the hospital with him."

"He's very lucky to have you. We both are," she added.

"Hold that thought," he said, releasing her long enough

to get a jacket from the closet. "I think I'm going to need this. It's going to be cold out there without you." He embraced her again.

"It's going to be lonely in that bed without you, especially now that I know you love me." She smiled up at him. "Say it again," she begged.

"I love you," he said. "But Doc Norman did warn me you shouldn't get pregnant again for six weeks."

"I have you scared of getting me pregnant now, too, don't I?" Marisa laughed.

"I can hardly wait," he said, kissing her one more time. "But I'm going to be terrified of touching you until he says another pregnancy is okay."

"He insisted on giving me all sorts of things to prevent it," she said slyly.

"I *can* wait," he reassured her. "I'd be happy just holding you every night for the rest of our lives."

"Yeah, sure," she teased.

"I didn't say it would be easy." The familiar glint came into his eyes. "But I have a feeling I'd do almost anything to keep you as my very own wife, my sweet Marisa."

She touched his face lovingly. "Just as long as your idea of 'anything' matches mine."

Josh just slanted her a smile that said their thoughts were a perfect match.

Epilogue

"Josh, are you coming?" Marisa called from the bottom of the stairs of their wonderful house.

"In a minute," he called. She could hear him giving Ryan a list of instructions.

She sank onto one of the lower steps and looked around the great room, the large open area of Josh's dream home that connected to almost every other important room in the house: the kitchen, formal living room and dining room, the loft above, the huge deck that ran the entire length of the house. The grove of trees beside the little creek that ran through the development separated them from view of their neighbors. Hundreds of the fall flowers they'd planted last spring were in bloom and there were splashes of color everywhere. They were ready for the party—except for one last stop at the grocery store.

And you could get in and out of the bathrooms with ease,

Marisa tacked on in her mind as she decided she should make a precautionary visit there while she was waiting.

Josh and Ryan—the boy had grown half a foot since this time last year and probably an inch today—were coming down the stairs when she came out. "You ready?" Josh asked.

"Ready and waiting," she said with a grin. She loved to rub it in when she had to wait on him. He'd taken to wondering aloud if her tardiness gene was contagious.

"You're sure you're going to be okay?" she asked Ryan.

"Dad gave me a list of things to do while you guys are gone," he said, rolling his eyes. "He's trying to keep me busy so I won't get into any trouble." They'd been letting him stay by himself occasionally, as long as it was during the day and only for a couple of hours. Josh worried every moment of the time they were gone.

"You know you can call or run over to Brian's if you need anything." Ryan mouthed the words with her. Evie and Bob had found a smaller house a block and a half away, and moved to this neighborhood only two weeks ago. It was wonderful having them near again.

"I know," Ryan said.

"Mom and Dad may get here while we're gone," Marisa reminded him.

"And we'd better get going." Josh put an arm around her and glanced at his watch. "Or my parents and Janet's family are going to be stuck waiting at the airport."

"See you later," Ryan called.

"Mmm," Marisa said a few minutes later when Josh finally drew away from her. She loved the little rituals that they'd established during the past year. Josh never started the car without kissing her first.

"Happy anniversary, sweet Marisa," he said softly, his

finger tracing her eyebrow. His hand moved to her bulging stomach. "How's my baby?"

"She's going to be here today," Marisa warned him. "You can ask her in person."

"No way." He started the van. "You're always late," he told her. "And Dr. Norman said she's not due for another two weeks."

"That shows you what Dr. Norman knows," Marisa said smartly. She was positive she'd gotten pregnant the minute they'd stopped the preventative measures, six weeks after they'd lost the other baby. Thinking of it now, she had a twinge of sadness mixed with joy. That baby had helped bring them together, gotten them on track. One year. It had been one wonderful euphoric year—give or take a few less-than-favorable days here and there—since they'd said their vows.

"Are you sure this party isn't going to be too much for you?" Josh asked, taking her hand.

"I keep telling you." She picked up the hand holding hers and kissed it. "I'm going to miss it. You and Ryan are going to have all the hassle of playing host to both our families and all our friends."

He laughed.

"I'm so excited they're all going to be here, get to meet each other. I'm so excited we're finally going to get to see Janet's baby." He was almost eight months old now. "Now your family—they're the ones who are late having babies," she teased. "I'm *always* on time."

"We'll see," he said as though he had some divine knowledge.

They were both silent and smiling the rest of the way to the airport, lost in their own thoughts and memories. It was as perfect a late-summer day as Marisa had ever seen.

Janet was the first person Marisa saw standing on the

curb outside the terminal with her beautiful son. Marisa was out of the van almost before it stopped.

By the time Josh parked and joined them, they'd already exchanged a very long and awkward hug, and oohed and aahed over little Stevie and Marisa's shape.

"Where's everyone else?" Josh asked as he took part in the hugfest and lifted little Stevie out of Janet's arms.

"They're waiting for the luggage," Janet said at about the same time everyone started filtering out the door. Soon all were talking at once; everything was chaos as the men started loading the van.

"We should have brought two cars," Marisa said quietly to Josh as they finally started to pack beloved people in around the mass of bags and infant equipment.

"We're all going to fit," he said, drawing her close to his side and kissing her nose.

"Yes, but they all need to go to the house. I need to go—" the first pain hit, bent her almost double "—to the hospital. My water just broke," she said breathlessly when she could speak again.

"This isn't on the schedule for today," Josh murmured, lifting her off her feet and into his arms, swinging her around carefully before he sat her in her seat. Joy brimmed on his face and gradually turned to confusion. "What're we going to do?" He nodded toward the back seats where everyone was getting settled.

"We're going to go to the hospital, then let them take the van home so they can be with Ryan and greet our guests," she said. "We have time. This doesn't happen in minutes, you know." She gripped his shoulder as another pain hit her. "Well, not usually," she said when it was over, starting to get a little nervous herself.

He kissed her stomach, then hurried to the driver's side. Explaining what was going on as they drove, he got her to the hospital, then sent their respective families home, protesting all the way.

Several hours later, about an hour after Mary Melissa Maxwell had made her appearance, Josh watched as the nurse settled Marisa for a night of well-deserved rest. Their families—and he suspected all forty or so guests from their party—were down at the nursery, admiring his beautiful daughter. With a few mumbles and grumbles about the chaos down the hall, the nurse left, and finally they were alone.

"Happy anniversary, darlin'," Marisa drawled sleepily as he moved closer. "Do you like your present?"

"I love my present," Josh whispered, laying the most tender kiss he could muster on her forehead as he smoothed back damp strands of her hair. "And right on time. She must have gotten Maxwell genes."

Marisa laughed softly. "Since you're late more than I am anymore, you'd better hope she got mine. And if you wanted someone who was *always* on time," she added softly, "you should have asked for it in our marriage contract."

"The contract?"

"The list," she corrected, and he almost groaned aloud. That list was going to haunt him forever. She contradicted the assumption. "Don't you remember that night in the restaurant? Our first date? The list you sat there and told me about—all the things you wanted in a wife." She looked smug. "With the birth of your beautiful daughter—" she lifted a hand to his face "—they're all done. Every last one. In only a year. Aren't you impressed?"

"I'm impressed." He sighed contentedly.

"There are some things I'm always on time with."

"Weddings and babies. The most important things." He

wanted to hold her, knew she needed sleep. ''I love you, Marisa Maxwell.''

''I love you, too,'' she whispered.

''So we're up for renegotiation, huh?'' he said after he kissed her one more time. At her slight frown he explained, ''Of our marriage contract.''

''No way, buddy. Now you're stuck with what you get.''

''As long as it lasts forever,'' he said.

''Forever,'' she murmured, savoring the sound for a moment before she agreed. ''Deal.''

''Deal,'' he answered. It was the best contract he'd ever made. They sealed it with a kiss.

* * * * *

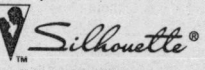

If you enjoyed what you just read,
then we've got an offer you can't resist!

Take 2 bestselling love stories FREE!

Plus get a FREE surprise gift!

Clip this page and mail it to Silhouette Reader Service™

IN U.S.A.	**IN CANADA**
3010 Walden Ave.	P.O. Box 609
P.O. Box 1867	Fort Erie, Ontario
Buffalo, N.Y. 14240-1867	L2A 5X3

YES! Please send me 2 free Silhouette Special Edition® novels and my free surprise gift. Then send me 6 brand-new novels every month, which I will receive months before they're available in stores. In the U.S.A., bill me at the bargain price of $3.57 plus 25¢ delivery per book and applicable sales tax, if any*. In Canada, bill me at the bargain price of $3.96 plus 25¢ delivery per book and applicable taxes**. That's the complete price and a savings of over 10% off the cover prices—what a great deal! I understand that accepting the 2 free books and gift places me under no obligation ever to buy any books. I can always return a shipment and cancel at any time. Even if I never buy another book from Silhouette, the 2 free books and gift are mine to keep forever. So why not take us up on our invitation. You'll be glad you did!

235 SEN CNFD
335 SEN CNFE

Name	(PLEASE PRINT)	
Address	Apt.#	
City	State/Prov.	Zip/Postal Code

* Terms and prices subject to change without notice. Sales tax applicable in N.Y.
** Canadian residents will be charged applicable provincial taxes and GST.
  All orders subject to approval. Offer limited to one per household.
  ® are registered trademarks of Harlequin Enterprises Limited.

SPED99   ©1998 Harlequin Enterprises Limited

Coming in May 1999

BABY *Fever*

by
New York Times Bestselling Author

KASEY MICHAELS

When three sisters hear their biological
clocks ticking, they know it's
time for action.

But who will they get to father their babies?

**Find out how the road to motherhood
leads to love in this brand-new collection.**

Available at your favorite retail outlet.

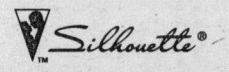

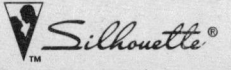

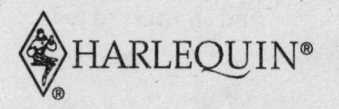